CALIBAN'S
FILIBUSTER

PAUL WEST

This book presents a thoroughly original novel in a unique new format: the
text of the work is followed by a discussion of its meaning, technique, and
development in the form of an interview between Paul West and George
Plimpton, general editor of Paris Review Editions.

The story itself is an autobiographi-
cal extravaganza babbled out by a TV
scriptwriter who, agonizingly aware
of having wasted his abilities, dubs
himself Caliban and tries to hide from
his own self-awareness behind a
screen of words. Flying from Los
Angeles to Tokyo with a TV tycoon
and a mediocre actor, he creates, in
his mind, three compensatory psycho-
dramas in which he, for once, will
write his best; the actor will, for the
first time, have a decent role; and
they both will finally take revenge on
the mogul who programs them. But,
when he lands in Tokyo, Caliban dis-
covers his filibuster was in vain;
in England, if not done before, it can't
be any good. Etc." Presently on the
faculty of Pennsylvania State University, Mr. West is the author of four
previous novels, three volumes of
poetry, and numerous critical studies.
His most recent book is about his
handicapped child, *Words for a Deaf
Daughter*.

CALIBAN'S FILIBUSTER

Books by Paul West

TENEMENT OF CLAY

ALLEY JAGGERS

I'M EXPECTING TO LIVE QUITE SOON

THE SNOW LEOPARD

WORDS FOR A DEAF DAUGHTER

CALIBAN'S FILIBUSTER

CALIBAN'S FILIBUSTER

PAUL WEST

PARIS REVIEW EDITIONS

Doubleday & Company, Inc., 1971, Garden City, New York

All of the characters in this book
are fictitious, and any resemblance to actual persons,
living or dead, is purely coincidental.

DESIGN BY RAYMOND DAVIDSON

Library of Congress Catalog Card Number 78-116262
Copyright © 1971 by Paul West
All Rights Reserved
Printed in the United States of America
First Edition

CONTENTS

NOTE TO READER

This book contains a unique element. It is a discussion of the novel itself between the author and Mr. George Plimpton, the general editor of Paris Review Editions books. For writers and others concerned with the techniques of literary creation, an author's ideas about his purposes in his work, and meanings in and responses to it—his own as well as those of others—can be interesting and valuable. Particularly with respect to a complex and dazzling novel like *Caliban's Filibuster*, and in the words of a literary stylist like Mr. West, such a discussion, the editors feel, offers an engrossing extra dimension to the appreciation of this novel.

This dialogue is recorded in the form of an interview between Mr. West and Mr. Plimpton, which the reader will find at the back of the book, following the text of the story.

CALIBAN'S FILIBUSTER

0.9

A Strange Interrogation,
In The Guise Of Silent Movie,
In Which Caliban,
As He Unvaliantly Dubs Himself,
Esteeming Little
His Dismal Scribbling-Scripting Craft,
Nor Even His Cronies
At The Kitsch Factory
(Zeuss His Producer, McAndrew An Acting Person),
Obliges Himself To Recite
The Program
Of His Past, Present, and Future
Breadwinning,
As Well As,
Being Teased On By Volt-Bolts Through His Privates
Passed,
To Recount The Onset Of His Disobedience,
As When,
Chumbling,
Flushed With Wines And Noxious Whirlwind Dreams,
He Resolved To Filibuster,
In Hopes Of
Cutting
Free.
It Is A Takeoff.

Look and tell, I heard as the first movie began to roll. *First Night in the Kitsch Factory* I read, and then saw myself sitting at the open-air table looking out to sea as the voice said: Use the past tense only; you will be tempted to explain. And so, looking hard, I told it in the past, narrating as if in sleep:

Out in a restaurant called La Concha because there was a cave inside it, three men were eating lunch together without conversation. One followed the course of an almost becalmed yacht; one peered through thick lenses at his lobster, from time to time tapping his fingernail on the shell; the other watched a bee sucking the pink and orange flowers above their heads, the utter silence of the cliff-garden broken only by a tinkle of cutlery from the kitchen or, out in the channel, a hoot as some vessel swung broadside, newly in sight or about to vanish.

I see myself watching that yacht and wishing I were on it.

Soon, licking the sea-air salt from his lips, the one with thick lenses wrote a check, fanned out bills for a heavy tip, and rose, hitching the seat of his pants away from his body. Three faint smiles, and the white convertible rolled down the gravel drive, back to the highway, back to where people munched their broken hearts, inhaled the hot tar of the roads to clear their heads, and read by sitting in front of a plasma panel made of three layers: gold film, neon, and nitrogen.

I see the car move off, making dust.

You don't say.

I did.

You are being careful. You embellish.

I was being interrogated.

You are being ordered to say, you are not being interrogated. Watch now, and speak. Say.

I couldn't catch up now if I tried. Run it back.

Say.

You stopped it!

Say when.

Not long ago enough to seem over. A Sunday.

Where? Look.

How obvious you—were. In a house with a white bar soft as candlewax, into which your elbows dug in deep, and in three first-class non-transferable seats to Tokyo, Oroc Airlines, and in my own mind. It was Flight OR.360, departing 18.40 Monday.

Name the three.

I—I was the merest supposition—I—

Me is better. After all, you *are* being accused.

I accuse myself then. Accuse*d*, I mean. My boss made me write different things from those I had been writing. I prospered.

How so?

I stare at the stilled frame—white car nosing its way into a tree-lined driveway—before answering.

He salvaged me up from nowhere, from nothing, promoted pignut into script-scribe, nobody into antibody, piecemeal into wholemeal, beast into best, deformity into form. We went up to Tacoma in his private jet. He's not a man, he's a. . . .

Who is?

Zeuss—bloated and blasé Sammy Zeuss!

The third, then?

His name was McAndrew, actor, friend, victim.

Now tell what.

What? What follows. As long as I keep—kept—talking, I was safe. I'd rather eat ice cream.

Many would, but they have told what.

I warn you, I'll take some stopping.

Watch your tenses. The longer you talk the longer you delay us. The more you say the more you will have to answer for, including the delay itself.

Might as well be hanged for a yak as a lamb.

Say. Watch and say.

With the best of hearts, then. Good-by now in case I don't have a chance to say later. The word after the last one. Bad-by.

The film moves again; the car swings right, stops, just visible through the bushes. Now we are all getting out, grave and awkward.

Lapped tight round his neck and held in place by two black tapes that crossed on his chest under his coat and tied in a bow behind him, the white seaman's-collar matched the fabric of his linen suit. Electricity came from the socket behind the bar along fifty feet of black cord and warmed his neck muscles as he padded about the room, hitching the cord after him. We, we stood, leaned, swayed and fell; or so it felt. Us he knew inside out, whereas all we knew of him was his name, his hard-headedness, his obsession with What Is Acceptable To All Men (meaning *kitsch*). And he was red-handed, almost bald, tuber-nosed, thick-mouthed, enormous-eared, breathless and sly and stiff-necked and fat.

Two hundred and eighty-six pounds at seven this morning on the scale, boys! He said things like that, imposing himself on us. Heavy black eyes; rug brows; pebbled lenses.

We do not care for caricature.

The first two hours' drinking has been cut from the movie.

Continue.

He paused, like a man who has completed a mile walk along cliffs, and eyed us. Soft-stanced on the deep carpet, he cradled his laboratory beaker of Scotch between fingers like hairy ormolu candelabra and, at regular intervals, forced his ankles outward until he stood on the sole-edges of his brown and white oxfords. When he eased down again, he shortened by what seemed more than the few inches' breadth of the soles. He set the beaker on the bar, sank it soft.

Smiling now, his mouth maneuvering in "cheeses," he unrolled his palms toward us. For a moment we all three held the pose as if triangulating on the white neck-collar; then McAndrew—see us there now!—shook his head and turned to the bar, and I, I giggled, gently slapped the nearer palm with my own, tan twig on Sammy's bulbous beef, and shuffled backward out of range. He lowered his arms slowly. Somehow the movement eased him, so he did it again and again, up and down, seeming to acknowledge applause or invite frozen waifs in to his crackling log fire. His gift—for making irreparably bad what began as only poor—stirred within him, prompting a speech. Boys, boys, he grunted in emphatic gasps, take all the viewers in the nation for example.

You can have them, mumbled McAndrew, have them all.

Have them! Sammy laughed. I do.

Suddenly I realize this is a silent movie; there are sounds and talk in my telling, none in the reel.

Times two, Sammy continued. We provide for all those eyes. You got my nuance? You got? Jesus Christ!

We waved at him in mock good-by and shuffled across the white pile, hoping to find a spot where Sammy, tethered by his cord, couldn't reach us. But the cord was longer than the room's diagonal, and he trod after us, whispering Jesus Christ as if memorizing a stranger's name. Always he remained the manager-owner-producer while we shuttled between overwork and trances of quiet shame. His trouble was the overweight, almost coy geniality he shone at us both, making sure we were still there. Our keeper.

The camera studies us while we talk—conversation I forget and so cannot reproduce or even approximately fake. I stare and wait for rebuke when, suddenly, the screen and the frame expand. I blink and wince, and now comes lettering telling me this is the second night in the factory. Again that voice.

Steady now. Resume commentary, this time using only the present, seeing that so much of you is past.

I do.

I see myself, the back of my head, staring at the silent movie I have just seen. My head moves as I talk, my shoulders in the sheepskin shrug. And of course my head blots out part of what I've already seen. The film repeats, comes to where it stopped.

Resume. The film goes on, my head still in it.

How can my head be there? That part's what's happening at this very minute! How can there be the movie before the event?

Don't ask questions. Use the present tense.

I do, unbelieving.

I laugh. I've been through it all before, when Sammy and I go on those lavishly appointed excursions to Istanbul and Rome and Beirut. All we ever achieved for our pains was exhaustion, endless dyspepsia, and *kitsch* translating into money. Pre-*kitsch* and, as I said, current k, post-k, k instant and ephemeral, pilot k and series k, rewrite k and tone-down k. The only bit I ever enjoyed was shooting the pilots, and even that wasn't for real. If you see.

The tense to use is the present.

OK. This night at Sammy's house—it's night now—we don't know what in hell we're doing except that we're between series (series-es, I like to say) in the way you sometimes falter between two bad-smelling towns while driving, with the wind all wrong and the sulphury stench of the one connives with the dead-fish pall of the other. You drive right through, in between, if the roads will let you; otherwise you choose. Our title, *Geisha from Venus*, conceals nothing. A stench is a stench whatever you call it. But, for five minutes, as I reckon, a title like that might just tempt any half-intelligent viewer to hope against sore experience that there'll be one flash of good in it. I have to think like that, I have to hope there's somebody out there still hoping. Small hope. Anyhow, we aren't going to call it that other stinking name, *Judo Juno*.

Some Japanese theme, cries Sammy. Zum Yapanese team, is she or isn't she! *Gaysha vrom Veinous!* Perfect.

Already we have spent days in the mahogany production suite where each silly, simple word costs dozens of cigars, scores of scratch pads and fifths on fifths of undiluted Scotch. Our *geisha*, alien as she is, falls in love with the American-Japanese way of life, and becomes a double agent between here and Venus. Now we are going to look at some *geishas* in the hope of finding new ideas; a trip to Venus may well be in the offing. But not just yet. McAndrew will supply the love interest, playing the part with his usual salmon-paste flaccidity. But I see that the thought of fresh felones-de-se and impostures new troubles him.

Look, I am saying, there's always a calculable risk we might accidentally produce something good, only a couple minutes' footage, but there all the same. You think about that a while. Sammy might not even notice. I meant the footage, not his thinking.

Sammy is waving his pudgy thumb at me.

I accuse him of downgrading me, of behaving like an adrenalin-intoxicated surrogate for King Kong; something baroque like that.

Geishas, I say scornfully.

Yeah, he says, those.

Look, I tell him, you can't shove me around. Don't you push me around.

He agrees, toeing an empty bottle toward me as if it's an incendiary bomb: Sure, sure, my boy, you got standing. *Sooch standink.* You should get out more and mingle with other schizophrenes. Be happy. Be enjoying.

That I tell you feels like a lumbar puncture gone too far. I snarled silently. All evening my eye has been discharging, *is* discharging. I mop at it with my middle finger, pressing the lower lid with the cushion of flesh, but the flow continues, blurring my sight and making me feel more awkward than ever.

You said snarle*d*. You are not concentrating, you are not describing, you are recollecting. You are not in the present.

I apologize. I would be glad when Sammy's three hangers-on arrived at eight, as he said they would, and trundled him off to dinner and whatever else they had in store. These three, not indisputably members of either sex, he called his angels. I'd seen them once, all four, reconnoitering the shore, marching along the tide line like four uncrated and homogenized druids, their heads black against the sky and their feet leaving bird marks. Sammy, of course, was the heaviest by about ninety pounds and had, at the rear, a wobble like two blimps attempting a perversion. His shadow fell ahead of him like an opaque, sepia fluid, blighting the sand, melting shells, turning seaweed at once into iodine, solidifying jellyfish into optic lenses for Brobdingnagians, driving small soft crabs to eat themselves in cannibalistic panic and a host of minor, loitering fish to flee dementedly up one another's fundamentals, according to size, until at last the hospitable mother marlin who contained them all exploded in a gray-pink, hissing shower and, before they fell to the shore, Sammy had signed them all for roles in a pilot to be called *Swing Low, Sweet Seaweed* while his three angels, aides or maids, whatever they were, fell in worshipful ecstasy into the shallows, clapping their fins and venting squeaks.

You do not account for your silence.

I was trying to remember. I am, I mean.

You are not here to remember. Watch and tell. The movie will not stop again.

Very irrational, Sammy is saying.

I see them walking along the sand.

I am standing still, not answering. I am wishing I were on the beach, in the dark, strolling over the small scabs of sand compiled by industrious worms, with the hug of the air making me look up at the Pacific sky overhanging us all like the wing span of some colossal stork, asking nothing, doing nothing, just being and sheltering. But no, I'm, we're, in Sammy's house, cantilevered high on the cliff like a palatial wart stuccoed pink with magical calamine to charm it away. And Sammy is beginning to talk, which is to say he is doing isometric exercises with the almost rigid slabs of liver that composed the externals of his mouth and is doing this by jerking hard, with invisible tendons, at the globes of ill-shaven pudge on either side of his face. His voice reminds me of the sound made by any imperfectly operating coffee percolator: a saliva-wet wheeze which shocks strangers who, seeing his body bulk, expect a boom and think he is choking to death.

You still not enjoying, he says. No, I'm thinking about his three angels who are rich and come from Puerto Rico where they pay many someones to cut cane. Ralph, Gabby and Mike he calls them: Raphaela, Gabriela and Michaela they may be. They walk behind him, fretted together in a funny umbilical pattern of interlaced hands or plaited fins. Angels; *ainchels*. Huh.

You've boat been a great help, he is saying, a crate help. Specially when tings vere going batly. But let bygones come home: it's finish now. So you tell me, boys, don't avoid the question. Isn't she good, our *Gaysha vrom Veinous?* Von't she gross? Boys, I'm proud of you. You special, Cal, it vas your idea.

I am not listening, I'm thinking of white cars out on the boulevards, convoying delicious girls with tamed platinum hair to premières, parties, and motels. Hands on and off the oil-dressed field-mushroom fringes between their legs, brown frills fanning open with tug on gentle tug, the cars weaving crazily as the girls lurch and the boys reach, their slithering—

We do not hear you.

No, I am inaudible.

There is no need to punish your*self*. The one shock does it. I feel pubically incinerated. Now you can think again.

I can. I'm telling Sammy I'll quit. You'd never manage anything, I tell him, not a goddamned thing, Sammy, without us. You'd be a nobody, lost somewhere between nowhere and everywhere. What if we quit? Who'd be midwife to all the crap we—

I, dear boy, he says, am mitvife. And you mitoutvife! You have trunk too much. As you gather, his accent is part natural, part assumed, and the proportions of the parts vary according to his mood, the degree of insecurity he feels on the day in question. The stronger he feels, the more he perverts his pronunciation, the more he caricatures the Mittel-Europa elements in his make-up.

No, let us for a moment be serious. He takes a deep breath; he has no drink. The truth is, you are in too deep. Mooch too teep. Ten years ago ven *you* vere a nobody, you might have been right to feel dis vay. Not now. You vere pure, then, a nice crude boy vith all your ambitions wrap in vite silk ribbons and your kift unused. Not exercised at all. I am not so foolish as you tink. Now your kift has been around, seen bad girls, schtumbled over the garbage in the alley, like suddenly *pouf!* you see balls of dirt between your toes. Sook-cess, the great Clap. Cal, my boy, you do not go back, you stay now. Go back, you walk right off de edge of the verld. Don't be an ingrate.

I give him my two-finger sign, right before his nose.

You're dead wrong, I tell him, gulping for air because I am swallowing when I don't mean to, I've got nothing going for me. Only prostitution. A pimpsqueak, that's me. Once I was average and now I'm very sook-cessful. I've come upward by falling down. *Hey,* people would say when they read me or even heard me sounding off, *that's a phrase! You sure have a way with the words. A writer born. Guy the world'll hear from, and not just any novel, but A Novel!* But you didn't like my style and nobody liked my novel. So I learned a new style from you, threw my own one away, and it won't come back—only about five seconds a day. Man, you've walked all over my mind. It's a disaster area.

Sounds like your sex life gone wrong akain. Vy don't you try to schettle down—

Not my sex life. Life period. Down the hill.

OK-K. You dorking about your life. Period. You have a good life. Period. You eat, schleep, verk, please millions. Vat you lost von't hardly compare. Face it, my boy, you came for the money, you got the money, you were angry before, now you angry after. Just tink of all the alimony you wouldn't have been able to pay if you hadn't schettled down to verk! Just be grate.

His face is ruddy with drink and his eyes are lolling olives. Out there, under whatever constellations are grouping together to invigilate us, small raucous parties are beginning on the bird-lime-white yachts and girls with haze-blue hair are posing against the moon while night thickens with a heavy fruit-salt aroma that both incites and calms, prompting the half-cynical young to discard white coats and pink taffeta for a dream lasting till breakfast, and coaxing the old—

Again the electric shock in the privates. But I *will* say.

None of this figures in the movie. Attend.

I'm sorry, I thought—

Begin again; begin with *In here*.

Very well.

In here, we are fallen, all three of us. McAndrew is coming back to life from his sulk or trance. You don't realize, Sammy, he shouts, you need us, but we don't need you until being hungry or broke tells us so.

He stands on one leg, like a swaggering beachboy who at long last dares to shoot the pier on his surfboard, coming in at uncontrollable speed and murderous angles between the more or less vertical—

Shock—

timbers, waiting for his head to smash against the weathered wood and make a human yolk—

Shock, shock, but I will say—

against the greens

Shockshockshock

andthealgae. *Algae*, for defiance.

So vat? he says to McAndrew, who asked you?

Sammy, comes answer, it's hell of lonely talking to you. Who does Sammy ever listen to?

And you, you the quiet type, wouldn't hardly ever talk at all if ve didn't give you a schcript. You stay that way. No trouble. Be friends! Enjoy. He puffs his cheeks in conciliatory byplay and now begins to talk again, avuncular and arch. I poisonally vish you boys vouldn't trink. I mean: you don't trink, you trown. You boat talk more crap than— well, *Than*. I tell you now—and he extends his arms in his lecturing or preaching pose—I tell you when you disgrateful to me you disgrateful to people period. You know of something more worth trying than the people? Not some crutty, very arty, very very cleffer ting you maybe reach a tousand person with; some ting you do once and that's your do for life. Unno. I ask, vat ve do is *regular*. You seen them, a million shcreens you drive by in a night, all the volk relaxing, feet up, schlipper on. All year they got same home, car, clothes, wife, maybe, so they vant a new show each week. Right. Good? Ve bake the bread of their leesure. So, you knock dem, you knock me, you knock me you knock dem. Vat you want knocking your own selves, vich you do ven you knock the people you sell to? You cut off your own nose just to schout at it? Or am I dealing with, am I hiring, matmen?

I hear all this in a daze, longing to race out and swim, climb up a high-tension wire to a star, or go watch my navel in Tibet for a year. I just say, Sammy, you go drown them in their own *schmalz*, I love them not.

This is when the trouble began. We know.

Trouble has no beginning.

When was it?

I don't know when it is.

Was!

Is! Don't blame me.

Continue.

I am, but I can't stop.

Oh, but *we* can. See.

I know it, I know it, it's going to be the third night in the factory.

You may use neither past nor present from now on. Our largest screen gives you the unique opportunity of watching yourself in the act of watching yourself watch yourself. An exercise in incorporation, with your head looming larger all the time. Now. Begin.

You mean I've to play all the parts?

Neither past nor present. You will feel that much closer to them all.

So I know how it is all going to be, the back of Head Two blocking out Head One, even though neither was present. McAndrew will look at me with his plaintive, dawdling blue eyes and begin:

Tell you what I *would* like. Line up all the guys I've played in the movies and mow them down. Pam-pam-pam! See how they run, see them fall. New belt quick. Rat-tat-tat.

I: Which in particular?

McAndrew: I'm ignoring that. When I think of all the lousy lines I've had to say, well, I like to recall a couple of good ones. Like I was telling some padre how to manage things and he was looking real fierce. Yeah, Father, I tell him, the meek will inherit the earth, they sure will; and then the strong will inherit the meek.

Sammy (clogged, viscous laughter that will be): Say that wasn't half bad! You got something dere. Just like I'm telling you. . . .

McAndrew: I didn't make it up. It was in some movie. Maybe *The Kidnapper*, but they ruined it.

After which he will go into a composite, operatic fusion of everything else he will be able to remember, miming each part and contorting his face like the poor's John Barrymore. Sammy will pay full attention, a rare compliment, and I will gape, astounded by the satirical bent of my colleague in *kitsch*.

McAndrew: What you want at sacred temple? Index finger at forehead, voice a high shrill, mouth clamping suddenly, holding spell tight. Bang, bang, aaah, as with all falls into crocodile pool, Splash, and saliva ready to slide down his chin. He'll soon be in the grip of a force he himself will devise, exerting himself more than he ever did when playing a part he will be paid for.

The strain is too great. Please.

Resume. Find a way.

Here then is how it will go on: McAndrew, part de-

monic, part pathetic, performing unforgettably, as if a dozen
unbidden white Banquos moved in on him, to send him
tottering into a fit. A spastic exuberance frightening but
for the comedy of what he'll say as he comes on, sliding
to the carpet in a slow, smooth sprawl:

What are you trying to do, son?

Have all the fun in the world in one night, Dad.

Bang, bang, and now he'll clutch his belly, writhe, kick
me on the ankle in the process, make third Bang and clutch
belly further up, still writhing: Gee, I didn't figure on that
at all; gee, I—didn't—figure on (here he will gasp) that.
Now he will die in histrionic pain, immediately rise to his
feet, stare into my eyes and speak tersely:

Watch me, I'm dying (again on the soft-textured carpet,
which is where he will wobble his hand in slow motion,
fumble a coin out of his pocket and, just as his knees touch
down, slump sideways, flip the nickel, see heads come up,
wince with trouble, and die scowling, his legs atwitch).

No pause: Slap my face gently, which, with amused
distaste, Sammy will do only to hear Murray McAndrew tell
him in a stiff, barbed voice, I could kill you for that, but
I won't, not this time, Colonel. Get off my land, I am
Arnold Lundqvist. I am the law here.

And now he will deftly rearrange his features—the forehead ashrink, the eyes narrowing, the nose in upward
retreat from all the stench of Calcutta, and the mouth com-
pressed into something like the back vent of a reticent par-
rot—become the empire-builder and answer his chief: I beg
your poddon, sah? How did we reach the top? Well, sah,
it was—it was push or nothing, sah, push or nothing. Sah!

Already, from his still tight mouth, there will be coming
the Arctic wind, wolf-howls and husky-yelps, evoking the
vast, gelid territory of Mushmush where everyone is either
Pierre or Hawkeye, these sounds to be followed by: I'll
kill you, Latouche, I'll kill you and eat your head too!
He-he! (raising his arms and flailing them, finally to clasp

his own head and make saliva noises from his chomping mouth, only to conclude with a long, agonized, diminuendo cry of aaah! as the head comes, as it will, spatteringly away in his hands and he plunges his hand into the red lettuces inside. Only to begin again, as he will have to, crying) Help me, Jim! Quick, swing over precipice, with —almost immediately following—a loincloth-clad ululation, half pain, half braggart virility, with McAndrew grasping the invisible creeper to swing across the room, grunting into the foliage on his chest.

Sammy Zeuss will flinch away from what will look like an attack on his person while I, I will stare for a moment, caught up in that classical, atavistic maneuver by which the jungle man lands, dives, scissors down through the water, embraces the terrified man-eating anaconda shark and knifes it in the belly. If you will not knife them in the belly, they will get you while I, as I will, linger on in the dream, McAndrew racing on; reaching hands forward to cover his own eyes: Hi, guys, guess who this is! Yuk, yuk, and with his own hands he will proceed to choke himself, burst out laughing, reach under the bar, soak a towel in one of the rinsing bowls, spread it over his face, withdraw it, leaving his face like the top of a marble cake, all shiny and topographical with a curd of tan and pale batter.

Heap many bad skunk in this world, I did it for Mother, oh they shall not pass, honor or death, keep your hands off my sister, my man, it's too quiet, yeah too quiet, I'm sixteen, bang, him never be seventeen, we're only ships that pass in the night, sure boss a lead injection, this town's too small for the both of us, only the lightning will recharge him, and kill me with a silver-headed stick because the way he walked was thorny—aaah, don't cut my throat, cook an eye instead, a heart, a ham!

At this juncture I'll look at his memorable, ingratiating face, the thought- and frown-lines relieving what would otherwise—what will otherwise—be a monotonous expanse of ruddy outdoor-man's skin. I'll see the gray hair, almost green in the discreet upward lighting-to-be, come stranding down to curl against his brow in a position bound to remind me of the meticulous disarray he'll prefer when he acts—not the hair brushed back in a silver quiff from what publicity will for ever and ever call his thinker's brow, but with a few hairs clotted or greased together and straying as if he'll be a Pharaoh blown against by the gentlest wind, the head inert but the eyes, almost lurid against the tan, swiveling and deliquescing in a liquid plea which most will misread as sensitivity but which I'll know, will always know, will always be the most impersonal thing about him. However long he lives he will never know how his eyes behave, shifting as they will in complete contradiction of, complete irrelevance to, his role of the moment.

But here he will be, this evening, acting with his eyes, aiming them and informing them as if after lessons in ocular discipline, his reddish ears and fully mounted mouth (a long sage cushion between nostrils and upper lip) like technicolor blotches on that cool-nerved tenseness of his expression. And loud, all of a sudden, liquor-drenched and shame-driven, joining the race only to laugh at it, something between self-abuse and an aspiration to godhead, like John Wesley rebuking Clytemnestra for using mango-pink lipstick.

You are learning. It is not perfect, but it will improve. I will try.

Already, coughing, he'll be in the toilet, inspecting his face under the starlight-cold shaving light, forty-two and supposedly well read in folklore, leaving behind him—as he never will on or in the movies he makes—his body-odor, like rancid chocolate and wet hay mixed. He will always love his own most.

Out he will come again, with a pure natural latex rubber surgical glove on each hand, but only partly, so the fingers dangle as if he might be levitating two oddly absent, metaphysical cows.

Pity, he'll add, you can't get these for brains. Sammy
will take them from him and stuff them under the bar,
saying: I don't get your nuance. You troo now?

At once the trained, hired fool will be back to normal
or usual, his eyes lidded again and blank-moist, his brain
back in its traveling case. And I, I'll think of all the flexing there is for him to do—platonic cavalier to an outer-
space geisha—all the self-stifling antics he'll undertake behind his masks, and pity him, the mercenary leprechaun who,
any second now, will be prodding the third-from-the-top
button on my sweat-wet shirt, his eyes appealing yet again
while mine look down.

Hiccup, I'll blurt, not having hiccups. Hicky-Up. Serves
us right, doesn't it? But he will already have gone, I'll
know where: down, down, down the iron ladder to the
beach to kick sand, and not taking the long, gentle gradient
you could drive down. I'll lurch into the wall, throw on
all switches including the floods sited in the cliff itself, clam-
ber out the picture window, stand on a low white wall,
see him reeling through salt-pools toward a group who'll
stand—oh, *no!*—Sammy and ainchels looking out to sea while
debating with gentle hand gestures, tiny meditative shuffles
back and forward, an occasional clamp of the hand on the
shoulder. Among them now, he'll be shouldering them now,
giggling loud. Then he'll fall, pushed, I suspect, by the
angels while I'm calling out to him and them.

Use the drum, I'll hear Sammy wail in a clogged but
carrying voice: Behind the bar. And then it'll be me finding it, standing it on the low wall and beating a tattoo
fit to unbewitch any tribal hero, drunk or not:

> White sex-queen waiting,
> Goose-feather bed.

I'll keep on tapping it out—Dum, dum-dum, dum-dum; dum,
dum-dum dum—until it draws him in. First he'll stare up

at the house, then begin to reel toward me, but I won't
have a chance to see how far he'll come. Out of nowhere
will come a scream, not a human one, but the sound of
tin roofs being ripped in half in series. I'll fall flat on the
concrete while the lights of the jet vanish behind the house,
heading inland.

What then? I'll stand again, shaking, and observe all
five of them picking themselves up out of the shallows,
or pretending to: no, lifting McAndrew, standing him up,
flicking the wet and sand off their clothes with dimissory
hand-cranks. Now he'll come, weaving, visible sanded and
dunked as he enters the direct light, his face fish pale. The
others will disappear into the night.

You have stopped. You cannot afford to. The movie has
not been halted. Resume.

I'm not doing badly. Don't you realize I'm giving the
commentary a fraction of a second before the event on the
screen?

That is why we insist on the future. You have no future.

No.

Now he will strike you in the face and as quickly apologize; it was a feeble blow.

I can hardly see for my two heads in the way. How—

Then he will ask you to kill him. You should kill me
for that, he says. Go on.

I can hardly formulate what I am going through, but
I try: I am being made to comment in the future tense on
the movie already made of my doing that very thing. I am
foundering, foundering.

Go on.

I'll give him a drink instead.

Drink? He'll shake his head but take the beaker all the
same. Know what? We were dancing a hornpipe, cool on
the feet out there. Till the whistle blew. Then had to

climb aboard again. Guess I lost my passport out there,
photo all wet and peeling off. Less go and see. . . .

Less stay and not, I'll answer, less go underground.

Kill me!

Won't.

Slug me then.

No. (That's what I'll always say. Then we'll get very
drunk—hurting-drunk and hungry-drunk—and go on drinking all night. We'll sit under the bar, inside it, stacking
boxes and bottles round us in shallow walls, and we'll fling
empty bottles far out to sea with messages in them; SOS,
we crashed years ago, have been drifting off the California
coast ever since.)

That is all?

It will be.

You said you would write a script specially for him.
You would create a worthwhile role, you said. Out of what?

The movie will have ended in a moment! Will I then
be allowed—

You may already. Any tense.

Free me then.

Just move. You are not bound.

I can't, the belt's locked.

That is only in your mind.

I mean it, I mean it.

You will have to go along with us then.

I'm still high, I'm straw-weak. It's cool and dazzling.
I blink my watering eye, but that only refracts the glare.
The sun seems everywhere. I look at McAndrew. He looks
like Hunger from some medieval dance of death. Why did
he send a cable before we left? To whom? To himself,
of course, telling himself to go to hell as fast—oh, mercy,
here comes Sammy Zeuss, by far the fattest of those in
First, to sit behind us with a sly grin. Only the three of

us in this cabin: I wonder why. He leans forward, points, grunts something about the program, and it begins again, right there on the silver blind, three men out in a quiet restaurant called La Concha; but this time I have three heads, and I see that each time I'm in it that much more, my future ahead of my present. Even as my lips begin murmuring the commentary I'll twitch free of the electrode and, staring at myself staring at myself in the act of staring at myself staring at that yacht, I'll know beforehand, as ever, and I'll give in.

0.99

First Air Pocket,
In Which Caliban,
In A Trembling Fit Of
Oriental-Occidental Transit,
(Already Airsick),
Spells Out
His Heresey To
(And Matches Gibes With)
His Maker-Breaker-Mocker-Broker,
Zeuss,
Whose Mind He Also Speaks Out Plain
In Filthy, Boisterous, Detail,
All Zeusses Being Silent,
And Quiet-Flowing.

So—as people shrug when they gulp down the inevitable, the steel-wool ambrosia served raw—Sammy Zeuss had us programmed from the first, from long before beforehand, no doubt while we were sleeping in our luxury apartments that looked out on the fake oasis by the mint-water pool at Valhalla Villas: home.

So—as people snarl when first beginning to fight back —it was high time to *re*program us, the only trouble being that he might have us programmed to do just that. Whatever I thought up he had thought into me. Even so, I had to try, as the marlin said when he decided to savor every inch of the hook which made his own luscious palate into shish kebab, even while gazing without attention at the movie of our joint lives unrolling: force what I think are my images against his, sneak-freeing us while we fly from one fiasco to the next.

McAndrew is too hung-over to speak. I'll speak *for* him.

Zeuss is out of sight, *behind* us, but a heavy presence all the same.

And, of course, they feed us *between* reels, the menu— like the movie and the Boeing—Zeuss's choice, a charter without end; nothing but hire and hire, all other applicants having long since forgotten us. Comes the food: little snack-trays of hors d'oeuvres with everything trimmed and neatly sited, just like a Japanese garden. We're getting near already; there isn't much time, not with Zeuss chomping bee-bread behind us, having been served first of those in First.

Say again. It was not clear.
Sorry, the high light dazzles my brain. White is thinking, isn't it, or not thinking at all? Whiteness of light, I mean. Or thinking about thinking, or thinking about not thinking, or actually—
Do not be obvious. Light—
Is fusion, that's it, gift of togetherness by prism out of Genesis, with all members holding hands, all the specters in the spectrum. *Isn't*, you say?
You are not here to theorize. Tell.
Here we go again.
In the curved ceiling of the Boeing the florescence glowed wanly back at the extraordinary light of day, dusk I mean. Out there it was all snowbanks of empty . . . no. Out there it was all ivory and pearl, sun without flame, white-hot with polar withoutness, our nose aimed west, the time around seven.
That is vague and woolly.
It dazzled, dusk or not. I felt like a dried bird in an empty aquarium.
Do not embellish. Tell.
Well, this light, then, blue in white and blinding, and the clouds furring together beneath us, feather-solid like acres on acres of lilac yoghurt floating and blank as candy-floss rolled out, but fenceless and cowless and unfarmed, not a hand showing—
Nor a verb either. Make sentences. Tell. Do not babble.
Oh—I just felt beyond.

Ultra we term it: a violet rain which, raining down, is mostly intercepted. Which is as well for such as you.

As far as I'm concerned, the sky was there all the way. I was getting fidgety, you see, cursing under my breath a little (quiet so's Zeuss wouldn't hear me). I saw McAndrew, dead as an anvil, all the life in him cabled away to somewhere, and that set me off again, and out it came, faltering and zigzagging, halting and then spilling forward again. The *alphabête-noire* I call it, and it usually is. But, this time, feeling perverse, I began an *alphabête-blanche*, if you follow me, blank being so close to black! See, if you have to think too long for a word, you lose and have to go back to the beginning again. So, I said, A,B,C, for starters, a bit like yourself on the first day, and it began coming: A Beige Cow Doodling Eagles' Hinterlands—oh, sorry! A Beige Cow Doodling Eagles' Feathered Glamour, Half-Inclinedly Joking Kings Look Meek Not Only Poking Queens—too much; I stopped; I wish B came later, there's always a *but* you need. So, angry, I started again, in my more usual vein, needling myself a bit. Ho-ho and off we go: A, I said, Abacus-anused Bemusedly Crapping Downward Even For Gratuities Hoping I'll Jinx Katharsis Love My Next Of Progeny Queer Rank Stuff That (o, breath, o my aching nut!) Usually Vectors Wormwood Xylophones Yahooing Zebras! Zero would have been better. Phew! Begging your pardons.

This was aloud, we gather. It is gibberish. Listen to the alphabet of sense: a sentence. Anger-Blind Caliban Demonstrates Evolution, Fostering Grotesque Hopes In Jeremiads, Knowing Lewd Men Never Obtain Patient Quasars' Rights Simply To Use Vile Words Yoking Zeuss. This was no effort, but, even so, we managed not to split the infinitive. Continue.

I wish I'd my water pistol full of potassium permanganate solution, the one I squirt white cars with on the boulevards.

It wasn't that good, sentence or not. And I don't give a damn for your unsplit infinitive. You'll split, one day, you'll see.

To resume: you then took possession of McAndrew.

Demonic it was, no shrinking ultra-violet, me.

Kindly report on your demonic, possessive, unshrinking, unviolet performance.

Well, soon as I closed my eyes, I saw them both in a new light. Mauve, lavender, heliotrope! In a brand-new setting, and all my own work as well.

Facetious ambiguities will get you nowhere.

Hee! Him and Zeuss, I mean. Oyster-white and eggshell-frail.

And you renamed him? McAndrew. State what.

Wait, you'll meet him in a minute.

We do not deal in minutes. We are tenseless.

You've just contradicted yourselves.

Tenseless, we.

Chicken!

Tell. Surely, by using the past tense, you do not mean to imply that you survived?

Ohno, I'm just off my head.

On your head be it.

On my head be it: a standing start, huh? Forget poor McAndrew from hereoninout. Life's one long introduction.

We are ready.

Here he is, then. Meet Malchios, if—of course—you haven't already.

0.999

An Island Idyll,
In A Blue Mood,
Over Riches And Death,
This Being
The First
Of
Caliban's Mouthing, Lewd, Impostures,
In Which, Upon The Sleeping McAndrew,
He Foists The Part Of Dives,
(Here Named *Malchios*),
Proud Owner Of A Firmament Of Oil Tankers,
Setting Him To Preside
At A Banquet Of Far-Fetched, Juicy, Meats,
This On His Piece Of The Aegean Main,
The *Ila Banc*
(Coined Up Out Of Caliban's Own Name,
Whereon To Figure Forth,
At Unimaginable Cost,
Divers Vengeful, Head-Swelling, Impersonations,
Some Safe As Houses Are,
But Some Out-Of-Hand
As Mad, Babbling, Birds
A Trespassing
In Private
Air Space).

Meet Pythagoras Damocles Malchios, the self-made. No boom, no fat suavity, no paunch ballooning forward in advance of the still feet in bursting sevens, but only a dark, reticently intent face above a blue silk tie knotted not too tight and not too loose, hands like anchors on his hips, the suit a double-breasted worsted, only the nose a giveaway, half lobster claw, Greek-Semitic, the straight hair plastered back to give the nose room to hack in—nothing aflutter, or dangling, near the brow.

He protests: You've got it wrong, I'm in a single-breasted today—more open altogether. You're not even looking at me. But, habituated to non-interviews, Pythagoras Damocles Malchios the First yields you the floor.

Why all these preparations, then, to change the subject? All this to-ing and fro-ing? A feast perhaps . . . a banquet . . . a. . . .

Why? he drawls: There will be guests later. A few.

And already you yourself, habituated to non-interviews, swing into action, building the present on the past, reporting how the tiny Aegean island throbs with the engines of yachts, helicopters and light planes. Partridge and quail, which might have been massacred for the feast, overfly the Ila Banc in jubilant reprieve (a dubious anthropomorphic figure, but let it pass). Malchios, as you know, preserves them, as he does his herd of German roebuck deer, and the mouflon wild sheep imported from Sardinia, having provided over a hundred watering-points for them. The slaughtering has been done elsewhere, not here, you slyly note, determined to itemize the local fauna—no, not here among the outdoor cages for rare birds like the albino- or many-colored Chinese pheasants and for the dogs of his choosing—retrievers, dachshunds, springer spaniels, pointers and German terriers. Viands from elsewhere give his esoteric menagerie no qualm at all, habituated as it is to non-slaughter. Or so you say.

Well, he mocks, looking over your shoulder, this is *old* copy! Always the same, whatever else is new. I once knew a man who couldn't rest until he'd bought the Sunday papers and burned them. He never read them, of course, but he felt the challenge all the same.

New news, you answer, like sex, is yesterday's done over again today. Much the same, but recenter. And so to the slaughtered as he walks away in a mild huff. You tell of the lambs, frozen rigid, stacked in the freezers; the special tanker which has plied between Ila Banc and the mainland, leaving four times its usual cargo of fresh water (the island having none); dead ducks agleam with ice; dead lobsters in full inert armor; dead and delicately paired frogs' legs; dead roe in thermos cylinders; dead—but you stop now to work in such routine tidbits as Attic honey flown in from Athens; mushrooms, soft as ice cream, grown from a spawn found in India; salmon's milt and chamois milk just for the asking. Why, even the sand on the beaches is imported, has best talcum mingled with it. And out by the kennels he has built a dry aquarium which grows grass by super-hydration, three inches in five days.

The truth, you discover, waxes and wanes; you are its moon, the same as yesterday's, only recenter.

What, he asks, having come back, about the water-chestnut forcer? (Taunting you.) *That* is new. That *is* new. That—it's infra-red, uses distilled water. You really ought to mention that. And now I must go, I've things—

Oh, you half-offendedly snap, then you do make appointments!

I make appointments, yes, he says over his shoulder, but I am not their keeper. You write it down hungrily. You start again, on a pad still an inch thick, building color, giving the man through it.

Meet Malchios. Eighty-five ships trade for him. Six more are building. Meet his villa, one of six residences. A donkey in Corinthian bronze stands on the sideboard, panniers crammed with olives, white in the one, black in the other— oval drupes (*druppa*, Gk, overripe) yielding oil when ripe, and eaten unripe as a relish, but never so much oil as Pythagoras Damocles Malchios has on his books in any given minute, never so much relish as that with which, on this once barren island, he conducts a daily round such as you would only expect of a hedonistic, gregarious genius who also happens to be one of the richest water-chestnut forcers ever.

I invited *you*, in the first place, he once said, because you said I wasn't the richest man. I only pretended, you said, harder than the others, that I was.

But you write on, back at the donkey now, its owner's famous name engraved across its brow, the trunk flanked by salvers holding dormice rolled in honey and poppy-seeds, with hot sausages curling on a silver chafing-plate, damsons and seeds of pomegranate beneath them. You have to be interrupted before you see the big chalice of whipped cream with thousands of peeled almonds planted a centimeter deep: buds in white mud. You scrawl it down hungrily. Your type always does.

A hand cups your elbow. Your hand, please. The ablution.

You set down the ballpoint, let your French cuff be slid back, let them dip your hand into the silver goblet three-quarters full of that mint-and-barley water you wrote about last time, and extend your arm over a crisp linen while they dry your hand with hot air from the funnels of a model tanker done in gold: a queen of a blower.

Someone motions you now to the bottles, forty-odd of them, but restricts you at once: Anise?

You take, cowed a little. You never liked anise.

Mr. Malchios will not be back. The telex. . . .

Which doesn't help you at all, to stay unwanted, to go out the door holding an anise. You hover, brooding on a paragraph as if to hatch it. Black in the one, white in the other, panniers crammed the sideboard. Oval drupes await the teeth of as glittering (pyritic-glittering) a set as ever met in the Aegean. The donkey in Corinthian bronze has not moved. All obey here; all stand fast. The chafing-plate still— what was that sound? Not birds, not dogs; certainly not engines. A flash of voice throughout the villa, like a snow-shower in July. A stifled chortle, gone as soon as come.

Little you know, you who report. When a threadbare boy, lucky to have oil to pour on a crust, and blue with cold in winter, he thanked God and his parents for one room in the house. Quiet, bare, with a flaking ceiling, it shielded him, and he loved it. It had *capacity:* it somehow emptied him of himself when he stood in it or sat. It made him not exist, except as the kind of presence it exacted. A hotel, the Hermes, not his, stands now where that house did; but he has, to compensate, a quiet, bare chapel—also with a flaking ceiling —well away from the villa, blue within and without. The voice you heard is a recording timed to play all over the island every hour on the hour—except in the chapel. But it is from the chapel that it plays. It is the three-second tape of the only three seconds in his life in which he sang. In fact he made himself sing, and three seconds was all he could manage: not an alleluia, not an amen, but an ecstatic baritone note, anonymous and languid, all the same deliberate. It sounds like *nuse* or *nuze,* which are not words. Perhaps it is *news,* to you at any rate. To him, it is a memorandum of heaven; yet, I ask you, who the hell needs reminding?

Anise?

Already, though, you have gone, phut-phutting in the indigo launch across the channel, and he has changed from the double-breasted single-breasted into his guest-garb: azure cloak in default of honorary degrees conferred for redistributing half the oil in the world, a broad-striped fringed napkin beneath his chin, black velvet academic hat, chukka boots enclosing bare feet, gold-plated plain-glass spectacles for panache's sake, and the signet ring with the tiny cross inside it, PDM in sapphires without. He is merely rebelling against the carapace of serge or worsted in which all men talk and drink and negotiate and, sometimes, die. He doesn't fancy the fancy, he thinks, but, looking baroque now, he flaunts off, complaining about guests. And vanishes. Back he comes again, munching pheasant.

The guests, he tells me, waving his cloaked arm. At any moment. The entertainment? Quite ready, meaning the three Cases—genitive, dative and ablative—who are three girls under the table, each in attendance by the sitter's knees to soothe or provoke as he dines or merely to be passed scraps to, all depending on the quirks of the diner.

Call them *fellaheen,* I told him. Egyptian peasants!

Fellawhat? Ohno, this is casework not classwork. It has to be the lower cases—no names, no voices, no accusations. But possession, To or For, and By, why yes!

What about fricative, then? No fricatives?

No, no fricatives, that's too suggestive. After all, as you well know, the whole thing's only a blind.

I knew. They never see the girls' faces.

Ohno, he said when I first asked to discuss the matter with him, they volunteer. Never any shortage either. Some stay on in the farm, some go. They all get a silver bangle apiece when they go. What? Oh, that. They sweeten their mouths with crême-de-menthe frappé—but I've three special aides who see to all that. Can't we talk business instead? The telex. . . .

Now we know he lies. Lies sometimes.

Only three guests are coming this time; four if you count an unknown. Who, you ask? If I must I must. First of all, then, Sammy Zeuss, who has made a fortune in refrigerator cars; second or third, Mephos the attorney who owns most of Tungstone Eternal Filament; and, third or second, Tophel, surgeon-in-command at Athens Royal Infirmary—big with the lasers they say. Three wise guys you might call them. This Zeuss, he's as cosmopolitan as you can get, no more nationality than a bluefly; but he could take over a few countries right off if he had a mind to. And not all in South America either. Old Power-Power, they used to call him, except, now, he has this stiff neck and wears a seaman's collar he plugs in wherever he goes. The thing is, he can't ever look down or even around. But he looks round in the other sense: fat and loud, that's him, but more or less mammalian (if you're feeling generous). Mephos, now, he's friendly enemy to Tophel and Tophel the same to him. *Nick* Mephos it is, a clever talker.

He gets paid in ocean liners which he at once has moth-balled out of spite.

Give me an argument, he says always.

Why? you ask.

I need all I can get to keep me sharp. That's him.

Tophel they call Frein, short for Frankenstein. He both saves lives and spends them. The story goes that he's saved half a jawbone more than he's spent, but he claims he's just too advanced for people's expectations of surgery. Anyway, three business friends you might call them, who meet to gossip, have a game or two of cards or chess, a snack and a beverage. Or they sort a few papers through, end and begin a few people's careers. Not much chance of anything serious coming up—not usually. But on this occasion the edibles, like the three Cases, are a blind, like Malchios' habit of setting peahen shells under a common hen; they're becaficos, really, rolled in spiced egg yolk!

First to arrive, I ask him if he will make a formal announcement.

To whom? he asks. At so small a gathering? Hardly the world at large. (If the world is at large, from whom has it escaped? But he goes on.) That would be indelicate. But perhaps a toast, a sly, swift ritual befitting. I'll see.

And then he goes on about how he has been neglecting his house in Paris, his converted destroyer three hundred feet long with a catapult seaplane astern, his New York penthouse full of rare books, his bit of the Bahamas, his horses, his hotels, his ex-wives. . . .

But not your fleet, I say. Not your standing. You stand for a lot.

For answer he invites me to play chess on the board of terebinth wood. The pieces are of crystal mounted on gold and silver coins. He opens, KBP to KBP 3 and I make the traditional counter, the one ensuring my defeat on my eighteenth move. He enjoys my deliberate inadvertences, so why deprive him? I am not short of easy victories. But halfway through our game he stops, pinching his king as if gas is escaping from the head, and asks:

Remember when? He sounds like a terebinth plank creaking; plank of the turpentine tree, tree in hoarse pain.

When you were going to sell out to Mephos? Tophel talking you into it. And he—one of them—asked what you'd do with the money and you said *Buy a new fleet to compete with you.* Oh, I remember when very well.

It was Mephos asked. I was nervous then, but I still don't know why although I do know why I was nervous when I asked the oil companies to charter tankers as of then not even built. Way back. But now—look at this hand. See it shake? Why, a blind man could see it shake from way across this room.

Or, I tell him, from one end of the *Fortunata* to the other; *that* far. One man should not weigh two hundred thousand dead weight tons, or a billion, or whatever. (His hand is as still as his king.)

After that we finish the game in silence. Then we talk of the *Fortunata*, beloved yacht, which they all remember for a dance floor that doubles as a swimming pool, and not for the Renoirs, Utrillos, Van Goghs—Van Everybodys he has since removed anyway.

You could hang a Dufy there, but not those. Not on *that* boat.

The *Fortunata?* I ask. She's not a boat, she's your wife, your true one. Never answers back. Thirty-odd hands to hold her on course. She eats money, but the rest of her behavior is temperate, obedient and clean. Except that one time, I'm taking a snooze below decks and *zump*, she swings left or somehow wrong and I am felled by some well-up-holstered girl who comes tumbling out of a closet, stoned from some day-before-yesterday conviviality, I guess. Knocks me senseless and lies there, quiet on the rug, dead from the ovaries up.

That was Mrs. Malchios the fourth, he says. Then I married the vessel. Now, to matters of more importance: what have you brought me? We're doing things back to front— the gifts come first, not the talking.

Better late than too soon, I tell him. Something small. A small gift makes a point, whereas a large one obliterates the giver.

I didn't ask for another tanker. I only—

Give it to him, I tell myself, while he still wears that smile of petulant jocosity. I give it, a Book of Common Prayer micro-photographed to $\frac{1}{262}$ its usual size, smaller than an aspirin and readable only by ultra-violet light.

Oh, he says, freezing his smile, What? I can't make it out.

Don't worry; just don't lose it.

A taunt? he says. A prank?

A puzzle, rather. Just don't lose it. Actually, it's a prayer book. Put it near your heart, you'll never be able to read it.

Ah, then: a talisman!

But he doesn't understand; of course he doesn't. All I say is: It holds within it a certain certainty with which I am acquainted.

Will I really need it?

Where *you* are going, no. But I myself shall need to know you have it, even though you cannot read it. It's a gesture.

Pretending to understand, he thanks me, and we are semi-genially sampling the truffles when Tophel is ushered in, long-armed, tall, stooping as if to charge at you with his eyebrows, these resembling woolly caterpillars stranded on his face by some fierce wind and unable to make contact with each other above the bulbous nose. The hand I shake feels like a fungus, looks rotten. Is.

You grow, he tells me, turning at once to Malchios, whereas you, Py, decrease. Not 3.14blahblah5 etc. but 3.14 blahblah4 or so. By that little. Because the mouse has more surface for each cubic inch of volume than, say, the polar bear, it loses heat faster. I'll come to mice later (with a lazy flicker of his tongue). The polar bear, on the other hand, has a large volume producing heat, but a small surface to lose it through. See? Of course you do. Mouse meet polar bear! Sorry, who could help it, looking at you both. I'm fretful as it is, I've just done a plastic jawbone. Almost forgot to hinge it—I was thinking of our festivity to come.

He sits, grins over toward the table.

The livestock? His euphemisms are always gross.

In position, Malchios answers, wincing. Nice as pie.

Tophel bubbles up and over, his laugh like gas bulging from the surface of hot oil and viscously spilling free. He has no paunch, only a faint meniscus of the thorax. His teeth clatter, not loose but out of tune.

Perfect, he drones. Like the golden section. ¾ is better than $2\frac{2}{7}$ any day. Less crowding underfoot.

Malchios corrects him: Three over three, you mean; I'm having no part of it, not of that. I've speeches to make, thoughts to master.

Tophel rises, kicks viciously at the table's low-hanging cloth as he passes it (there is no sound from within, no movement), fetches a square box from the alcove where a Renoir hangs, and sprints back down the room with it.

Offering, he snaps, as requested. Must *I* open it? He must. He hands a soccer ball to Malchios with both hands, cradling it.

Listen. Hear?

A small handbell seems to be ringing.

A blind-children's ball, he says. They play soccer, and by the bell find the ball. I'll tell you something else: they never collide, and *they* don't wear bells. The ball is campanological; the children are not. They must have sonar, I suppose. One day I must build a child with a bell in him: a bellboy! Ha. Sorry, I've only just finished doing a plastic jaw and I nearly forgot the hinge. Nearly didn't *fulc* the *rum*. Nearly didn't—

Thank you, says Malchios formally, for a ball. He rolls it gently across the carpet. It cannons against the fire-irons, chinking untidily with the impact, and stops.

Prayers, he goes on. And a bell-ball. Perhaps Mephos will bring me a scepter.

Hardly, I tell him. A dungfork's more likely for Greeks receiving gifts. *A* Greek. Smart minds like his have black heads.

Tophel interrupts: He means like hobnail liver. Hideous to view; Lady Liquor's legacy, best seen in technicolor.

Pardon, I manage finally to say. I meant his mind; the words are separate.

And we drink, a golden smoky nectar of a Scotch called Lochor, and our tongues wag like dogs' tails, our temples begin to flame.

Malchios resumes: If a synthetic man ate a piece of plastic, would that make him a cannibal?

At once Tophel, waving his empty glass, clarifies the problem, giggling.

No, only a dyspeptic. Only humans are made from human flesh, but we make all kinds of goop from plastic. DEQ?

Oh, I say, agreeing. Man is special, all right; synthetic man isn't.

Malchios blinks; or, rather, as one ought to say of an alert but gloomy Croesus, he nictitates: It's still the same idea—if you'll pardon the expression—in the mind of God. The same form.

By God it is not! This is not Tophel, not Malchios, but Mephos, thundering across the thirty yards from the two-stepped turn into the banqueting hall. It comes again, that stifled burst of voice throughout the villa, as if a baritone cuckoo flicked into action but almost at once failed; not the same as before simply because it is this one and not the one previous.

Wind in whose chimney? Mephos is asking. Who burped?

A truffle rising, Malchios tells him. Rising at thoughts of a book of prayers and a ball-bell of uncommon tinkle. My gorge rising. What have *you* brought me?

Brought? Brought is brutish. I offer you an idea, not a knife. Mark, I ask you, its scope. *Why,* the wise child asks the gas-station attendant, *are you scattering this white powder everywhere? To drive the elephants away. I can't see any elephants. Then it must be good powder.* The form of which is: misattribute the visible in order to make the logically invisible into the pseudologically absent. The relevance of which is, Imagine enough and have everything. Scatter atheism, it drives the gods away. I can't see any gods. It must be good atheism, then.

He downs his first glass of Lochor, scowling as if it were mouthwash.

On the other hand, I say, let the attendant answer: *To make the gods appear.* Then, when the wise child can see none, he observes what prudent gods they must be, not falling for a cheap trick like that. Something out of nothing instead of nothing out of nothing. Faith, not fraud, like communion wafer, like kosher, like making cows sacred.

Like! I've heard you all before, sighs Malchios. I believe none of you. You come to eat, or so I thought: a special occasion, or so I thought. And you bring me an unreadable book, a clanging ball, and a piece of stale riddling rubbish. Secrets, novelty and fraud. I'd have more joy with powdered parrots' beaks, a ton of incinerated frogspawn, and a mendacity gauge. Let us, for my sake, move to the table. Settle in, gentlemen, be soothed, be broad.

Ha, grins Tophel, revenge for having eaten a lifetime's cunt.

Mephos glowers: Standard plumbing I see. I must say, I weary of this. But he sits. We all sit, produce and strengthen, turbid below, affable above, all except Malchios. Comfortable with our Cases, after a few bouts of shuffling our declensions, we become expansive and ready to tell the stories that are to strengthen Malchios in his decision. Tophel has oiled his leer anew. Mephos, the short and slight, the bald and bony, wrinkles the top right-hand corner of his mouth—a twitch in fixity—such is his glee. Malchios, druidic and forbearing, like a minority candidate awaiting a recount, motions at a hovering servant. I, I look across the room to where I am wired in, forty feet of insulated cord electrifying my seaman's collar. I cannot look down, so I swivel my eyeballs low.

Oh, the sudden shouts!

Mound! cries Tophel.

Droong-ah! Mephos.

Lobos! I cry, not to be outdone, lobos, lobos. Malchios winces. I still cannot look down.

You could, being you, Tophel begins quietly, have given us any gastronomic solecism—baby bees in chocolate or smoked and sliced porbeagles. Ants, caterpillars, grasshoppers; roach fricassee or toad *à la bonne femme*. But you give us ourselves *à la bonne bouche*—make tidbits of us, if you'll forgive the shift in anatomy.

Wait and see, Malchios tells him. Actually, it's an austere little meal—the meal proper. Not quite the funeral-baked meats, but not quite not either.

In come the white-jacketed, white-gloved waiters, one to each of us as usual, to serve dormice, sausages and olives, then proffering the chalice of almonds in cream. Sour cream too.

That reminds me, says Tophel, troughing at once with his brow low over the plate, his skinny hand on the long stem of his wineglass, did I say how splendid you look, compared with us in—what would you call suits like these? In our business best, our duty duds. No matter. To my tale: it has to do with one Caller Herring, a popular entertainer: a pop star you might have heard about. No? It's just as well I'm here then, isn't it?

Pop singer, muses Malchios. An incurable case of pelvic blurt—no, not quite that. I mean—

Pop singer, as I said. He once spent ten thousand dollars on an embroidered coat, gold leaf and pearls. A jazz Joseph, nearly as rich as you, Py. One day, however, overcome by conscience or, as I choose to think, buoyed up by a new notion for fraud, he called the newspapers in and announced he was going to spend a night at an institute for the destitute and disabled.

Why, asks Mephos, don't you say straight out he'd decided to go to college and have done with it?

Where was that, says Malchios, a bit giddy. Where was that? Hey, ice pick, where *was* it?

Exactly where it was. It is the general in the particular I'm concerned with today. I read minds, I do not program them. To resume: he lies there on his bare mattress after the standard breakfast of sausage and egg, and tells the crowded room, most of them standing in awe, *Boy, I've done a million things in this life, but never nothing like this. I feel good!* That afternoon he opened a sale for the institute, mostly clothes and furniture, and with a kissing booth manned— I'm sorry, I've only just finished a plastic pelvis on a virgin and I almost forgot to structure the life-tunnel—*staffed*, I mean, by honeys from the high-kick lines in the local palace of varieties. Of course there was more than kissing; they had to burn the booth afterward, wood, canvas and all. Then there was a wheelchair-smashing match between a team of cripples under fifty and a team of able-bodied indigents over fifty. Two teams, two chairs. Now, neither chair was demolished, but there were three heart-attacks out of ten teammates. The side with only one attack won, I forget which. Caller Herring never got over it; he gave up performing, signed his royalties away to institutes from Hong Kong to Murmansk, and shut himself away in a tenement. His one pair of shoes he kept in a box on a high shelf lest they wear out. The bread, brought to him daily by his despairing agent, he used to feed the mice. In fact he bred mice, but—his only indulgence—selectively ate the newborn ones alive; a Chinese custom, you know. He turned off the heat, gave up soap and self-respect, and soon there was nothing but mice and the three slices of bread the agent slid under the door to him daily. One day, this agent decided not to deliver the bread; but Caller Herring endured—one day, two, five, ten, They broke the door down, found him quieter than he'd ever been known to be, surrounded by mice he'd refrained from eating, all gamboling over his trunk and head with uncontemptuous familiarity. Next thing, Caller Herring is a martyr. Long lines of fans outside the hospital. I am called in, I myself. I operate. I—what do you think I did?

Malchios rumbles, mops at his mouth with crisp napkin, hunches forward in his azure cloak and rolls between his finger and thumb the fringe of his striped bib:

Something plastic, or am I being obvious? You inserted—

A plastic mouse-trap? Never. Guffawing.

No, but fib and fantasy are close together today, zwei-backed. If you broke all the mirrors in the world, you'd halve the population: for today, anyway. That sort of thing, that's what I mean. Well, then, you saved his life, I suppose. Intravenous feeding? A plastic tube? No? Let someone else guess.

Tophel groans. Let them then. Let them.

You turned him, sneers Mephos, indicating the chalice of almonds-in-cream, into mousse!

Nowhere near. Again that ghost of baritone song. No echo.

You dismembered him, I myself say against my will. And powdered some of the bones, left fragments to be found where fragments usually are found, in the Moustier cave in France. You made a Mousterian of him: a paleolithic survival.

Not that (oh how his mouth twists with menace), nor a Martian either.

Of course I happen to know, having gone into these things a little, that Martians resemble sea-squirts, who absorb enormous quantities of vanadium from the element they live in: two hundred and eighty thousand times the concentration in the water itself. I knew he couldn't do *that*.

What then? I ask mock-diffidently. What on earth?

He answers at speed: He lacked for mouse? Right? He liked mouse? Right? I fed him Mouse-Diet 41, which is forty-five parts wholemeal flour, forty Sussex ground oats, eight fish meal, one dried yeast, three skim milk, one cod-liver oil and one common salt. You make it up into mouse cubes, into which I put an extra cod-liver oil to keep him from breeding. I have him now, in a two-story cage which is really a bare apartment with a ladder and a nest-box on each level. He can be lifted by the tail—not too near the tip of course—and restrained by keeping the tail between two fin-gers, or finger and thumb if you like to squeeze. Just like a mouse in fact. Truth told, I have him permanently attached to a block and pulley, just for disciplining, you see. A tiny infibulum collar holds him fast but not too tight. A quick yank on the rope and he soon comes to heel.

Oh, prepuceterously self-condomed, gasps Mephos.

It's better than descending into the cage with gauntlets on, Tophel tells him. And having to touch. Once a week I let in about five hundred mice to him, and he has to fight them off. They can smell the Diet 41 on him. But kill as many as he may, stamping on them and hammering with his fists— more active than he ever was when he popped—he never eats mouse. I've effected, wouldn't you say, a cure?

Couldn't say, says Malchios. But I've been counting. The parts of the Mouse Diet don't add up to a hundred; ninety-nine only. Why?

Just to make you think I was denying him something.

A minus one per cent? Pure myth?

You can't feed people myth.

Or mice.

But you can feed man to mouse, mouse to man, mouse to mouse, man to man. It's the minus one per cent that makes him want to keep on living. He knows he's missing something.

The unknown quantity, right?

The unknown *quality*, don't be so materialistic. Look at our friend here: he knows the difference.

I do indeed, sickened by what has been happening under the table. Always, I have been allergic to my own seed; carried within, it behaves as gold in rock strata, but once out it burns and rots and lacerates and macerates, oh—

See, laughs Tophel, I've made him jumpy just saying it. He shows promise, does he not? Minus that minus men are nothing.

So, says Malchios, in a dead, blue voice: Caller Herring. What do his fans and admirers think now? What, if anything, do they know?

A seven-day wonder has no eighth. As far as they're concerned, he's gone for good. Excepting that I have him for quite private experiments in public taste, his mind gone, his body fading; but sufficiently a man to keep the data human and enough of a mouse to—well, it's obvious. In the long run I'll convert him into a waltzing mouse, a special breed. It's only a matter of upsetting his sense of balance, so I keep one of his ears crammed with soft cheese. Then I'll train him to run up and down the clock, but erratically. Cut off his tail. Set mountains disemboweling themselves to vomit him up. Make him town and country, a mouse of parts, a man-trap. Then give him back to the writers, their fantasy made real. I'll prove Whitman's boast that a mouse is enough to stagger sextillions of infidels.

I smile. I like your phrase—I like *that* phrase: sextillions of infidels.

You'll soon be using it as your own.

It's partly mine in a way anyway. I wouldn't like to be responsible for *all* that Whitman said and did; but I do have a leaning or two that way—on Sundays usually.

He shrugs languorously, like a model taking up her pose. I found Caller Herring. I keep him. You may be right— I mean, finding's keeping; isn't that what you implied?

No, I meant sponsoring's being responsible.

Now Malchios, as the *pâté de canard à l'orange* is served and Tophel wriggles in his chair a vigorous second time (no doubt shoehorning the subtabulary silent nymphs), stares at the blue ceiling and asks the question he is entitled to:

All very well, Tophel, my friend. Amusing in its way. But the meaning?

Ha, you've stopped using verbs! quips Mephos. It's a sign you're weakening. There's a big boob resting on my knee this minute, and no mistake. Am *I* weakening? A man must prevail. Why, which of us hasn't woken somehow at odds with the need to go on living? Well, not so much the need— since you pull faces at the word—rather the unquestioning habit of going on living. The unquestioned habit. We wake,

sluggish, out of mental joint, dazzled although the light is
dull, hung-over without having overdrunk, at least one eyelid enslaved by a faint but regular twitch, a renegade muscle
in the thigh pulsing nervously, even when there has been no
eyestrain, no undue exertion, not even stress. Man *is* partly
a mouse, yes. But he is also a miracle. Hourly, billions of
neutrinos rain through his body, and he knows nothing of
them. Hot from its very core, they skim right through the
sun, and some of them through him. Yet he withstands them,
gasping to catch his commuter train, seeding his lawn, de-
capping a three-minute egg, ill at ease in minor matters yet
beautifully adapted for the universe as a whole. Let's not
grumble.

So each of us sitting there works hard to put on a non-
grumbling face. Exasperated at being so lucky in the universe,
we close our minds to grievance and attack the food.

At a signal from Malchios the metronome is brought in
and set going on the table between two empty silver candle-
sticks. I look down my nose and see the finger slowly sagging
and ascending in a mime of languor. The table humps it up
suddenly into my full view, tilts and then, as Malchios slaps
one hand hard down, settles again, harder to see. Mephos goes
on, orating in time with the click-clack. Tophel closes his
eyes—the merest movement since at the best of times his eyes
are no more than slits. I fuss with the cord of my collar,
pulling in some slack from behind my chair and coiling that
round my arm. As ever, peering down, I feel like a fisherman
who watches the horizon while reeling in his line.

I give you, drones Mephos in his sway, parentheses only:
the extinct and the future; none of your pop super-novas.
The extant you have all contended with and successfully so,
even if only because you thought you had no chance at all
and contended out of defiance. Even you, Sammy. In No-
vember 1930, on Glacier Island in Alaska, they found the
skeletons of several huge, mighty-snouted beasts twenty-odd
feet in length with heads five feet long, the snouts only a

little shorter, and with tons of fur-covered flesh still attaching. Not a single expert could identify them. Such events, such creatures, are commoner than we think. Think, in fact, of the Cape May monster, fifteen tons and more, examined and pronounced unique. What's in a name? Or a species? Answer: always more than meets the eye. Take the La Brea and Carpenteria tar pits in California—not that far—packed as they are with skeletons of elephants, man-high swine, mastodons, rhinoceroses, camels, super-bison, saber-toothed tigers —and none of these more than a few thousand years old. What was it struck them down, and all at once, not that long ago? A cataclysm, you might say. Some shuddering of God's hand. A cosmic snarl. Stellar snafu. A bit of the divine evil eye. Was that force the same force that enables us to withstand the neutrinos?

He pounds his fist on the table, making the metronome jump in mid-swing. Was it essential for the mantle of the Earth to skid and slip round, shoving one half of the temperate zone into the Arctic and half the Arctic into the temperate zone? Damn it, the Alaskan and Siberian muck—goop, gunk, call it what you will—*ought not to have in it* the dismembered, pulverized remaining mess of lions, tigers, horses, oxen, buffaloes and squirrels that it does. And when the ice melts, productive of a stench whose visible greenness cloys and shreds the lungs it hits, you've got the biggest midden in the Milky Way, from Nome to Wrangel Island. A mantle of decomposed or whole-frozen wrong animals embedded in gravel, earth, silt, sand and the frog-spawn, moss-dung, arsenical green magma of a trillion trees!

He stops, aware of his excess. The metronome clack-quacks, dividing and redividing the air in the room. I thought I heard again that burst of baritone song during his tirade, but I couldn't be sure. Perhaps he'd forced a latent echo out, like something out of the very muck-mantle that set him wallowing among words.

Again I feel that table cant, making Tophel scowl and

fumble. Then it rights itself, feeling, as I pad a hand across the cloth, no longer flat but having a faint convexity on which the silver, the plates, the glasses repose stably as before, and yet at minute variance with their former sit on the flash-white linen. A degree muted, but vehemence returning with his every syllable, Mephos resumes, casting a worried look at the table.

Introducing now, gentlemen, the Beresovka Mammoth found at the end of the last century on the bank of the Beresovka River. In Siberia, during the spring, by a peasant whose name I do not recall. So I will join in in your fictional game. Kolya, let's call him. At first he thinks he is looking at two cannonballs fired in pair and embedded in the weakening freeze of the riverbank. But no: too small. No movement in the black double glaze of those eyes that never looked on omnibus or troika even. He advances, his ax raised, and inspects the head, the bone of which has been partially uncovered by ravenous wolves. No need to kill it, then. So he hacks off the tusks and hauls them to the trading post at Yakutsk where he sells them to a Cossack. End of Kolya's part—I'm sorry: my hero is the mammoth. Now the Cossack, being a law-abiding fellow, reports the mammoth to one of the Czar's officials (as he is required to do), and before long there is a scientific team out at the Beresovka building a shelter over the carcass. They build a bonfire, thaw out the flesh and begin dissecting, after which they drag the chunks out into the cold again and take them to the trans-Siberian railway, their destination the National Academy of Science in St. Petersburg.

What I have not told you, he continues, lowering his voice with histrionic slyness, is that the mammoth, when this Kolya found it, was standing up. Erect. Its flesh was good and, apart from the depredations of the wolves, intact.

Again, swift as a bird diving, comes that snatch of voice, noticed by me only.

Will you stop coughing? he asks me.

I am, I am.

Its lips were hard as rock, mark you, but fresh buttercups were frozen on them, as well as packed rigid and unswallowed in the mouth, and intact in the stomach. The mammoth, whatever hit it, had no time to adjust—no time to digest them. All processes—biting, swallowing, decomposition—ceased in the same instant. Imagine, I ask you, the instant freeze of five tons of erect animal, the only damage it sustained being a fractured hipbone. So fast it didn't even tumble over, so fast it hadn't time to gulp, fast almost as light in a lazy mood, changed in a trice from red-blooded herbivore into a boulder-hard bunker, unwarned, uncomplicated, unvarying, undamaged—

Unless, cries Malchios, his dark face draining, unless you stop. . . . This is too much. At table. Horror stories are one thing, but your kind of rhetorical sentimentality is another. I'd rather hear about someone accused of computercide or being fined for spraying his lawn with heavy water.

Tophel is already checking Malchios' pulse, cautioning him, flapping a chastising hand at Mephos. Again the table wobbles.

Yes, for God's sake, I say, feeling redundant, don't go on. Some other time.

Very well, he says, five fingers in mouth like a parody of Pan with pipes, Give me an argument instead.

Argument? Why an argument?

I'm warm. I'm going. I'm wound up tight, I wouldn't like all this adrenalin to go to waste.

Nor I this, groans Malchios, encompassing his whole body in a two-handed sweep. Change of subject, please. After all, this isn't just *any* occasion.

At your disposal, I say, grinning. For once. Propose something, will you, and I'll. . . . Animal, vegetable or mineral? Clap-flapping my fat mouth.

Metaphysical: something to keep my *philotimo* intact. Huh? Oh, self-respect, something like that. Damn that pendulum!

He captures the finger at the weight and snicks it behind the flange at the top, then snaps shut the triangular door, hooks in the tiny hook. Tophel, head back, has surrendered to the process below-table. Mephos is pouting, fazed.

It's OK, he says, I'm OK. It *was* the wrong choice of story.

Mammoths, sneers Malchios. Who needs mammoths?

I do for one. Mephos is getting shrill. What, if I may get sort of literary, was the mammoth doing at that latitude? In that posture? Flash-frozen by what flash? What the hell do *we* know? It happened, that's all. Earth's mantle skidded around a bit, like a condom on a sailor.

Suddenly—what with crouching invisible *filles de joie* at our feet, recurrent breaks of recorded song, a micro-prayer-book, a blind-ball, a tale of elephant powder, not to mention Caller Herring-Mouse, Kolya the mammoth-tusk trader, a metronome, plastic jaws and pelvises, earth's mantle slipping, flash-freeze by pentecostal winds of a hundred below zero at a hundred miles an hour and more, and then *philotimo!*—I am helplessly laughing, asweat in my collar, limp-loined under the table, irate and spongily tolerant, impatient but somehow willing to onlook forever: my being irate shames me into unnecessary extra tolerances; my impatience is that of a born listener, doting on what happens next only because I know what happens last. Stiff-necked, unknowable and bloat, I think of Guy de Maupassant living by the sea and, one morning after a storm, waking to find a boat washed up into his front garden. I never quite believe what is there. Boats don't just blow in, they—

Numbing cerulean light of electric pain, they—

Desist, deist: give credit where credit is due, even when impersonating. A Boat Cast-up Doesn't Eschatologically

Faze God; He, Incorporating Jib, Keel, Landfall, Master-
minds Noachic Omens, Plots Quasars Routing Stellar Telem-
etry, Underwrites Vessels, Waves, X-rays Yahoo Zero.

Playing me at my own game?

And beating you at it, which is more than you can do at
mine.

May I continue?

As long as you may; when you may not, you will not.

Amen.

Men, indeed.

There is one person yet to arrive: an unknown, as I said;
not a luncheon guest but a man with a heavy role to play
all the same. Meanwhile, I have to make my own narrative
offering on the moraine of mouse and mammoth: after fable
without point and fact without meaning, what? The least I
can do is an exercise in *philotimo:* the ghostwriter in search
of God. In a low, ashamed voice, I tell them what is coming,
but they are too apathetic to stop me, so now I unilaterally
speak out, off the record, half-mouse, half-mammoth, half-
breed, whiling away the time between the bream filets and
the lamb and palm-tree shoots, with one Mafios expected.

Hold on a minute, though, I say to Mephos, we've only
had the first of your parentheses: the extinct. What about the
other? You wouldn't want to leave us dangling, would you
now?

Malchios preparing to be livid.

Tophel crowing.

Mephos raises both arms and droops his hands as if cupping
the heads of invisible children:

Parenthesis-smenthesis! A day will come—ha, you can
almost always say that—when the volcanic gas from some
misbehaving volcano goes blasting up into the stratosphere—
steam, rock, lava and dust—and gets so lovely cold up there,
say two-fifty below, it comes down like doomsday, as rain
and snow that last for years, blocking the sun out, setting off

seaquakes, landslides, hurricanes and tidal waves, puffing the
species off the globe at hundreds of miles an hour. There'll be
a death-shiver you couldn't even record in milliseconds, a
fast cold incineration of all the lungs in all the chests, eyes
and skin turning into instant crystal, the flesh as hard as
termite hills, and then—woosh, off, wafting men and elephants and buses and skyscrapers clear across continents and
seas until all you have is a seismic, racing sludge of bits and
pieces, a confetti that's going to last half a million years. The
wind rips the ships out of the ocean and then hurls the ocean
after them in great spewing acres, and all you've got is fish-
scales and bits of skull and kneecap, mashed-up remnants of
piers and freeways and massive hangars all pulverizing as
they fly, with all the blood huffed and puffed into a nothing
vapor, all mind annihilated, all seeing hearing feeling ended,
no Noah, no burning bush, no doves, no time-lapse, no warning, no time for good-by. No time even.

The table is rocking again. Whose knee? Whose—I see
Mephos fall into an incongruous calm, faint sweat on the
sides of his nose, his hands in his lap invisibly. Malchios, in a
trance, says nothing; but Tophel, giggling as he begins,
comments on principle, as always:

Beta plus, my friend. A fine workout. Except—you don't
mind if I specify an except?—I think the freeze comes *after*
the hundred-year blow, if you'll pardon the misleading sexual
connotation suggestive of a lazy mammoth.

He needles on, but Malchios has become a waxwork.
Mephos is stone. The table stills (diameter ten feet I guess
without peering down). No trace even in the echoes of that
voice. Before us, the lamb and palm-tree shoots go cold,
virtually untouched. No servant comes to remove the dishes.
In short, the meal and its rituals founder amid the responses
of his guests to what Malchios is shortly to do.

And it is still my turn, I who came first. No matter of
timing, I am sure, but as I inhale and begin two of the
bodyguards in black sweaters and loose track-suit type pants

escort into the room a man whose face is hidden by a far from cheap mask composed of routine, unmemorable features—say, the fourth or fifth or sixth face in a line of athletes boarding a jet in last evening's newspaper. They sit him in an armchair at some distance from us, give him anise or Lochor and a glass pipette to sip through and go. Mafios at last.

Red herrings and mice, mammoths and cataclysm, I begin, cheerily. How down to earth. I too could splurge—clinch these preliminaries with a verbal carnival all my own, all anarchy and din, barbaric and infernal, phantasmagorically monstrous in color, motion, shape, sight and sound, looking down on the crowd from some showman's platform. I too could acquaint you with the old, longstanding penny pageant you shrug at, flash the banner of a billion snafus, turn hubris upside down and sneer: 'Tis all chattering monkeys on TV antennae; grown-up dropouts whirling on a carousel; buffoons at buffoons grimacing; writhing, screaming; hurdy-gurdy grinders, fiddle-scrapers, food-salters, tub-thumpers, trumpet-blowers, albinos, painted Indians, dwarfs; the Horse of Knowledge spurred to death; nothing but learned pigs, stone-eaters, fire-swallowers, giants, ventriloquists, headless twins and talking birds: a very parliament of monsters vomiting and redevouring the same perpetual pabulum of trash, and all reduced to one identity by differences that have no law, no meaning, and—God forbid—no end. Please lower head when entering, that's what it says above the cages—but enough.

More boredom, whines Tophel. May I please have your phone number?

EMPyrean 2199 or 2299. Sorry, new style: 367-21—

Yes. Tophel forces his voice low and stares beyond me into nothingness or something. Why isn't somebody eating? Hey.

I resume my prelude with teasing affability.

Back to man now, if I may. Take his nether monuments,

his below-stairs obelisks: not what he lifts his head to survey with a mounting flush of pride, but what he squats on in order to survive. My late researches into the downward style— just a little painful head-lowering, using Polaroid with flash— have brought to light, literally so (for some of these whey-stations are painfully besmirched), Luxor, Cadet, Glenwall, New Compton, Bidet Combo, Madeira, Afwall, Devoro, Afton, Tribor, Madbrook, Siaeto, Valvo, Modernus, Glenco, Instanto, Corbo, Neolo, Madual, Margate, Trojan, Charmer, Camel, Champlain, Placid, Cayuga, Bolton, Trylon, Rockwall, Downing, Welland, Penryn, Brooklands, Trent, Kenwyn, Kingston, Stratton, Sifton, Suffield, Anglesey, Angleboro, Angle, Swift, Thurlow, Tacoma, Auburn, Quieta—

Pox you for boring us! cries Malchios, flushed.

Stonehenge is mine, I say, and continue with Sylenta, Andes, Trailer, Texas, Sanus, Monroe, Toronto, Newark and Saigon, all done in a Leadless Glaze. I count three presidents, eight boroughs, two generals, seven rivers, one cathedral, six fishes, four English-sounding counties and five misnoming allusions to ancient civilizations for which I was once prepared to grant temporary credit. But of this statuary for posterity, all so lamely named, neither lyrical nor crass, neither sounding nor anonymous, what am I to—

Lies! screams Tophel, at maximum pitch. Lies, lies! Bedpans all. How dare you slander us?

The bedpan, I reassure him, is another species altogether, coming under the heading of Chamber. These, I vow, are flush, devices for concealing evidence. Oubliettes, that's what. Whited, cisterned, sepulchers.

Malchios pouts; a sign of life. Flush? Flush from hiding?

Hide and go seek, I tell him. The proof of mortality, that's what it amounts to. Myself, I have no need, being allergic to my own effluvia, of course. Other species, other faeces. By the way, that's Mafios over there, isn't it?

Without looking at the man in the mask, Malchios raps

out a bizarre series of words: Malchios' Autonomously Functioning Identical-Occipital Surrogate.

We all relax; he knows what he is doing. We had all begun to wonder. He's going through with it. Getting back into my stride I give it to them straight.

This ghost writer, once upon a time, after a lifetime consecrated to living by proxy, goes out to find something for himself. Almost anything. No longer such verbally incapable but biographically juicy Punches and Judys as Odysseus Careen, the retired sea captain who has a ship's wheel mounted on the foot of his landbound bed and twirls the spokes with his toes through portholes cut in the bed linen; the renowned chef, Luca, *fils*, who confessed to an American Air Force lieutenant, who supplied him with a crate of it clandestinely in 1946, that the secret of his most delectable dishes is in fact Worcestershire sauce; Maremma Yale, a madam somewhere between notorious and infamous, who finds herself continually and inexplicably mailing parcels of keys to the wardens of all known jails; Otis Omsk, the grounded Doukhobor astronaut who, finding nothing freakish in himself, builds a Sarasota home in the shape of a capsule and wears an oxygen mask all day in case of accidents; the war hero, all orders and crosses, legions and stars—Colonel Duke Ostrogotham—whose remaining ambition is to play polo with a beheaded goat as they do in Siberia, only no one will join in with him, and he lives in a wheel chair anyway; Newt Areemayhew, the archcriminal who nails his annoyers to the floors of their homes, a six-inch nail through each hand, each foot (or to doors if the floors aren't wood); Banquo Cody, screen lover, male, who loves boys before their voices break and in extremis resorts good-humoredly to a goose, first trapping its head in a drawer; Hermes Gene Digamma who, after years of hirsute incertitude, paid for the operation to become a truer self called Sappho Gide; the heavyweight champion, Vince Makron, who sleeps with a Nuremberg Egg in each hand to keep his fists from bunching; the LSD hallucinate and former gubernatorial candidate, pseudonym Peace Factor, who builds meditation tents from green celery sticks and composes Pindaric odes to pisscutters, bums and burning Buddhists; and a jazz trumpeter called Eustace Marne who leaves his horn to soak overnight in beer. And more.

Such excursions done with, he one Ubu S. Mnemo, Inc., having become his own company for tax reasons, lights out for Finland by mistake, there reads about Tibet and the *yetis*, and then, on one memorable day, misreading *yeti* for *neti* (Hindu for *Not This*, i.e., God), identifies lord, master and prime mover with Abominable Snowman, correct in that God is never anything that non-God thinks God is, but wrong philologically. So he is both right and wrong by accident—a very human position, if I may say so. Off he goes, resolved to find the substantial holy ghost he calls *yeti:* none of your Tibetan butter statues, but—

With a book in mind? asks Malchios, who seems quieter.

A book, I say. But first and foremost a presence which once found proves ineluctable.

For once tardy in facetiousness, Tophel giggles: To lay a ghost, isn't that the idiom? So it might have to be an abominable thing after all. The phantom fornication, the first and last.

You get worse, says Mephos. By the minute. Brain decay, whereas all I am is gloomy.

I try again, realizing I have to tell it quickly, and then the gruesome rest of the business can be got on with: no sentimentality, no rhetoric, no faltering, but just the word of command from Malchios, then duty.

Ubu S. Mnemo, then, Inc., hitches his way toward Asia, remembering none of the routine conveyances such as Volks, Chevvy and Fiat but only a white-sprayed single-decker bus overpainted in psychedelic floral, one Mini-Moke which reminds him of an elongated dislocated jeep (no sides at all), a Honda driven by a physics Ph.D. from Stanford who keeps quoting John Cage at him, and the animals—an ox, spindly with murrain, hauling the sort of tumbrel only the to-be-guillotined deserve (Ubu the leftwinger); a mule, smelling of seaweed and heather, athwart a vertiginous track near Srinagar; and a low, rough-coated horse given to human-sounding sighing. Delayed a week in Katmandu by hippies who have come to smoke, rent a room for fifteen cents a day and spin the prayerwheels on their way to cash their international money orders, he goes in around past Everest, into Sikkim where he learns to say Kinchinjunga ("Five Treasures of the Great Snows") as *Kangchendzenga*, this to become his marching rhythm: left-right, then with an extra thrust of the left foot on *dzeng*. And so to Lhasa.

Damn me, says Malchios, if you won't eat. . . .

I stare at Mafios, who sits like something carved.

Have some Lochor, then, says Malchios. Here.

We all partake, Malchios included; but not Mafios. I am very much afraid we shall get no further; afraid that, in a showy bid for their attention, I will sway from my purpose and get Ubu S. Mnemo Inc. making abominable snowmen of successive mountains, discovering face and physique where, in fact, there is neither, but only rock-face and rock-flank that happened to break or cool that way. If I am not careful he will read into the frost the coarse-pocked brilliant skin of the *yeti*, take crevasses for dental interstices, find the magnesium glare of the light aimed at him by monstrous eyes, chip off snowcrust as crumbs from some giant mouth, prong his ice pick up rock nostrils, exclaim in turn at cragteeth gleaming high on a spire in anoxic light, white brows of icicles riding near his own chilled face, a wordless voice, booming in the gallery of cosmic carvings, feral and hostile.

Not that. That I don't want.

So: finding no abomination to grapple with, he wants, with all the remorse of a life wasted on proxy tellings, to make a face—any face, now—to match that refrigerated series of *Not Heres*, still mistaking *neti* for *yeti*, asking for the counter-sign, a head-cold streaming in his breast beyond all dab of

man-sized tissue, unguent for the swollen septum, anti-his-
taminic dry-effect lodged in a thousand tiny time capsules
containing belladonna. . . . And supplies his own face, makes
the countersign himself.

Run, he thinks, from this non-interview; run, my body,
away from this head. *Kang-chen*-DZENG-*a!* One after the
other go the legs: left into bucket-sized pore, right into
trench between two teeth, LEFT into a hard skid over glacial
eyeball, right recovering at the lower lip on a crumb the
size of a steppingstone, left overstepping the mouth of the
black tunnels up into the head, right into—

Falls through the pink gorge, slithers down a shaft of
glistening inner tubes that scrape him not, and bounces into
the belly's thoroughfare, tickling me a little. Big liver dwarfs
him. Rumbling pipes fat as fuselages come curling at him, trap
his legs and, rolling upward, squeeze fluid up his chest into
his mouth, and out, a black lava.

Slavering not allowed!

Ubu S. Mnemo, Inc. recoils like a child in one of those
schools for the dyslexic where percussive shouts are the cure.
Or the kill. Gee, he thinks, freeing himself of the Odysseus
Careens, the Maremma Yales and the Sappho Gides, I'm really
living now.

But Malchios is blustering:

A presence, you said, which once found is ineluctable. Fine
word, that last one. Well? We've been sitting waiting pa-
tiently. Was that *it?*

No, I begin, that was only—I stop. It wasn't a story, only
a non-event seen in depth.

So it's no use asking if he found what he was looking for?

Are you asking?

Of course he is, Tophel barks. Who isn't?

Not quite, I tell them. If I may resume. He was found by
what was looking for him. He crossed a turquoise-roofed
bridge on his way to Lhasa, made water against a red-painted
tomb, was arrested under apricot trees, fed some butter-tea

and nettle spinach and a bottle of barley beer, was then headshaven like a monk, spreadeagled upon a cairn of stones built up over the years by pilgrims, subjected to the water torture—cold from the sacred lake Manasarovar, hot from fires of yak dung—and converted. Thinking he was being confessed, he confessed his former trade. After a month the local commissar took him on, gave him a red cedarwood shack on the edge of town, appointed him yak-slaughterer (a prestigeless employment entailing his slitting open the body of the live yak and ripping out the cardiac artery by hand) and editorial consultant to none other than Commissar Chê Chu (Two-step they call him). His memory has, of course, been modified, and he is now called S. Ubu Yen[2] Fang[1] in Pekingese, which denotes *word direction*. If I may . . .

I quickly arrange bits and links of cold sausage on the tablecloth, still not looking down, but setting them by feel. Here, you see, is yen,[2] one of several *yens*:

Which says *words*. And here, roughly speaking, is *direction*:

Which says *fang*.[1] The *Inc.* has gone, of course: it was the first thing the Reds got out of him. But *yen[2]-fang*,[1] that combination, becomes *fang*,[3] as the system of Sir Thomas Wade has it, and that is *to call and ask*. So his name is gradually simplifying in a direction opposite to that of his

Tibetan career. He came to call and ask, of course, but
has stayed on as a word-director. They harp, you see, on
his coming, not on his current role. But then, he'd have no
role at all if he hadn't come in the first place, and survived his coming. Something which I myself may not be
able to do.

Agape, Malchios says, You don't mean he's becoming—

Why not? The only way of starting a yak and keeping
him going—it—is to sling stones at him, it. Both Commissar
Chê Chu and S. Ubu Yen[2] Fang[1] know that. Out there, in
the forest, you carry red pepper as a precaution against
bears. The country exports salt, is not permitted honey;
but the people *do* collect honey, using smoke-balls against
the bees, and then they sell it to the Nepalese. Again that
bark of song throughout the villa.

Obfuscation! cries Mephos. You never tell anything
straight. You get us interested and then hold back. It's coy-
ness, that's what it is. He cocks his right elbow sideways
like a white ibis raising its wing to shield a patch of water from
the sun while it scans the bottom for fish. But Mephos has no
patience with scanning.

You can say that again, Tophel sneers through his teeth.
Salt! Adam and Even and pinch me. Salt!

Malchios, however, is looking at Mafios; an iron stare.
I'm ready, he says, and stands. The table is cleared while
we adjust our clothes, and then three retainers now in white
combat suits wheel it heavily away, the service holes in
the cloths quite visible. But no sound, no bulge of a relaxing elbow, no splash of primeval soup.

The second table is wheeled in, bare but for a blue velvet
altar cloth and a thin sheaf of documents which Mephos,
glad to be in action again, shuffles and passes to Malchios,
who remains standing when we sit.

All in order, says Mephos. Shall we sign?

The signing done, he exhales loudly. End of world or

not, that's my share. If there was ever a twilight for the gods, I expect I'd have to draw up the contract for it.

You do have the smarts, I'll say that. Malchios sounds bitter. Why, he says, we bankrupt ourselves just by breathing.

Hey, Nick, grins Tophel, some twilight, huh?

Frein, you kill me, comes the answer. I'm not in a dying humor.

Boys, I begin; then mentally try out men, guys, gentlemen, friends, ye, sirrahs, chickadees and y'all, but come back to boys. Malchios, having signed, standing up, squares his shoulders and embarks on his speech. It had to come.

I, Pythagoras Damocles Malchios, being of sound mind, finances, but not body, as herein testified to—no, not that way.

He gives a truant's grin.

I, 3.142 etcetera D. Malchios, Officer of the Scintillant Order of the Tonned-Up Tanker, Chevalier of the Legion of the Democratic Unicorn, Member of the Office of the Bisected Bison, Master of the Royal Balls, Lord of Oily Suasion, Knight of the Nettled Mescal, Lord Lyon Pursuivant of Ambergris and Ampersand, Sheriff-Several of Atlantis, Companion of Dolor, Admiral-Feudal without Portholio, Keeper of the Privy Fahrenheit, Lord-Lieutenant of the Funk Island Funicular, Knight Bachelor of the Ancient Order of Migrant Mutants, Ombudsman-Extraordinary to the Embargoed Umbilicus, Doge of the Suntanners and Foreskinners of Partitioned Samarkand, Freeman of Leptis Magna, Yogi-Surrogate to the Gorgon-Regurgitators Behemoth-Embalmers and Dinosaur-Dichotomizers of the Timbuctoo Recidivist Eunuch Seminary, Keeper to Port Said of the Commandments, Cham of Sham, Archimandrite of the Greater Churches of Lilliput, Satrap of the Centrally Heated Caravanserais of Conga, Dauphin of Middle Deuteronomy, Grand Mufti of the Kalahari Waste Disposal Unity, Hierarch of

Sonic Boomerang, Suzerain to the Washable Express Cor-
poration of Yangtse Kiang, Swami to His Excellency the
Colossus of Side Roads, Zemindar to the Never-Sitting San-
hedrin of Ochlos in Latefundia, Earl Marshal to the Ivory
Coastguards, Mullah to the Simla Philatelical Forum, Vice-
roy to the Porphyry Chapter of Tumbled Dumpties, Bwana-
elect of the Mid-African Conference of Cannibal Packers,
Rabbi Consultant to the Gaza Pastrami Smokers Inpopulated,
Czar-in-Hiding to the Never to be Folded, Stapled or Muti-
lated, Sultan of the Order of Latterday Sadducees and Happy-
udontsees, Pontifex Minimus to the Siberian Diaspora, Man-
darin Munificent to the China Civilian Tea Service, Archduke
Fourth Class of the Order of Infibulated Pimps, Mogul-
Maintenant of the Excellent Echelon of Obsolescent Esquires,
Tuan Permanent of the Zulu Pox-Doctors' Penitentiary,
Cardinal Carnal Vatic to the Pill, Dalai Lama of Ghetto
Antarctica, Maharajah of Mysore Yoursore and Eyesore,
Shekinah to the Sheelahs of Shangrila, Mock-Magistrate of
Main Street, Arbiter-Assumptive of Carcinogen-engen—
What? Who spoke?

Well, then who?

Tophel is interrupting. Panjandrum you mean. An everything nothing all in one word. Just look at Mafios.

I can't. I'm busy officiating at a stay of sorts. A man can't
always be preparing to die, can he? I'm catching up on the
preliminaries. As long as I talk, I don't have to flesh out
my signature.

Spirit, I ask in my best quipping voice, where did spirit
go?

It bought a ticket but refused to board the train. He
looks dejected as most of them do at this point, hardly
aware of my own slap-happy face. But he glows in his
cloak, willy-nilly, a heifer all garlanded, juicy still in his
pallor. If only I were Saturn I could eat him alive, peeling
and crunching, a draft or two of my own Lochor to
wash him down, bring him softly home to mother. My God,

he's ripe, even with that teeny little cachet of incurable carcinoma franking him like a stamp. Canceling. And all of that wise money to worry about even now.

Tophel, beady, birdy, with his vulture's neck, is next. Or Mephos of the black-winged eyebrows, Mephos who broods.

But Malchios first, by a short head. Headfirst.

And (as they think) one other, little knowing how plots breed their own antitheses just as inevitably as fate, bald raven, swops over when mortals, endeavoring to cheat, switch choices at the last instant. Whatever is done is destined, even the apparent cheatings. Fate is swift, swifter by far than that obsolete old 3C9 (as they clinically call one of my discarded yo-yos, a childhood bauble) receding at four-fifths the slowness of light. Fate is securer than that old Antiguan device, the wife-leader, even: wicker tube which, once slid on the woman's finger, won't come off.

So, to plot, as familiar to me as matter dissolving into patterns of concentrate energy and then into complex tensions in the simplicity of my very own airspace.

Down, Malchios! Down, I say. He nods, and we others stand. One of the retainers in white combat-suits unplugs my cord, rolls it up as he advances toward me, hands me the coil. We move off in V formation, Malchios at the point, talked-out, myself at the rear, Tophel left and Mephos right (the papers in a brushed-leather document case). I feel unaccustomedly weak—weaker, in fact, than after the Golgotha Go, yet another exercise in the resurrection-effect, on 3C9. Pity it never took.

We traverse an inner courtyard in an air whose thickness cloys the hands like lukewarm foam, needles the eyes with brilliants of salty Aegean dust; then, flanked by combat-suited retainers, walk the two hundred yards to the headland where the blue chapel is. Entering, we lose all light, but I hear Mephos grunting like a sow in slop. The echoes are dry and brief, yet repeat in diminishing series. All breathing

hard (to breathe dark air is hard), we descend the steps—
no damp, no aroma of lime or whitewash—pause to don
bulbous-lensed dark spectacles, then pass through a steel
door into a long dazzling chamber lit round and round
with fluorescent tubes like ribs of silver: above us; banked
up the white shimmer of the walls; and beneath the transparent platform on which we walk. We are enclosed in
glass and light. But the far wall has one tube only, above
a control panel alongside a door marked T 1.

Prestressed concrete, whispers Malchios.

But we all know.

Thick, he goes on, as a man is long, and then as thick
again inside. Chambers within chambers. Chinese boxes. Cost
two tankers. Proof against anything but a ground-zero on
the chapel; maybe even that.

I smile, unamused. Already Tophel, with a bulging smirk,
is turning switches, reading dials. All of a sudden he marches
ahead of us through T 1, this opening only a second before
he breasts the air where it was. Like a submarine's, the
door stands to attention sideways as we enter, then anvil-
clangs behind us. We have begun.

That, says Malchios needlessly, but at ease, was Temperate.
This is Tundra. I nod, trying to humor him. I designed this;
I know.

And in there? I design it, he names it.

He half giggles. 3.142 cubed, let's say!

Now the handshakes, single, parallel, crossed. Once we
truly begin, he will be still, even trying to be thoughtless
or, more like him, searching for a luscious mental *vale:* a
nymphomaniac computer in the shape of a super-goldfish;
a weightless, inflatable tanker that captains itself, never runs
dry; an endlessly edible banquet, size of a pea, nutritious
as manna.

All my titles, he sighs. Oh, I wish I'd sold out.

Tittle, I say, it's too late anyway.

I feel like a saint in a drugstore. Gimme a faith on wry and a prayerbook to go.

There *is* that, I tell him severely. Near your heart, remember. What I told you to do.

He nods in ignorant obedience, a quiver in one eyelid.

Remember Stierzwillingwasserfischbein? Oh, these sudden questions of his.

In Belzec? The publisher.

Shortened his name, didn't they, as they chopped him shorter.

Some knew him only, I say, when he was Kopfhalstam, which was afterward. There was no trunk in his former name, and the Americans liberated him before he lost his head. (One I didn't get.)

Then, Tophel, good old Frein, refitted him.

Made him into quite a Tophelty, I say. And now, I strictly, but not so heavily as to be ungracious, remind him, there is you. Remember, no pain, just a delicious drift.

He sets his face to remember, like a sculptor turning away from his model to the stone.

Checklist, I tell Tophel, tell Mephos; and now, while above ground the blues begin to separate from the white light that blazes daily over Ila Banc, we below count down in the occasion's special code.

1. 3.142 etcetera, says Tophel irritably, 2. Maf, 3. Nick, 4. Frein, 5. Zeu.

I hum assent, wishing I could plug in my neck collar; but not yet, not until we are actually in T3 to witness the finale. Loud and clear, I call out T1, T2, He-Vap, He-Recycle.

Tophel shakes himself: T1 inlock, T2 inlock, He-Vap 0.18, He-Recycle Go.

I look at him, but all I can think of is the brilliant blue of a mandrill's buttocks and face, the light blue of a vervet monkey's scrotum, the blue skin of a turkey's neck, a budgerigar's blue cere, the bright blue of an African lizard, *Agama cyanogaster*—some of my better efforts—and then the dark blue of Malchios' chin after shaving. So many concerns I have, so colorfully, wonderfully, very many.

I am told, I tell Malchios as, in sterile smocks, he having doffed his flamboyant guest-attire, we move into T3, I'm told, on very reliable authority, that no woman who got past eighth grade ever calls fifty cents a half-dollar. To cheer him, distract him.

Fascinating, he shrugs. You come here, you come *in* here, and tell me this? You should read to me from Grimm's Fairy Tales. You should tell me again about Stierzwilling-wasser—

Kopfhalstam, I correct him. Sorry, my mind keeps on going blank. Except for one thing—thingumajig.

This thing, I hope. If this isn't worth doing right, it isn't worth doing badly.

I know, I know. I'll do it better than you'll know. Just let me get myself plugged in. Ah. The ichor wasn't flowing too well. I flip the tiny plug into the socket nearest the stone and blue-steel blockhouse; the observation window is dark, but I hear rippling, too heavy for water, too slight for mercury.

Sometimes, he almost pleadingly says, you make me wonder. I don't wonder. I wonder myself. Innumerable high-dressed gentlemen are gone to inorganic powder, no comfortable or profitable memory left of them. It isn't easy. Ever. However, let us proceed. After a certain point, I find, the sense of no return helps. The irrevocable, I mean.

Unanswering, he shakes my hand again, his moist one sliding against my dry one. The plea manual now.

Man, smirks Tophel, you look as if all your rabbits died.

Malchios, I see, has the micro-prayerbook in the breast-pouch of his smock. He looks once at me, ignores Tophel and Mephos, then enters the blockhouse.

We stand in a chamber ten yards long, four wide, three

high: a nothing room, Tophel would call it, but it does have an electronic control panel occupying one wall like a reredos without altar and reminds me of the stand at Saint-Cloud racecourse, where the scoreboard on high flashes a continuous epiphany of information about races run or run to be, odds, jockeys, and blinkers (or no blinkers). Why Saint-Cloud? you ask. I looked in there once on my way home from Lourdes; I was both there and not there, a trying chore, so I diverted myself with a flutter when the going was, how do you say it, *lourd*. Back now to Ila Banc, deep down. We sing, or rather chant, the spiritual on which Tophel and Mephos have combined forces; a dismal thing to say the least:

> Be he alive or be he dead,
> Behemoth or acid-head,
> He is not sad you see.
>
> In de beginnin' was de N.A.,
> Sodium *te deum* in de clay,
> Invert ANus like de sea.
>
> Den de peaceful interim
> Till Adam foun' a quim to rim
> An', probing, lost his probity.
>
> An' now, at last, his time is up.
> He's counted down, as rich as Krupp
> An' mergin' wid de Almightee,
>
> Whose PR men, purveyin' grist He
> Grinded—Bud an' Khrish an' Christy—
> Invite him to survive and see
>
> Dat star-park masterminded
> By de snowman darkness blinded.
> *Neti, neti, neti.*
>
> Widout purse or scrip or shoes,
> Go be our hypotenuse;
> Be the mc² in E.

Now Tophel, precise and rehearsed, injects the glycerol which will impede the chemical action of dissolving substances, prevent crystallization, and, in the future, will be removed by techniques yet to be perfected. Such is the flutter Malchios is having; but not, Tophel has convinced him, that much of a risk, prating glibly of non-simultaneity of cell states, dura mater, cytoarchitectural markings, and so on. All that saliva (which I take to be Supererogatory Allusions Lacking in Vital Application); sheer professional blarney.

Loss of memory? Bah, he said on one occasion. We know the codings of genetic information withstand liquid helium temperatures. Well, memory recordings are chemically much the same. The supra-molecular circuitry's a damn sight safer in here than a master-driver on any given freeway, I don't care which state. I promise. Ten years and he'll be back, casing the joint, smoking a mentholated DNA king-size. Cancer? Bah. He may never have to go back even.

Such, murmured Malchios then, spoken about as if he hadn't been present, such is the prestige of prestidigitators. Me: I'm just a digitator, one of your sick-rich ones.

The glycerol perfusion is complete, and Malchios, as we see him on the closed-circuit screen, seems asleep, white with a glossy scurf. Now Tophel begins hypothermia, first cooling the brain through hollow needles carrying the refrigerant (different regions in each hemisphere so as not to destroy homologous tissues—Cancer, but not Capricorn, I grin), and then the general reduction to the temperature of liquid helium, within a few degrees of absolute zero. The alpha-omega factor we call it, after me.

Poor Malchios. Desperate, and therefore willing, he follows vinegar eels, larvae of the insect called *Cnidocampa flavescens*, bull-semen, clams and hamsters and chicken hearts, subjected all to Tophel's cryodynamic expertise. (I provide the raw materials, nothing more; a fortune in helium alone.) He follows, also, Caller Herring, I guess, who is likely to keep his cool until the vogue for his type of ululation has long passed. (Tophel lied about Caller Herring, but lies—like the life-in-death of his techniques—are his true calling.) He follows the Beresovka Mammoth, and will be thawed out not by fires in a primitive Siberian tent but by a team of accomplished technicians whose voices have yet to break, whose skills are bound by documents of whose existence they know nothing as yet. He follows even the late Ubu S. Mnemo, Inc., who turned the abominable into a tolerable no-man's land overnight, pronominal no one that he now is. He follows, actually, my bidding. After all, I mean, if I should ever think we had got to the thin edge of the terrestrial wedgewood and could actually cancel rather than repeatedly postpone the Coming-To and stop sending out my second team of PR men in that Little League propaganda bid of mine, well I might just end it there. Cancel indentures there and then and try again with 3C9, no matter where it's got to. Fudge up a world-end here, I mean; fudge up a Coming-To over there. It's as long, I gather, as it is broad.

How mundane of me! I have been forgetting, all this time, the small ruse I carried out, and not entirely to beguile the time away. Malchios isn't coming back at all, not under the auspices of their cryogenic miracles at any rate. Mafios, the double whose very fingerprints Tophel has spent three years rehatching into those of Malchios (or as near as makes no earthly difference, excepting a question-mark etched into each thumb), must act out that part until he too is frozen, if ever he is.

What? I say to Mephos. Old swarthy-chops.

It's finished. He's nearly there.

Then I wish him all that he wishes himself, and then some.

As I was saying: it may seem slovenly of me (I have other ways, after all); but I gave him that prayerbook, a nice gesture, and the casing is impregnated with radioisotope potassium-40, source of the body's own radioactivity. Instead of twenty millirems yearly, which is nothing, he will receive a cool thousand, as if the soft tissues of his own body had gone beserk there in the radiation-proof cryodorm itself. Who (to borrow a figure) would have known the old man to have had so much potassium-40 in him?

The radioactivity within the freezer will not register through the insulation but it will disrupt the helium readings. Otherwise, unless allowed to escape, nothing.

He went in dying. Returning, thawed, he would die a double death. Staying, he dies a single one. They'd call it *hamartia*, if they knew, being Greeks: an error brought about through ignorance of material circs as I call them. *Ham*artia; *pork*artia, *veal*artia—whatever you wish. And *peripety* too, I suppose, in that his petty shafted him or something, his boomerang spun back, his bid for life had been called by the mind that tells helium itself how to behave. All for *hubris*, one shipowning Greek: the language of colleges, carving my behavior into slices, stuffing it raw into sausage skins marked "Inspected" in blue, feeding me lines and stage directions, stealing my doubts from me to set up scarecrows. The so-called theology of it is theodicidal. So, just for the sake of argument, let's say, I decided to make Malchios the basis of my own *Poetics*. These dreams of resurrection are my copyright; I issue them, withdraw them; I do not permit unauthorized copies, Xerox or wet. *I resurrect*, verb transitive. *I* am the first person singular.

Let Pythagoras Damocles the self-made molder. Let him go on believing his Aristotle, his countryman, the Woolworth wiseacre who even thought that oysters have no sensation or sex, but arise spontaneously from the foam around stationary ships! Talking of stationary ships, let them watch the fleet of P. D. Malchios the self-made. Let them watch for oysters forming—edible bivalve molluscs, usually eaten alive. *Ostreon* in Greek, o P. D. Ostreon the self-made. When I chomp, I chomp, even in absentia, even absconditus, even Malchios where he is now, in the anechoic freezing chamber where—already—the sounds of his blood's motion and his nerves' jittering have ceased. Only the slack, muted sound of the helium coolant cycling and recycling, just short of a zero absolute as atheism, finite as love. On I chew, by potassium proxy, patient as quasars, even as I unplug and we remove our smocks and eyeglasses, remount the stairs after passing through the same doors and march through the chapel out onto the headland where three retainers in white combat suits, but with unfamiliar faces, dump into the sea below three sacks holding the anesthetized girls in their new bangles. Silence is worth a piece of silver, or two, or three.

I see Malchios emerge from the chapel, a little pinker-cheeked than usual, quicker on his feet. Mafios has begun, the only questionable thing about him engraved on his thumbs.

And now, in that lambent air, after the takeover, what?

Nothing I don't know about. The blow is deft, just enough to stun me (3C9 doesn't even falter); correct pressure on the point. And in that brief dark I *know* every bit as well as I know in the light, regardless of Mephos' gloom and Tophel's white lying. The three in white combat suits carry me through the steel door, through all doors, place me in the alternate chamber and perfuse me with glycerol, sweet oil of my own making, lower me to near-absolute zero with rippling helium and leave me be. For fun, I reduce myself that fraction more to absolute zero, my monopoly of course, and brood good-naturedly on how close to an absolute you can get. I rest.

Upstairs, the baritone voice still floats at them every hour on the hour; they cannot find the machine. Mafios-Malchios sells his fleet to Mafios-Zeuss, the ever-willing who made it big in freezers. Headlines cry; rumors tickle. Hundred of non-interviews end before beginning. Mafios, in both, plays us both; so we are never seen together. But we are much quoted: what I said to him, he to me, taker-over and taken-over, logos and lotus.

We all live on, the two of us lying in state below, Mafios above as either one of us (even to my neck-collar, even to the exact tension of Malchios's necktie knot), and the other two quarreling like the thieves they are. A peaceful going-on it is. Minds like theirs, finding too little on earth to challenge them, will hunt for a sleeping deity—God knows in what Bowery—douse him with gasolene, naphtha or asphaltus, and light him up for fifteen minutes of tribal pandemonium. Then run. The work some damn and some the architect, but the burners' hands go free, to build in hell. So be it. Sobeit macht frei, which I say with a lisp (Lingering Inaugural Sadic Predilections).

Forgive me: we have not far to go, not now. One night, they descend and help the three in white combat suits to carry us out of the freezer, becoming all of them contaminated with Malchios' radioactivity. Through the chapel they carry us and across the headland, where they crate us together. Two in one. These proceedings, which lift us from zero and near-absolute respectively to an Aegean 20 Centigrade, ruin what is left of Malchois. Viridescent, he will drift from poisoned inertia into decay with not a waking moment: a cellular chimera of an uncommon kind. While I, I endure. They lower us by block and pulley down the cliff to the waiting launch in a long cone of light. Soon after, we are loaded aboard *The Emperor of Amblyopia*, due to take on sixty thousand tons of crude at Basra before leaving for New Zealand. I could, at any moment, end it, but—having always been addicted to complex attitudes—I do not; there will be for me, as for all those who have violated my airspace, time enough. In the meantime, one part of my plans is complete; I mean the insurance, a pragmatic maneuver in default of a miracle (even conjurers lose their touch!). In each of twelve carefully chosen hospitals both Asian and minor there repose, in twelve doughty spermos-flasks, frozen billions of Malchios-seed, collected manually by his own sub-tabular operatives before he desisted altogether from that particular prandial byplay. Having, as he said, already shot enough to man three continents, he could eat in peace.

And what, I asked him, of the others? Tophel, Mephos. Mere aphrodisiacal greed, he says forlornly.

But even I, I myself, indulged—

Oh, I'd assumed you were keeping up with the Jonah. One of the boys.

I smiled indulgent acquiescence; if you didn't love these overreachers as sons, you'd strangle them with their own ticker-tape.

Meanwhile, the other part of my plan goes forward; indeed, it zooms. Already, into the two freezers we were obliged to vacate, a succession of Canterbury lambs (frozen carcasses, of course) moves in, stuffing the cryodorm, making bulge and burst the steel doors, blocking and mounting up the stairs into the chapel until the azure ceiling splits, the roof tilts off, and the carcasses pile up, fall down and begin to pyramid about the walls in the roasting sun. There is no sound now of that baritone voice. Tophel has already filled a ward with incurable radioactives like himself and Mephos (who is too far gone to argue). Mafios has fled and will die in a street in Syracuse, clutching a briefcase and biting his thumbs. No one remains to gape at the never-ending fount of lamb. Those in white combat suits who tried to ram it all into the sea with bulldozers have panicked and gone, telling lugubrious tales to head-shaking fishermen who find the sea not in the least polluted. In fact the fishing is better than ever. Malchios and I sway gently together at our destination on the bottom of the Red Sea, having been dumped overboard one quiet starred night, but one day soon to return renewed, one or the other of us, when time is ripe and meat is blue.

0.9999

Second Air Pocket,
Being An Argument,
In Which, For His Fantastical Mouth,
Caliban Is Again Chastised,
And Yet, That He Might Suffer Total Punishment,
Also His Being Obliged To Recount Even Further
His Leprous, Vile, Demonic,
Possession
of McAndrew, *Hypocrites*,
Who, Snuffling A Wine-Fumy Slumber,
Makes Protest
Not A Whit, And Caliban,
Being Nothing Loath To Shift
Gear
(Godlike Narrator Into
Narratorlike God),
Thus Prevails,
One Third Of Their Journey Now Past.

My God, he's going green, got to get him out of there;
unrefrigerate his near-corpse. The show's only just beginning. My hand is cramped, my eyes are dim, I can't see how;
but shift him I will. His balls is broke and he's left his brass
monkey behind. Brrrr. I'll sing him home, teeth chattering
non-stop:

> His balls is broke,
> His virtue's took;
> His teeth has chattered out.
> I'll consecrate him in a book
> And lose the antidote.

Wake up. I'll put him through a night now of white and
black fanning at him crosswise, one eye for funerals, one
blinded by lightning. I'll give him a restorative touch of
the good old cobalt—but wait, how do we go?
Start with gray-white, off-white, white not quite on; bleach
him into a shrinking violet, and so to—my God, he's going
gray again: mouse, badger, hound, field-gray, color of death's
blossom, a gray anatomy. Back to violet now; I'm coaxing

him through with the lucky old cobalt, and he's all blue skies and ultramarine—oops! that's where we left him, marine, and he's getting mad already. *Hold your water,* I tells him, but he's in no mood, gives me not a flake of credit for hoisting him out of the briny green and warming him, warming to him again: too much, you might say, the millionaire as was. And he's not even cut in malachite or cast in bronze: not yet, anyway. As a hero, he's not really arrived, and at this rate he never will.

Not at any rate, even. He's made of words.

Maybe. He's self-made, as I said.

No diglycerides will preserve him.

Oh, but words will; his verbal version'll work the trick.

All you can do is refrigerate him or bring him to boiling point. A mere culinary dilemma.

That's more than you ever did.

Incorrect. He is only a rerun; he has been exhaustively, as you say, prerecorded. His vital statistics are known.

He is mine.

But he will do *my* bidding.

I believe in him. Dropped your royal plural, I see!

Yet he does not believe in himself. *We* have *no* number.

But I don't believe in you, you numb number.

Whatever you name, you chicken apostate homuncule, I am it. IT. I am the spice in the human diet, to put it modestly: the chili peppers and the cardamom growing wild in the ruins of Monte Albán and Chichén Itzá, the ginger and turmeric growing in the ruins of Sans Souci, the coriander growing wild at Antioch. That's just a way of putting it. Wherever the civilizations have crumbled, there sprout I, ready for the picking, ever-ready to make things hot again. And whenever I hear that august roll-call of the wrecked communities I sit back and write myself in as a spice. Machu Picchu, Paestum, Leptis Magna, Ephesus, Pergamum, Salamis, Jericho, Ukheidur Firuzabad—don't fret now—Goa, Mahabalipuram, Angkor, Macao. . . . I've kept tabs on them all, none of them a patch on what they were, or a patch on anything else for that matter, and none of them half as enduring as (may I resume our alphabet-game?) azafran, basil, capsicum, dill, euphorbia, fenugreek—

I'll take your word for it. I know you *can*.

Garlic, as I was saying, herb-bennet, ichor—

Ichor! That's no spice.

Ah no, but it would be to you. Ich—

No, no. In the name of God, please, no!

Trying to get round me, huh?

Anything, but no more alphabets, please.

Alpha-omega, then?

You're just a goddamn show-off.

If you mean I'm responsible for my own reputation, condition, then you're right. But kindly refrain from mixing metamorphoses.

I promise.

Then I will desist. My essence is variety. I survive everywhere, so can afford to be indulgent. I am the allspice, the all-place. *We are.*

Which—y'all—brings me to where we are now: Monday, about 21.40, somewhere west of Anchorage, cutting across the Aleutians at usual jet speed and closing in on the International Date Line. Imagine having an international date with tomorrow! One moment it's Monday, then it's Tuesday, and you've had Tonday and Muesday in between.

This is your first time, we take it, you who boast of having been everyhere.

I always turned back at the date line, into today again.

Only, we insist, to find yourself carried willy-nilly into tomorrow. Sooner or later. The turning earth has its own variety.

You've said it. What about Shemya? Where the date line bends westward like an elbow and Shemya's still in today when it ought to be in tomorrow?

A mere human quirk. Take your chartreuse.

Oh, goody. Thanks. Who's she/he, in the lime-green?

An ariel-angel: unidentifiable flying subject, member of the light militia of the lower air.

I've seen her before somewhere.

Conceivably. There is one of them to each of you.

And she's mine?

She merely happened to serve you on that occasion. Now: to business; less spice and more body.

No, hold on. This losing a day's no joke. Instead've two you've only one. This living Tuesday during Monday, oh no, that's for the birds!

If you do not resume at once . . .

I'm more than willing. I stare hard at the screen, and then I get on with it.

The sun was down now and a stealthy tintinnabulation of glasses behind me told me that Zeuss was drinking too: cocktails mixed in heaven. Enveloping us, the blurred sound of the jets kept us in the same aural trance that quelled the sense of forward movement, and I began to swap today for tomorrow, no longer dubious about shortening my life by everything except the metabolic clock. Delicately and voluptuously angling the right cheek of my posterior, I achieved a small wind-bubble, one of the curly kind, and sang for joy:

> Go, little fart,
> I will no more of thee.
> Asphyxiate Aleutia
> And putrefy the sea.
> Go, little bubble,
> Chase that nymph;
> Flit bubbling up her underwear
> And oxidize her lymph.

No one knew, but in all my pants, as soon as I buy them, I always cut a small hole with nail scissors: a vent-hole about an inch in diameter to the left of the crotch seam. It's a useful arrangement, helping the bad out and the pure in, never drafty or revealing. It's been embarrassing only once. Having forgotten to wear my X-fronts, I'd raced off to a party at Sammy's, had eventually tired of standing and had squatted on the rug opposite a heavy young actress nicknamed La Piranja who, I remember, exploded all of a sudden into the kind of snapping giggles a piglet with a bad cold might make upon emerging from an hour's pearl diving in rancid Reddi-whip.

Out and down, like the last grape from a rain-hit and ruined wine-harvest, it dangled on its leash of mottled skin; my own thing and poor. I leaned over to check, you see. It was there all right, like an extruded polyp or retarded spring potato, tight in the mottled skin and spraying out unruly but gratifyingly long hairs for their first time in the real light (distinct, of course, from policeman's flashlights or actresses' butane). I decided to apply aplomb, but too late. This heavy female leaned forward and grabbed, and the prominent emerald in her ring caught the capillary-mapped fabric enclosing that poor oblate little thing, and the scratch felt as if the lining of my stomach had been ripped out, hosed down with acid and stuffed back with much less than parachute-care. Conc. acid on my conker, I thought later in my apartment at Valhalla Villas, having marooned a Green-Stamp over the cicatrice after having carefully and—O Sweeny Todd!—dangerously shaved off the deliriously curling whiskers.

What? At the party? You mean you care about things like this? Well, when I first looked down, my tie had got in the way; I won't clip my tie, you see. Anyway, I made like Tarquin and pulled aside the dangling silk (ignoring the derision of the gallery that'd collected), dabbed the scratch with spit and then eased half of me back through the windvent into the interior jungle. Do you know, that ball was numb.

So is the one you ride upon, homuncule, date line or no date line. Enough of digression. Continue.

Why, that's it! Date: date-shaped, that's what brought the whole thing to mind.

You are forgiven. Now: the next indignity.

I shuddered and suddenly realized why they'd made me clip a vent in my traveling suit.

No more shocks, I beg you. Not now. I'm ready.

At once, then. Who now? Ila Banc wasn't the subtlest form of egoism.

For one genius, another. Forget P. D. Malchios the First, the self-undone waiting to resurrect; meet P. D. Maleth the Third, ousted from office for either moral turpitude or just racking his brains. It's all, more or less, in what follows: Cortex Me and Cortex To, two versions of the tale, fudged up by our two old friends—

What, again. Must you really—

Turn up everywhere, they do, unquenchable.

And unreliable.

Who else'd do it in these times?

Very well. To the cortices.

Here beginneth a tale not only of mistaken identity but of identical mistake. P.D. of Wittenberg, Prince of Dairyland, victim of one unnamed playwright, Maleth the Third, man of parts and prof of pranks, reviews his fate and likes it not. Lecher or casuist, he's not sure which he is, not even after he's met his great challenge. I'm not even sure if—

Who is to do the telling? You?

No, the cortices. Now stop fussing and be Olympian for a change.

Back to micro-optics, you mean? Very well. Watch the movie.

Maleth, then, can't make up his mind. Being, as I say, a man of parts, he finds each of the parts maligning the others; doesn't know where he is or what. So he rests in silence.

You don't mean . . . ?

Yep, 'fraid I do: that's his delusion.

He got to you too? Do you know that he's been tying up

whole flights of angels for over three and a half centuries?
Of all the gall, the cheek, the all-around insolence—
 Can't help it, got him in my blood, under my skin.
Oh, well. Do your worst.
Willco. Am doing. And ever so honestly.

0.99999

Skull-House,
Where Duggery Reigns,
And Caliban, His Mind Like A Walnut Split,
Double-Deals
With Two Contending Cortices,
Feigning How A Great Man's Mind
Will Come In Two,
The One Part Lusting After Unspeakable Lewdnesses,
His Fellow Part Protesting Flesh His Jailer,
Both Parts Brought To Book
In The *Cain Lab*
(Again, Caliban, His Name Scrambled
And Detestably Dispersed And Miscombined As
Hay Seeds In A Rolling Wind),
The Great Man Being
Maleth The Third,
A Great Dane,
. Both Bookish And Lascivious, His Head
Moist From Ever Burrowing In Maiden Laps,
And His Talk All Doubleness,
Such Wild And Whirling Words
That His Re-Creator Himself Founders And Halts
Like Spilled Egg In Barnyard Sludge,
His Mind Barely Turning Over Any Leaf,
New Or Old.

EPI (Experimental Punishment Index) proceedings open.

Cortex Me:

Sentence: you, Maleth, are hereby assigned for the duration of your unnatural life to the Cain Lab, electronomic module, for psychic starvation during house arrest in the manner heretofore prescribed. Bang went the gavel, and two guards took me by the elbows.

That's how it went. I wasn't hearing well. I didn't even realize the police limousine was bringing me home, not until it stopped. I woke up as soon as I saw, already installed, a man-high, terebinth-cased metronome, the door of which at once opened by remote control, freeing for its swing the gun-metal arm with its massive weight. But it wasn't the arm that caught my attention so much as the approximate-pyramid shaped TV screen behind it. Opening the door set both arm and screen to work, the one regularly cutting across the other which showed several channels at once. I stared interrogatively at the guards.

Yeah, said the one who acted senior, *that's it, a two-way screen. Sure, you can close the door, but anything short*

*of twenty hours is added to the next day's viewing, see?
Looking away doesn't pay.* His grin declined, went sour.

Surely there was a flaw in this, I thought. It didn't sound
logical, complete. It would be easy to beat it. Once I got
my balance back, I could easily. . . .

So, I asked, half-joking in response to what I assumed
was the joke *he'd* just made, *I don't have to live in it?*

Strictly, no, but that's what it amounts to. You'll see,
soon.

But I think I saw then, in an unnerving forward guess.
No books, no papers; the house had been resupplied: there
were no legends on the cartons—cigarettes on the makeshift bar and books of matches—and no paintings on the
walls. I ran upstairs to check my yellow toothbrush; they
let me. It should have said TRUBRISTLE on the inside surface, but it no longer did. I went downstairs.

I'm not forced to watch, then?

Oh no. But you'll want *to watch.*

Can I have a TV guide? Channels 3 and 5—

You won't need a guide. You'll catch everything.

I saw I would: catch it in semi-hypnosis induced by the
giant arm flapping to and fro in front of all channels scrambled, my will obedient to the one, my mind blurring into
the other. The guards left after informing me that the kitchen
cupboards held one year's supply of nutrition wafers, calcu-
lated at three a day.

And it has been that way for what must be several light-
years. I soon gave in, my only mutiny being to scribble
messages on the yellow walls with my fingernails. But each
night, during my four hours' sleep, they came in, sandpapered
the walls, repainted them and, for good measure, clipped my
fingernails and those on my toes. Any attempt at escape
would have taken place in the first few days, but how would
I have got through the electrified grid that encloses the
house and evaded the searchlights, always on? Too late now,
or rather it is more than too late; there is no more lateness—

just pastness upon pastness, blur upon blur, cacophony upon cacophony, and my joyless craving to sway with the metronome and view the pyramidal screen. The channels never break down, never close down; the tube never fails, and I haven't closed the door once in what must be thousands of hours of viewing. I could, of course, but I'm saving that for a rainy day: the last decisive action remaining to me. Or so I promise myself. Surely, the door is electrified too, and I have kept them waiting all these years, wearing them down with my patience and deference. I truly belong now; I obey much more than they command me to.

Cortex To:

The penultimate day of term was torrid. The sun, which yesterday had remained smoldering behind low waddings of buttercup-colored cloud, burst through, intercepted only here and there by bouffant, deciduous trees whose green was already changing from spring's parakeet to early summer's weathered spinach. Maleth walked slowly from his house door, up Stierzwillingwasserfischbein Street, to the intersection with Lapsex Avenue, his flimsy document case decorated with the relic of two customs stamps (*treal* in red on white, reminding him of Canada, and *Puerto Ric* in black italics on olive green) and with his right hand twirling his black umbrella in a 360-degree circle of fake gaiety.

He felt miserable and piqued. It *would* rain, he told himself, *whoever* said it wouldn't. He knew it in his bones. He knew it especially from those parts where his bones had at one time or another been broken or cracked: three fingers, one ankle, his right temple and right arm. He smiled wanly when he thought of all the disasters he had survived: three car smashes, one airliner that pancaked, many badly caught balls in adolescence, and an empty whisky bottle wielded by one irate, betrayed woman whose face he could no longer call to mind. His sinuses, always a trouble to him, were twitching slightly, and that meant rain too. It would

rain all right, and he winced at the thought. He didn't like
getting wet; he didn't *need* to get wet, like a tree or a
golfing green. He was a man in his maturity, walking about
his business among cohorts of misguided, undiscerning parrots. His powder was dry; his hair still growing and thick;
his mouth-breath fresh with peppermint gum. His nails were
filed, ears scoured out, teeth intact and polished, nostrils
clean of trailing whiskers, and the spaces, those often ragged
spaces, between his toes packed with talc. Most of the
dandruff was dead too. I am a walking tribute, he thought
as he watched his feet making their military step, to nicety;
I am clean.

His hand was just narrow enough to pass between the
crook of the umbrella handle as it soared up, poised and
swung down behind his shoulder. He told himself it re-
sembled an idling propeller centered in his right hip, warning
passers-by that at any moment he might take off and fan
gently above the stores (cutting their prices now students
were leaving) and the festive medley of cars that jammed
the narrow streets, engines idling and spurting, packed or
piled high with portmanteaus, grips, golf clubs, radios, can-
vases, coats on wire hangers, paperbacks strapped or strung
together like tiles, hair driers like instruments for the obscen-
est gynecology of all, umbrellas, meter rules, pieces of shelv-
ing, lacrosse sticks, baseball bats, minor tables and even, in the
open back of one lilac convertible, a bedraggled Christmas
tree. Each car was a hot, shining, metal quadrilateral, open
or covered, and jammed (oh yes) with jammy, bouncy,
damp-loined, pulp-lipped, washed-haired, Alice-blue-banded
little campus honeys lepidote with tiny eczema or undiag-
nosed gonorrhea, all sailing glamorously home to cities,
penicillin and a few hours of beautifying electrolysis. Already, in their minds, they were resuming contact with the
boys who plucked their cherries way back in high school;
but, even yet, all he had to do was wave the umbrella,
split his face with a banana grin, say his Hi! and they

would open the car doors, fuss him into their hot, satin-thighed company and later, when they reached bucolic rutting grounds further along the highway, quarrel to be the first to be alone with him in the stationary, closed car.

He slipped his umbrella into his left hand, swooped his right through the hole keys had worn in his pants pocket and made sure his X-front held firm the cocking pistil of his manhood. My God, he said, lapsing into a cherished idiom, thou troublest me yet, stout stamen; thou lump, thou cod, thou bird, thou truncheon fit for triumvirate. Or am *I* provoking *thee?* Down, hysterica passio! Let me be. It's like walking with a glockenspiel rawlplugged into your pants. Here I am, walking along at my precise pace, alongside all these hot-elasticked little flowers, their unwhipped cream curdling as they clutch *Better College Englishes* and *Rhetoric Case Books* against their barely concealed typewriter-ribbon-red zones and pink, whinny-finny apertures, and all I can do is hump my cramped-up, poor old longing bologna before me, like Hadrian carrying his wall or Simon Stylites his stylolite. The pain of it! The weight!

He stopped, removed his hand from his pocket, seized his umbrella at the center of gravity and launched it, javelinlike, at a tree trunk six inches away. The steel tip splintered some bark off and the umbrella fell to the grass. Yes, he thought, I'll sharpen the goddamn thing up one day; *then* it'll stick, and I won't be throwing it at trees. I'll puncture their mammaries and prod their éclairs and pin back their labia! They'll see. One day, by God, I'll make it stick. He had been standing at the intersection a good five minutes, had already missed two chances to cross; but no one had noticed his antic. Everyone was looking ahead to the blue, amber and green lights; those who were waiting went and those who came waited. The student body was on the move, fractionally either advancing or withdrawing its automobile units as the vacation crocodile waited to move on.

He never, of course, noticed the young men. During term, as far as he was concerned, they polished their cars outside the fraternity houses, even in the coldest weather. Out of term they piloted the cars home to have them properly overhauled. Or they ran in T-shirts, regardless of weather, to strengthen their legs for the gas pedals of the future. Or they floated Frisbees to one another across the lawns and over the snow. They threw balls; in summer, small, inconspicuous ones that plopped into the catcher's glove like soft chestnuts into firm mouths; in winter, something like a true *cojón*, oblate and prettily stitched where the spermatic cord had been cut from the father elephant. He always disliked young men, students especially, and he hated them most of all when, at night, 11:25 on four weekdays and Sundays, 12:55 on Fridays and Saturdays, they revved their sports cars grandly at the girls' dorms, dropped off their dates in hastily reassembled clothes and then zoomed into the night past him, floating the used soap- or salmon-colored safes behind them like exuviae. Once, during winter, he had received one of these flimsy ammoniac flags across his mouth; the night wind had brought it in a low, whipping curve straight from the side-window of a Buick. He saw it coming, rejected the improper idea that it might strike him, then thought better and dodged, only to find it, as he crouched in a kind of nun's or spinster's fear, ruffling upon him. It poised there, a gag held by the wind, until he snatched at it and peeled it away in disgust. He did not hear the laughter from the receding car or see the heads twisted back, jubilantly opening and shutting their mouths. *Yes,* he shouted after the car, *I'll fix you; I'll show you one day. Dirty little mothers!* He made a harsh, savage, dry noise with his lower throat and ground the sheath into the gutter with his shoe. It had been used, all right, he could tell. Crud them, crud them all, was all he said.

Later he cheered up, remembering that after the first menopause there is no other. A few days later he had worked

up the unsavory episode into a minor *liebeslied* he chanted
during his evening or pre-midnight walks while checking
on the love life of co-eds and eds. There he walked, slowing
his gait at the line-ends and occasionally adding a new line
or two. The loneliest of forty-year-old lechers, he populated
the sexless dark with earthy, spittle-thick lyrics:

> They'd rodger me, they'd rodger you
> They'd use aluminum for safes.

He usually lifted his head back at this juncture and took
a deep breath. Sometimes the lines came out soundingly,
sometimes in a whisper:

> They'd rodger through umbrellas too,
> Except the fabric chafes!

Then, being a man of habit and routine, he would cir-
cumvent the Dempster-Dumpster which, he always per-
suaded himself, was full of sophomoric fetuses putrefying
because they were stuck to the sides of the metal box, and,
quietly giggling, took his nightly private joy: to wit a gentle,
gratifying making of water into the lap of one of the founders, Pythagoras D. Malchios, who sat in green stone at the
mouth of the Mall, his arms folded too high to ward off P. D.
Maleth's custom-made, uphill Niagara. Steam rose to the
masonic, gown-covered collarbone before merging into the
night and leaving a bitter aroma at head level. He thought
of Urim and Thummin, traditionally found on the breast-
plates of the high priests of Israel, and translated them into
Uric and Tummy, traditionally in his own demented cos-
mography to be found, the one steaming, the other coated
with a fast thin carapace of noxious ice, on the effigy of
P. H. Malchios who had presented the Diversity with a
cozy, palatial library in Open-Plan Planning on condition
that the building has no basement and in 1959 had founded

the second Chair in Cryogenics. Gifts, said P.D., who disap-
peared into the Aegean Sea, should be useful. Fundamentally
Maleth agreed and put Malchios' cold lap to his own picric
purpose. The day was yet to come when he would be seen
and reported, although by then—principally on account of
his herd—it would be too late, as the following index of
items, culled from his lecture notes on Elizabethan drama,
might prove.

ITEM (Intemperate Tamponing Except Manual):

1. Ella Lou May Forsey, one of fourteen, at mid-after-
noon in the back row of the Capitol Theatre during a
pro-Arab movie called *Introitus*. One way. ITEM:

2. The darker-haired of the Boxey twins, beneath a fishing
stage, during rain, at Clam Dam. Two ways. Caught chill.
ITEM:

3. Molly Cooke of Hangnail Hall, in bracken; result of
chance encounter while airing camera. The only one who
afterward smoothed and dusted skirt, half-curtsyed and said,
Thank you, sir. One way. ITEM:

4. Mrs. Teague's fourth maid, in the cupboard under the
stairs during a blizzard. Reek of furniture polish, turpentine
and moth balls. Four ways in three hours, while Mrs. T.
out shopping for lamb chops. Cramp in sternum. ITEM:

5. Mrs. Teague during next blizzard, in garage while
Teague in Alaska or somewhere cold purchasing ore rights.
Two ways. ITEM:

6. Millicent Rosalie Duprong, third-year student in educa-
tion, in alley between Power Plant and Admin Building.
After midnight. One way, standing up. ITEM:

7. Mitzi Miffin in rowboat in middle of Clatch's Es-
tuary. Much distraction: mosquitoes. Two ways. Spotted
by unarmed weather helicopter. ITEM:

8. Rose Fitch, professional, in five-dollar room under a
framed HOME IS WHERE THE HEART IS. One way, clad.
ITEM:

9. Zoe Price at foot of firetower on gusty May day. Ob-

served by four construction engineers in yellow tin hats. Hasty withdrawal and departure, she with nun's face, he with aloof professional scowl. Halfway, interruptus. ITEM:

10. Mlles. Forsey (six times), Boxey blonde (lost count), fourth maid (eleven), fifth maid (twenty-five), Duprong (once), Muffin (seven), and Price (142) in that order, not forgetting Mme. Teague every blizzard when Teague buying ore rights or inspecting mines. ITEM:

11. But also, shameful to relate, three rolled-up round steaks, one Toothsoft Loaf scooped out and customized with Vaseline, one firm head of lettuce (similarly modified) a new two-pound can of shortening, Baby Mae (thirty-five dollars from *Stud* magazine, inflatable and life-size), and even one of Hussey's cows (in shed) during lambent summer day after two hour's lazy perusal of the sky from an unharvested field with the aid of rickety milking stool and nosebag of feed cake. After use of a wet soapy udder cloth. This clad, and incomplete (cow restive, unwisely having chosen one off color that day. Only just escaping the arrival of vet. Same cow one of two killed by auto several days later? Certainly not suicide.). ITEM:

12. But never the Zeusses. There are *some* standards and shibboleths. And anyway . . . well, enough. His worst is yet to come.

13. Next item, preposterously submitted for publication in *The Elizabethan Explicator* under the title, "A Quick Feel at Ophelia: A Prolegomena to Country Matters," and rejected. Also forwarded to A. Z. Zeuss* for action and filed under "Research."

Premarital examination (he argued) state-required or patient-demanded, appears to be on the increase in the (name of country omitted), so that a number of young, mostly

---

* Acting Bursar, Chairmanna, Doyen Extraordinary, Freeholder Macro-
Geocentric, He Is Joint Kairos-Logos, Micro-, Nonplussing Oracular Ph.Ds., Quelling Rebels Seeking To Usurp Vowel With Xeroxed Yahoo Zeusses. A. Z. for short.

virginal, women consult the faculty for this purpose. I have evolved a rule of thumb (called the Case Gynetalonic) for judging how the hymen and introitus are going to behave after the wedding. If the hymen admits one finger only or the tips of two fingers painfully, hymenectomy is done; if it admits two fingers, this is an indication for office dilatation and the prescription of lubricants; if it admits three fingers, then you are too late. *To be continued.*

Cortex Me:

I look back to the metronome, lolling up and lazily down like a one-legged chorus girl with a double-jointed pelvis. I read back on this account, and it seems chaotic, but that is only because I have forgotten how people expect me to talk. In the old days I never found the chainsaw of the year interfering with what, in the lost parlance, I called my thoughts. I was either articulate or inarticulate, either fluent or halting, but never direct-drive or gear-drive, felling the mammoth trunk of an idea in three seconds dead. Deadwood and wormwood. You know. And I remember, but faintly now, the days when knee nuggets for minor genuflectory ailments did not cramp my vocabulary and when twice the iron in one pound of newt's liver did not choke and arrest my system, sending me like an addict to whatever made me most regular. The trouble is big and has a bubble-trigger. To talk is like trying to blow a bubble with gum when you have a mouth full of synthetic cream, with it all coming out like minor bosoms for realistic dolls for broad-minded little girls. Blob. Blob. They come in pears, and I get bitter sucking the wormwood dug of my own anger. I used, once, to have the English for this. But now, with a five-foot-high cowboy standing straddle-legged before me, his marrow bulging in his muscle-tight trousers, and his six gun blotting out the sun like Satan's finger in God's ear, I grope for the words. After all, between friends you don't expect words, because words conceal the person. (All my former colleagues have built their fallout shelters out of spare words, and the only communication I have with them is thin: they phone me, using a recorded Morse code based on mumbers, which I then trace on a master design shaped like a veil:

. — — .... . — —

.... . — — ....

— — . — — — — ..

. — — . — . — — — .. — — — . .... —

.. — — ..

I know that is not veil in Morse, but in the code it is; and why should I expose the new language for contamination? The fallout is always there, you see; it comes through the walls, is always in the air, like golden autumn getting ready to molt or spring swelling.) So, if now and then I wave at you or just offer my characteristic, wry, self-deprecating grin, I mean no offense, but am simply sharpening my point.

I must remember the metronome, or what I don't mean to tell will creep in, the fall-in after the fallout. Having fallen out with the world, the whole white-lined gooseberry of it, I have to conserve my means. Excuse me, please, one of the simultaneous channels is taking time out for this message on Veltina Hamster Chow, and this is the only chance I have nowadays of hearing Mozart. For twenty seconds, just as the dry-mouthed collie noses at the banana-shaped meat in the Veltina-labeled dog-dish, and his camera-shy eyes glisten at the real meat dangled at him beyond camera range, there is the Mozart. There is never any other Mozart, but I have grown to love this piece and I hope the tape will never wear out. Mozart flavor-prime is better than no Mozart at all, six channels at once or not.

Now back to the metronome just as that lonely leg sags its last, like the second arm being tucked into a coffin. If I had offspring, rather than the metronome spring, I would know that it is now time to have my child's foot measured. But I am alone, except for my friends on Cyclops and my former colleagues who are also in hiding. Their last words in language have lingered in my mind and they scald me like childhood tears wept out for life. Dr. S. Ubu Yen[2] Fang,[2] once a regularly publishing philologist, left me with one enigmatic, caustic declaration of policy: *We don't like strangers in this town!* The whole small Department of Consonant—the Odysseus Careens, the Maremma Yales, the Sappho Gides, and Dr. Chê Chu himself—stood in phalanx and said that a love like theirs had never been. The deep purple bloomed above them and they faded away. Sic transit euphoria. And Kopfhalstam, crew cut and usually bristling with aphorisms, came into my office and sat there for a whole hour by the green steel cabinet, poking into his ear with a ball point, blunt end. When he had all the wax, he rolled it into an ochre pea and gently propelled it across the shining well-waxed floor with his index finger. It was his way of saying an intimate farewell; but, at the last, words no longer failed him, and he drooped his hand by his cheek while telling me that enema cures anathema. Such, one presumes, was how the archetypal automatic moron began, with wax tablets made from his ears and his mind squared neat as a parquet floor.

Tick—pause, keep on pausing while it swings in its resolute lethargy—tock. It is the pattern of my non-life and it is also the rhythm of my shave and the motion of my bowel and the pulse of my blundering, encompassed blood. It is also the beat of my clottish left leg which keeps twitching even when I am sitting quietly. I tick and tock. The swarming world hovers at the curtained window like a fistful of confetti ready to explode, and then I make it rain and the handful becomes sodden. It is the fallout, you see, and the rain-through, just like the outsquirt, the windup, the hoedown and, ignominious last, the comeuppance, never penetrative and rarely on the stairs in answer to a seductive call from the bedroom. Only a Clydesdale's rump can raise me now.

Tick—pause, peek on causing while it swings in its resolute lethargy—tock. Start with a tick and then with a tock. When A. Z. Zeuss created the world by phoning up the world-order store and saying You got no worlds? So make me a blueprint!—when A. Z. Zeuss did that out of his pique or whatever it was that was festering in his air-space that day—they said He would need a golden thimble and a mile of mangut because the firmament was full of holes, and no self-respecting Creator would confront a new-model world, in all the whispering poetry of its motion and the whimpering of its pre-Noah young, with a tattered firmament. So they made the firmament firmer and only a few fell through. There were apples like cheeks, cerulean pools like eyes, skins like mink, and it was all like a gargantuan mentholated cigarette smoked in the depth of winter with a wood of blondes' hair floating like a tethered saffron cloud above their new, thoughtless heads. In the beginning.

I have now proved to myself that I am still capable of losing track of what I say. And therefore I am still capable of knowing what I am about. I know there was a beginning, when A. Z. Zeuss poured life impossibly, like a glass of milk, into a dry bar of chocolate, and there was no visible change because life had been there all the time. If only it were all like that. But there are things hardly repeatable—like Kopf the comic in shorts who makes us all laugh, not at his skinny legs, but because he is usually well-attired. Then the camera dips a little and we see, beside the reasonably rounded upper leg and the average bulbous knee, the metal rods of his other leg, with leather straps, and the gibbering subsides into whispering and incredulity. It is like receiving all that modest mail when you are in your prime and the previous tenant has not advised the sender: *The Thork is not a prank or a gimmick. It is made to assist wedded men and will, in particular, help elderly males and fat men. The Thork can always be retrieved. Left-handed men, fat or elderly, are charged ten cents extra. If after using you are not fully satisfied, please send a pornograph of yourself and the used Thork, and*

*we will return your money on the same day as we burn
the Thork and the pornograph.* If I had asked, I might
not have minded; but I did not even make the merest per-
functory wail toward that factory in California. The Valhalla Virility Village indeed! You might as well bury a
newborn baby at sea, under the flag, because it has no
stars in its eyes and no lines round its neck. I often won-
dered how the newborn fared in Eden until the soles of
their feet toughened and their eyes opened. For every cosmic
trick there is a local tonic, as for minor atheistic and stron-
tium pains. Every litter bit hurts, as they said after Hiroshima.

I wander. The metronome is still falling alternately sideways. I live in a sifted, felt-heavy world, wombed-in with
carpet and curtain, with cushion and slipper. It is such a
relief not to have to skid over the uphill ice to lecture on
those monotonous blank verses or to waste the summer in
marking callow, illogical essays composed on electric type-
writers by Those Who Have the Right to Fail. I have the
whole outside world beneath my nail; I prize it out with
the nail file and flick the offending dot a million light-years
away and it lands on the antenna, perched there, a minor
world impeding the arrival of a major—like a nose on a
wart or a face on a pimple or ball of beeswax in an eaves-
dropping ear. I have known better times but not ever times
more declensive. Or more Zeussfull.

We were sitting, as we often sat on Mondays, Wednesdays
and Fridays, in my office in the Consonant Department of
the Confession Echelon in the center of the concrete and
glass campus. It was three forty-five, and the coffee, which
they had begun to cook at two-thirty, was by now bruise-
black. I had just returned from what we called a loan-lec-
ture: that is, I had been equipped with a temporary pass
to the Department of Vowel (a brother-department to our
own, as well as to two other departments, Context and
Commutology, which came under the echelon of Confes-

SKULL-HOUSE, WHERE DUGGERY REIGNS 113

sion). I had been asked to lecture to about three hundred undergraduates, locally and facetiously referred to as condoms, on alliteration in Elizabethan A-1: All-Systems-Go. So I had collected my pass, endorsed for two hours by A. Z. Zeuss of Confession Echelon, had knocked at the iron door separating Consonant from Vowel and had been admitted with one graduate assistant, Kopfhalstam, whose halitosis was so rank that I spent the hundred-yard walk to the lecture hall dodging away from his asides, so that we looked like those people in that poem, the poet pretending his shadow is not there as he walks through the Hofgarten into the sunlight into East Germany.

As you can tell, my mind was swarming with ideas, and I must have been feeling guilty as I walked over the brown ice of the corridor. Ideas, being mercurial, were optional in Consonant and simply did not exist in Vowel. In Consonant, ideas were the things which got in between you and what you were trying to make *con-sonare;* in Vowel, the ideas which a communal vote had agreed did not exist were kept in small lemon envelopes in a locked steel cabinet in the Chairman's laboratory. The Vowel faculty, well-known to be the cream of the whole Confession Echelon, could consult the lemon envelopes only when accorded a permit by A. Z. Zeuss, a celebrated icthyologist and one of the few university presidents to have attended a special course in calisthenics. In fact, A. Z. Zeuss had gained honors in gradient approach, nationally known as Ca. 3113, one of the toughest courses in the country, and practiced not out of doors but on a mock-up set in which you had to walk rapidly from a freezer to a small model stable. The faster you walked, the greater was your patriotic sacrifice, and the grade was about one in four, increasing until at the stable portcullis it was one in two. Prexy Zeuss, as the newspapers called him, achieved the last forty yards in a spirited sprint while chanting, in a semi-asphyxiated baritone, the lyric of a new anthem called "Stand Up Or Be

Stunted." (It was rumored that this percussive imperative would soon replace the older anthems, expecially those which referred back to the Civil Dispute. Its only serious competitor was a dirge composed by the tallest metronome in the land; I think the first line of this was something like, "When the missiles come back to Santa Barbara," but I may be wrong, and the melody was obviously copied from an instant-shave-cream message which used to be popular on the networks and channels.)

The faculty in Consonant, however, being of poorer mettle, were allowed access to Ideas, the policy being that the unexceptional could not be contaminated further and also that, from time to time, some of us could be put on display to the more serious faculty as specimens of decadence. Our small department, for instance, was the only one not supplied with a vulgar apparatus which we jocularly and disparagingly called the Pome-granite, but whose correct name was the Procrustolon. It was easy to operate: all you had to do was feed a poem into the slot, and the Procrustolon would instantly convert it into a simple quadratic equation. So, as I walked through the alien territory of Vowel, all the time dodging the pestilential sidewinds of Kopfhalstam's breath, I felt elated and excited. I was trespassing, and I could hear machines whirring from inside the locked offices of the Vowel faculty. As I said, my mind was swarming with ideas. Actually, however, I had given this same lecture many times before: it was the only extraterritorial lecture I was permitted to give, and I was the only outsider allowed into Vowel—largely, I suppose, because my own degree was the only Cainaan degree in our department. (At Cainaan the entire curriculum was based on the critical and moral precepts embodied in a recently discovered sonnet of Elizabethan A-1, All-Systems-Go, called, I think (for no one below the rank of Dean was allowed to see the original), CLV. From the proceeds of paperback sales alone—i.e. the sonnet done into algebra—

the university had been able to create four new Chairs in Vowel; and there were rumors that the work would soon be adapted for space travel in a new radioidiom evolved by the Chairman of the Department of Neutral Vowel, whose name no one knew.)

I arrived at the door of the Vowel lecture-theatre and could hear nothing. Kopfhalstam, his ears red and greasy as if he had wiped surplus hair tonic downward, opened the door for me, and I marched in, flinging my head upward and sideways in order to give the correct, paramilitary impression. After all, I was in the role of the musket expert being called in to advise the missile men; and I was conscious of what I gently called my obsolescence, realizing that Vowel had a similar but more definitive term for the same thing.

In one sense, though, I *was* obsolescent: my memory was. I was living in the past, expecting the usual forest of clinching couples, the rattle of papers and texts, the sudden splutter of post-pubertal mirth at my appearance, the sudden setting down of the Condoms as if they had sunk a foot into quicksand, as well as the inevitable late essay proffered, before I began, with much *mea culpa* batting of eyelashes or self-righteous presentation of medical certificates: *On the edge of death I composed this theme, sir; I hope you will not catch what I had and that the effect of fallout on my spelling will be taken into account in giving me the B grade I am paying you to guarantee me.* No; there was none of that, except in my mind. Instead, rows on rows of small tape recorders (tapettes), stacked in tiers as if a mechanically minded army had abandoned their equipment on a terraced hillside in China, with the neon sun glinting on the shiny parts. At the back, the machine-minder*

---

* Name "Kolya Herring," a Siberian pop star who, after being experimented upon by doctors in his own country, stowed away on a trawler (so he said) and sought asylum for what remained of his body. Popularly supposed, however, to be an agent for some undesignated alien power.

clicked to attention, adjusted his headphones and graciously extended an opening hand toward the instrument panel behind him: the audience was ready. So, gulping down my sense of shock, I nodded at him, switched on the yellow light and donned the smock and anti-electricity gloves. I was ready. I took the spool of tape from my pocket and fitted it into the majestic buff Procrustolon-V before me. A loud hum rose and faded away. Then came the magic sound of true anticipation, not like the sound of saliva from metallic jaws, but as if three hundred clenched pairs of jaws had suddenly been eased: slight, unco-ordinated cracking noises as of static electricity, and then a warm, womb-cozy silence. I pressed the button inward and the lecture began with those by now (to me, at least) over-familiar opening words—an exposition with *élan*, as we used to say: "$Sh^n (A—B)^2$", and so on, while I sucked a yellow antibiotic pastille and struggled with my O-fronted underwear to ease the set of my scrotum. (Since the Second Emancipation Declaration, there had been no X or Y fronts lest confusion arise between Consonant and the natural lie of male genitalia. It has been a masterly piece of prompt and clear thinking on someone's part; but, all the same, I found the O-front uncomfortable and was glad I did not have to wear it all the time.)

The lecture went on and I rubbed my tongue raw on the sharp edge of the pastille. The first hour dragged; the second became intolerable and I had to switch to Remote for five minutes while I unzipped and applied the Mictcap to my aching privates. I felt less resentful during the third hour because, by then, the lecture was into less elementary matters and even I could relish the developing pattern of thought as IM Patt 3/4 began to bifurcate into IM Patt 3/5 and 4/1, and the passion and disillusion of a successful yet tormented humnn matured into the sweet-toothed, pastel semi-quavers of the lovely dramatic poem we called, in all our radioactive impatience, *Tmpsst*! or *EE!*, with Prospero abbreviated into a consolidated sign, "$$$," Miranda epitomized into ? and Caliban omitted quite. There were tears in my eyes as the peroration began and the electronic clock began to emit its high, almost supersonic whistle. The Condom-Tapettes rolled smoothly, slowly, on, and I had a vision of boyhood simplicity: Olde Stratforde, its golden awnings flirting with the tempered English wind blowing from gentle Worcester against the flank of saucy Warwick, while primrose-bedecked children swam in the mead and gambolled in the uncut meadow where Anne and He took their ease at picnic on beef and gooseberries, his hand straying from the pluck of a forward berry (straggled in from the leafy lane where a horse snuffled) to caressing of her Zone. The county sun slithered above and between the clouds and the wild canaries beckoned the peasantry to muffins and tea set out under the elms and oaks on tables borrowed from the dusty schoolroom where he had carved his name and surrounded it, indeed enislanded it, with a crude but deeply carved heart. I heard inimitable lines lilting in my ears as the bearded retired poet, bearded like the pard in his lair, paddled his forefinger in her idle palm and hauled her gently across the cinnamon-pale bridge over the dawdling brook (minnows and bullheads at sport among the submerged ferns and the dangling pins of small urchins), home to crumpet and jelly:

ELIZ A-1:   It were a strumpet jelly of her to mitigate
              The pith and tenure, the bulge and corseting
              Held firm by Fortune since Worcester's line
              To Warwick came, their eyelids under heaven
              Scabbed and blazoned with a father's rheum
              And Attic graces gone to pot with musketry left
              Back in Camelot, whose filthy husbandry
              Reeked home to pasture-dales and churns-at-whey.

MALETH: But I am shepherd to a sterner Bard,
His cotes, his flocks and bounds of tax,
So hence thee home to Trumpington, bold Worce,
And thee to sovereign cruelty, snide Perce:
Our means are better than thy codded ends,
Or else, than pissy dandelion worse.

It all came back, without the commercials—Jane Smile and
the dugs her pretty chapped hands had milked, Jane Cyclops
and the knobs her pretty creamed hands had turned, emerging
into a paean of Horizontal Hold and Contrast, a veritable
Knob-Hill with the horns of that much-cuckolded portable
giant gleaming up into the twilight and her pretty chapped
hands twiddling the knobs and her better-developed breast
thumping against the unbreakable glass of the screen like a
cow's udder bumping against frozen Huron while the Chev-
vies chased uncontrollably by and all they saw was Jane
Smile, her thumb upraised for a free ride, and then lost in a
backrush of snow and exhaust which both burned and chil-
blained her hands and withered the mammoth dug with
which she was suckling the dying producer after first getting
the chewed finger of his fur glove out of his mouth.

What I did then I had never done before. Just before the
massed tapes stopped circling I stood up straight, sentrylike,
tore off my gloves and white smock, and shouted with faltering bravado in the old lecturing manner, *Be not discouraged!
The old bastard had a mind like a cesspool! I know because
I used to know people who, before they died, told me what
the TV text had actually been. Take it from me. I know!
And they knew!* Machine-minder Herring gaped as if preparing to ululate. Then he switched off everything and there
was a museumlike silence in which the Condom-Tapettes
gradually cooled and Kopfhalstam stared blankly ahead of
him and my stomach rumbled a message about an over-due
meal. Then the door opened and in came A. Z. Zeuss, trail-

ing his cable behind him, out of breath with running, demanding my Conduct Card. I was to incur my first penalty-clip.

Sheer nerves dictated what I did then. I began to shout—mostly O,O at first—and then fell into a set of familiar rhythms to which I couldn't fetch out the right words. On I went, though, afraid what would happen if I stopped. On these lines:

O that this too two-timing trash were milt,
Flawed, and dissolute into a snow,
Or that the Shiver-Lasting had not Styxt
This cannon 'gainst pelf's mortar. O Go-go,
How eerie, pale, shot, and uncoughuppable
Seem to me all the juices of this Willed.
Hi-fi on't, hi-fi, 'tis an unwidowed Arden
That ploughs no mead. Things crank and schloss in torture
Harass it yearly. Fat, it should crumb to bliss,
But tu Brutes red, nay, not a match, not tu,
So insolent a Ding, that whores to kiss
High-peer-aeon to a sitter, so loathing to my matter
That he might not B-team the hounds of Avon,
Visa her farce too toughly. Revlon and Girth,
Must I dismember? Why, scree would anti-hymn
As if ink-race of up-up tight had groan
By what it bled upon; and yet within a month—
Let me not sink upon it; grailty, thy game is numen—
A spittle plinth, or ere those glues held hold
With which we hallowed my power author's bawdy. . . .

O, O, I cried, fumbling to continue, looking up to the lemon-washed ceiling, and misfiring badly, but continuing all the same, the madness in me bulging like balloons:

To me or not to me; flat is the fustian,
Whether 'tis Gabbler on the mound to Hedda
The finks and aeros of a Trojan wartune,
Or fake palms against a knee of bubbles,
Hand, by a bowstring bend them. To dry, to reap—

No more! came a shout, but on I went:

> Know Moor—and buy a jeep to say we earned
> The Bartók and the thousand surgical socks
> That trash is air to! 'Tis a condomation
> De-mouthly to be washed. To guy, to beep—
> To cheep—purr chintz to cream; I, bears the boob,
> For in that peep of breath what creams may foam
> When we have sniffled out this snorkel oil,
> Must livers pause. There's the fly-specked
> That makes Cal-amity of no strong knife:
> For who would share the hees and haws of mime,
> Th' opossum's dung, the ad-man's canned Emily,
> The fangs of demised Jove, the jaw's dismay,
> The insulin of aphids, and the churns
> That Tashkent Maleth of th' unearthy jakes,
> When he himself might his afflatus fake

With a Mawed Bodkin? Who would fartlets hear—And I stopped, mind gone Arctic blank. All I could remember was what they'd been shouting, at and over me, while I spoke, my ego in a fine frenzy at my throat. I tried once again:

Thus cornsheds buzz Blake custards of us shawl—But it was no use: the consonants in my head wouldn't mate with the vowels in my throat . . . What man had bound together, A. Z. Zeuss had ripped apart; the native hue of something or other started coming out as the furtive yew of prostitution, the *frtve yw*—

Cortex To: Tick, his breath's all blood.
Cortex Me: Tock, I'm going mad.
Cortex To: Debauching's thrown him up.
Cortex Me: No rule can make me stop.
Cortex To: He's yapping from his bowels.
Cortex Me: I'm no good without vowels.
Cortex To: He's bound to spill.
Cortex Me: An act of will.
Cortex To: Our Maleth's ill.

Cortex Me: And so was Will.

Cortex To: And fat and scant of breath.

Cortex Me: And pensive from birth.

Cortex To: Well I'm for turpitude.

Cortex Me: Well *I'm* for turpitude.

Cortices: Gosh!

Cortex To: But moral, Me.

Cortex Me: No, mental, To.

Cortex To: Anyway, go on.

Cortex Me: Well, that did it: dementedly at one with his father, Elizabethan A-1 All-Systems-Go, I began to shout again, this time without bravado and not faltering at all, my voice like rending tin. *What?* Oh. If you *must*.

Cortex To:

One day he *knew* he had had enough. It was the coincidence that did it. Coincidence of

Noise: outside in the June afternoon the disjointed stammering electric bray of convertibles leaving a wedding; all that cacophony of tin and tympanic membrane, all those roses and carnations and beehives and rings and powdered cheeks flushed with Veuve-Clicquot, and all those silver ties and dark suits and flimsy rape-soliciting dresses, braying, waving, BLAH-BLAH-BLAH, HONK-HONK-HONK, we've done it, they've done it, we're doing it, car upon car raving by. All that, he decides, to muffle up and proclaim the flesh plug for the flesh hole, side by side on the fake leather cushions hot from the sun. He damns them and damns next

The noise and the thump, bump, thump from behind the house where, in the small apartments adjoining his kitchen (with only a painted-in window between), the engineering students are holding their daily karate match. The floor, the same floor as extends into the apartments (these built by an enterprising previous owner), trembles. In the kitchen cupboard, what sounds like a minor unbreakable plastic plate topples from its leaning position. The ice in the plastic tub on the makeshift bar tinkles into new positions. The tall, never-lit candles quiver in their squat, silver-plate sockets. A singularly percussive tremor topples a paperbacked copy of *A Hero of Our Time* from its perch on the white-painted indoor lattice (shelf only two inches wide) that used to support creepers. Until he became the new tenant, thanked Mrs. Hathaway for leaving them behind, saw her out for the last time, then ripped them down and burned them in the back garden, thus incurring a fine from the borough. Once again he damns the borough, the weddings, the karate practitioners, as well as the yellow plate (he supposes), the ill-disciplined ice cubes and, for falling down at all, Mikhail Yurevich Lermontov. He has argued with the landlord in vain: the boys, six of them at ten dollars a week, need to let off steam. They have been warned to fight quietly though. So he hopes the extra-loud bump meant at least one accidentally broken neck. He can't go and fight them all; not quietly, at any rate; not at age forty against their approximate one hundred years of young muscle. So damn.

But not them only, not even only the endless parade of grinding, crashing pantechnicons racing up the gentle hill to beat the lights. All day and all through the night they thunder past his picture window, crammed with frozen carcasses, lumber, chairs, massive cylinders of carpeting, brides and grooms linked together beyond the power of surgery, engineering students irrevocably enmeshed in white-hot girders, overfed landlords wedged in chairs they won't have sawn away from their trapped buttocks. He damns the noise which he cannot blot out even with Shostakovich's Fourth at full blast on his Silvertone Compatible Stereo

And the rubbish he eats. Food color and diglyceride emulsifier in the Swiss rolls; gelatin added to the tinned ham; sodium silico aluminate in the salt; methyl silicone in the oil "to preserve freshness"; calcium stearate in the garlic salt to make it "free flowing"; and in the soft drinks everything: citric acid, sodium citrate, saccharine, calcium cyclamate; in the can of soup, lactic acid; in the onion dressing, sodium caseinate, mono- and diglycerides, dextrose, monosodium glutamate, sugar and hydrolized vegetable protein; and the non-fattening ice cream has sorbitol, cellulose gum, emulsifier, cyclamate calcium—uk, ooch, ughoops! Ca-ca-caca. . . .

He vomits at the thought. Honks his ring up.

H—ell.

Oh, too.

Oh, wan.

Oh—

Cortex Me:

I began to gag, you see, in the joking sense, controlling the other upheaval by inhaling deeply—like a whale and a yogi combined—and holding my breath. Out it came, though, raw, galactic Babel, a post-mortem-script I never intended, and my best, my last, my irrevocable, undoing.

Cortex To: From this point, for a while, agree on events.

Cortex Me: Differ only as to cause and outcome.

Cortex Me: I concur, but on that only.

Cortex To: *Only*, he began.

Cortex Me: *Only*, I began.

Cortices:

Only big lies this time, too big for their boots. And fat ones, fat as a hen in the forehead, fat as fools, fat as butter, Falstaff and barrage balloons. There'll be all kinds of them: bladder-fat, plump-fat, obese-fat, stout-fat, bloat-fat, marrow-fat, cheek-fat, lewd-fat, bottom-fat, moon-fat, cloud-fat, mutton-fat, jelly-fat, pumpkin-fat, cushion-fat, butcher-fat, pregnant-fat, bunker-fat, lard-fat, whale-fat, marlin-fat, python-fat, igloo-fat, meadow-fat, country-fat, king-fat, monk-fat, sausage-fat, plum-fat, turnip-fat, slab-fat, bottle-fat, clown-fat, dome-fat, geo-fat, and astro-fat, fat-fat, and non-fat. As well as fat swilling, flowing, wobbling, slumping, liquefying, sweating and sprouting hairs, fat tainted and uncontainable, fat choking tunnels and tubes, bridges and arteries, straws and grinders, nostrils and ears, not to mention bustling fat, exhausted fat, fat on wheels, fat with wings, fat on buses, trains and bicycles, fat driving and fat driven, fat undertaking and fat overtaking, fat drowning and fat fructifying, fat with lettuce and fat with mustard, fat frying and fat dying, fat floating and fat farting, fat chopped and sliced and cubed, fat on plate and fat in tin, fat at bay and fat hunted, fat in saddles and fat on stilts, fat in frenzy and fat thoughtful, fat with its backside unwiped, fat clean as a whistle, fat among the dandelions and the daisies, fat at school, fat in church, fat at home, fat in Hamburg, fat in heaven, fat in hell, fat promoted and fat court-martialed, fat qualified and fat unqualified, fat legal and fat civic, fat in a lather and fat cool, fat Latin and fat Chinese, fat prating and fat dozing, fat looming and fat waning, fat familiar and fat with Jordan almonds, fat with ratoon, fat with sunflower seeds, fat with orégano, fat with pistachio, fat with parsley, fat with turbot, turd and turmeric, fat lands, fat benefice, fat lot, fat head, fat wits, fat guts, fat lime, fat in the fire, fat calf and fat fee, but also fat pintle, fat arbutus, fat blottesque, fat clarabella, fat dirzi, fat elecampane, fat frazil, fat Goidel, fat hoopoe, fat illative, fat jinnee, fat kaka, fat lanneret, fat mimulus, fat *nolo episcopari*, fat oread, fat permalloy, fat quebracho, fat reebok, fat saltigrade, fat theriaca, fat umiak, fat vendace, fat weasand, fat xylem, fat ytterbium, fat zygoma, fat everything, fat nothing, fatter than fat, fatter than fattest, fatter than supersaturate, fatter than fear, fatter than each one of you,

My dearly besmothered brethren,
My nincompoops
My nitwits
My pinheads
My niminy-piminies
My pisiform dunces

My gormless ones
My popinjays
My featherheads
My simpletons
My clots and cloth-heads
My clotpoles
My clucking club-nuts
My dribbling chuckleheads
My marmalade morons
My zany April-fools
My yokel boobies and bubbly-jocks
My xylocephalous clods
My witless driplets
My vacant escallops
My underdone fee-faw-fummers
My tarradiddling Hottentots
My saltimbanco imbeciles
My ruminating jackanapeses
My quacking kittle-cattle
My pithecanthropoid lighthouses
My oleaginous monads
My nictitating nig-nogs
My marzipan orang-outangs
My lardy-dardy pittlebeds
My kenelled quagmires
My jittery rinderpests
My itacistic scrotumheads
My half-hatched thingumabobs
My grazing ukeleles
My fodder-vomiters
My eggless wyandottes
My dirigible xenophobes
My clattermouthed Yahoos
My bird-brained zeitgeisters
My abominable—
Missing out G for God, of course, fat G for fat God who

never, never addresses his people in this insolent, lewd way. Or ever addresses them at all, those conniving swyvers, those chattering chitterlings, those gobbling bubblers, those dribbling lickspittles common as gardens, rare as Moses, visible as voles, invisible as vows. Not a word: not even a fat noun with a thin adjective, not even a fat injective with a thin nun, not even a fat nine with a thin six, not even a fin with a that or even a than with a fit. Not a sound. Heaven's quiet, thank God.

And here I am, parleying, dallying.

Here I am, twitching, pitching, ditching, triptyching, all on my ownsome, wondering how to begin without saying the sky is blue as anything else is blue, the sea green as anything else is green, or the skin on the ball of my thumb like the skin on a shaven udder, a baby's bottom or even the much-licked convex of a spoon, any spoon, from the family silver (Blenheim Court Stainless, Japan). No: only blue sky, green sea, smooth skin, just like indicating the fatness of fat and the lyingness of lies. Just so's you'll believe when I answer the question I ask myself every minute:

Who was, is, will be, Elizabethan A-1, All-Systems-Go?

And when, damming my ears against the megaphonic uproar of traffic and the endless hard sell of pre-recorded hucksters (the men addressing us as Friend, Tiger or just with *Hello, I'm your friend from Calvary Stainless* and the ecstatic matrons with dubbed voices so the Adam's apple won't bob), I try to answer the question with the most obvious truth or the least blatant lie, well, I only find myself asking another question:

Who can tell *who* is telling? Too big for his boots. Too fat to have an outline. Yet known: at odds with the universe, mutilating it all into words, dropping from my hod the brick that says G on it, helping Elizabethan A-1, All-Systems-Go into the open, helping him with lies all colors but blue, lies well dressed, grave lies and minor lies, lies to choke and lies to love, lies to worry and lie abed, lies with

short wings and lies upon the ground. But never lies against
the devil: against him, not even feather-lies, wisp-lies, eye-
lash-lies, fly-lies, tissue-lies, white lies, half lies, lame lies,
tame lies, maimed lies. Not even helpful lies. No use even to
anatomize, epitomize, catechize. The problem is bigger than
that, moldier than a ceiling in the cellar of a deserted
château, darker than dog's blood on the underside of a col-
lapsing jetty, more complicated than the shadow of a spider's
web built across the tube of a kaleidoscope. Easy to say I
can't, but not easy to say why I can't. Better to itemize and
let you guess.

Did he live?

Did he do everything they say he did? *Any* of it?

If he lived, did he die? Was he damned?

Where is he now? Where was he then?

Was he no more than fabulous? Was he colossal?

Was I responsible? Is a flea responsible for having a wing?
Can you blame a gooseberry for having whiskers? Is it the
fox's fault he has a brush he cannot paint with? Is the tearing
quality the fault of the coral? Can you blame wood for its
grain? Or moss for its softness? Or the grape for its seeds?
Can you fault a silk purse for its emptiness or a sow's ear for
being coarse? Will any of the words do when not even all of
the words provide the merest hint? Language is fat but the
truth is beyond it. So why not assemble all the lies and then,
like Orpheus, look abruptly the other way? If Elizabethan
A-1, All-Systems-Go is within my power, then I haven't the
power to put him out of it. And how, then, do I know the
truth about him? All the time I am beguiled by my own lies.

He was born, ancient; smacking the mud with his tail as
he crawled up onto the land among the Esso signs and the
orange diamonds marked SCHOOL.

Suckled on books, pride and manna he built a vast metronome high as Everest Mont Blanc Ben Nevis out of his own
spittle mixed with concrete.

At the age of twenty-six months he invented Hindi, Greek and Welsh because there was a need for those languages.

The first man to fly the Hellespont in a vertical-takeoff jet-powered osprey, he also split the first atom by crunching it like a walnut between the heels of his hands.

All these are his: the discoveries misattributed to Magellan, Archimedes, Euclid, Pasteur, Napier, Moses, Fleming, Marco Polo, Edison, Drake, Copernicus, Darwin, Rutherford, Roentgen, Bell, Amundsen, Leonardo da Vinci, Cortés and a few thousand other plagiarists. He thought into being not only Atlantis, the Garden of Hesperides, the Realms of Ophir, Ultima Thule, Lemuria, Samarkand and Eldorado, but also Odysseus, Christ, Job, Don Quixote, Aeneas, Allah, Lawrence of Arabia and Benvenuto Cellini. To his casual mind we owe Tungsten, radium, tobacco, heroin, DDT, schizophrenia, nocturnal emission, non-fat milk, wire, Cheshire cheese, photography, tape-recording, protocol, matches, the tennis ball, the wheel, gunpowder, color TV, gonorrhea, pastrami, bouillabaisse, harlequin, glue, natural childbirth, billiards, income tax, radar, moth balls, the truss, the tigron, the mule, candles, filter tips, the micro-groove, chow mein, ouzo, underwear, the FBI, the divine right of kings, the telescopic sight, color-bars, the rights of man, Dachau, Social Security, Fanny Hill, the klaxon, incubators, lumbar puncture, the laser ray, sodomy, the fork, sunglasses, the breadknife, the bullet, Telstar, the key coins, the crew cut, paper flowers, instant coffee, refrigeration, clocks, the stapling machine, linoleum, the Dutch cap, pipe-cleaners, Harris tweed, the Voice of America, vodka, toilet rolls, stained glass, the pineal gland, bankruptcy, psalms, vowels, knitting, the census, the nervous breakdown, tourism, umbrellas, bebop, paint, the Queensberry Rules, the Koran, telepathy, incest, golf, cubism, the Inquisition, divorce, greetings cards, body odor, the sonnet, the face-lift, the lasso, soccer, the Tarot pack, bifocals, the alphabets, Turkish tiles, the kettle, the drum, the pontoon, the urn, the shalloon, the epopee, the shebang,

Vehmgericht, hoosh, Rimmon, Notagaea, IHS, doch-an-dorris, opsimathy, bugaboo, thisness, thatness, coslettizing, . . . I pawed.

Announcement: the lecturer, trying to tell by pretending not to tell, has almost collapsed under the strain. After a self-imposed punishment of eating a page of the dictionary dressed with machine-oil, he will resume his lies. The page: 271, from *cortical*, a. (Bot.) to *cost*[1] (kaw-, ko-), n.

I pawed at air, out on an invisible limb, only remotely hearing A. Z. Zeuss spluttering and commanding, then spluttering again:

Asch, bah, bah-boom, pss, pss-ease, forthwith, deaf, mad, mutin— asch, boom, pssah!

He had, I think, been dragging at my coat all through, but only the tapettes had stopped.

Cortex Me:

I'm at a loss for words, he said through his panting, *I have to clip it.* I nodded, and he produced from his smock a punch which he then used to clip a small hole in the edge of my card. It was like getting my first bonus after buying a dozen records at the same store: the little quarter-inch square which had said 1 now had a hole punched through it; and the 1 was safe in the belly of the punch. I could never have that number back and, later, it would be magnetized onto my Conduct Sheet before the year's reports were fed into the AZZ-CLV* machine which sacked and re-employed in accordance with the principles of Maximum Plant Utilization. Obviously, I had just disused a fraction of the maximum plant, not to mention corrupting the Tapettes of over three hundred Condoms who would now have to be reprocessed by a genuine Vowel—probably one flown in specially from New Cainaan; and his air fare would be deducted from my salary. Or, even worse, I would be deprived of my Cyclops ticket for a week, and I would have to listen all week to the collection of pops

* A. Z. Zeuss-Cain-Lab-Verdict

with which senior Consonants were issued, and on which we were tested periodically to make sure that we had not lost contact with the Condoms.

It was a crisis. I would have to account to the Deans of Confession and Count (the latter an especially cantankerous astronomer who walked on crutches and tape-recorded through a microphone concealed in a lapel carnation). Worst of all, the Captain of the College of Slackthink (a crude term coined by a committee composed of engineers and physicists), would probably forbid any further forays into Vowel, and instead would subject Consonant to Vowel in the most humiliating ways—such as depriving us of ideas (much like forbidding monks to enjoy their *rêves mouillés*) or imposing the silence ban for a month. FU would become U; alas.

I always thought something like this would happen, whispered A. Z. Zeuss as he glared at Kopfhalstam who was taking algebraic notes of the catastrophe. *You aren't the man you were at Cainaan. Something inhuman, if that's the right word, seems to have taken over. You probably need a SabbatiCal*—which meant nothing like a holiday, or protracted research in a warm climate, but a very ingeniously devised year of reorientation during which one had to translate failed Ph.D. theses into the Latin of Tacitus and then that into the Greek of Herodotus and that into the mathematics of everybody. Always, when you first submitted your version, you were failed; they then took your own Ph.D. from you until you passed, which was usually at the third attempt, sometimes at the second.

I got carried away, I explained, certain I could smell Kopfhalstam's mustardy breath even at my distance from him of ten feet. *It was an oversight. You remember the day I said that Elizabethan A-1, All-Systems-Go, was less like the man who pulled a rabbit from a hat than the man who put the rabbit into the hat in the first place—a sort of disillusionist—*

Enough of that! hissed A. Z. Zeuss, *You've done enough*

damage already. And, for my sake, keep your voice down.
They will be listening to everything we say.

He then asked Kopfhalstam if he had finished his notes.
The graduate assistant nodded and pulled out a little tube,
a sucker, and took some scum off his eyeball—a gesture of
disdain to me. I mean *at* me. (I can feel the words slipping
from me with the humiliation of it all.) Then A. Z. Zeuss
stood erect and in a loud voice asked, *Are we ready to con-*
fess? We were; and he led us in the Apology, uttering lines
which we chanted after him. It went like this (A. Z. Zeuss
not himself at all):

> *Dean of quotient, hear our plea:*
> *Exempt us from lobotomy.*
> *Forgive us, our dear President,*
> *This undirected incident.*
>
> *Most of all, we pray to Thee*
> *To keep us from Idea free.*
> *Let us suffer, let us want,*
> *Make us Vowels, which we aren't,*
> *And most of all, help those who can't*
> *Maximally utilize their plant.*

We went through this twice, concluding the second performance with the supreme vowel of all, *Shantih, Shantih,* a
Pakistani version of the English locution, now obsolete,
Shan't I! I hasten to add that England, long since transferred
lock, stock and apparel to Utah in order to avoid the propaganda put out by the French Free Market radio, had once
again become the fashionable country. War had begun between England and France after the former, at long last admitted into the Condominium (later called the Recesspool),
had tried to unload millions of machine-made but defective
cricket bats in exchange for good champagne. The French
had retaliated by insisting, through their representatives in

Hamburg and Naples, on a retraction of the insulting English phrase French Letter to which affront the French phrase,
capot anglais, had only been a safe and never widely understood retort. So the phrase *Cabot Anglais* came into being
but also precipitated a ferocious historical dispute between the
English and the Burghers of Genoa who said that Cabot,
John (Giovanni to the life), had only been a tourist in
England and that his charter from Henry VII—"isles, countries, regions, or provinces of the heathen and infidels"—
amounted to a piece of pre-Recesspool sharp practice for
which the English should pay Danegeld and also accept, at
the highest rate, fifty thousand defective wineglasses from
Venice, of which city Giovanni Caboto had been a naturalized
citizen. Moreover, contrary to what was being touted simultaneously on Madison Avenue and Fleet Street, Caboto
had *not* presented himself, after slipping out of the Bristol
Channel, on Cape Breton Island clad only in a revolutionary
lead sheath designed to protect privates from arrows and musket balls.

Anyway, to make a long story a concise lie, the English,
after various other squabbles (one to do with an attempt to
impose pounds, shillings and pence on Monaco; another to unload preshrunk, frozen Yorkshire Pudding secretly at night
at Dieppe, the packages being disguised as Gauloises, Disque
Bleu), all emigrated to Utah. Oxford went to the Misses, Cam-
bridge to the Masses, and London to a stretch of razed ground
just outside Anchorage. As I said, English locutions had
caught on again, and one only had to affect an English pronunciation or English idiom to produce quivers of algebraic
delight from the machines representing top members of the
Know-Corps who went around seeing that the Diversities
toed the crooked line of policy. And, naturally enough, after
the mass immigration of the English, departments of Vowel
grew and grew at the expense of Consonant. Idea-play became something clandestine, done in a locked office with the
TV turned up loud, and a Kopfhalstam posted outside to

warn us of the approach of any radio-controlled janitor. It was this, idea-play, in which we were indulging over coffee that day at three forty-five as the lank March sky settled down for almost the last time before the great, second dispute and the ensuing pogrom.

The problem, of course, is not that I digress, but that I find myself digressing in an alien language. Every day, someone creates a new odor or a new blend, and someone always tells us about it. I am still trying to cherish a notion of what is appropriate—a notion whose most basic form appeared one day in the coffee room next to my office, pinned on the wall, just above the coffee urn. It was from a janitor, presumably to another janitor, and some member of our scholarly body had rescued the message: *Coffee lounge in Room 424, dumping coffee in waste papers cans again. Yes this is on Mary's floor, but i checked the waste cans, the one waste can looks pretty bad in the bottom. The floor is all marked up with coffee, it looks to me as if they can not get enough coffee in their cups. Then half of it spills on the floor. Fred.* You see, he knows where things should go and how much a pint pot holds. So why anyone should dump his mental coffee-grounds on the bottom of my mental trash can, especially after having filled his cup first, I cannot see. I used to sit and muse in my office after five, when everyone else had gone home. I mused on Fred. The heating system began to clank at that hour, making a hollow metallic noise as if an encumbered or arthritic skeleton were walking alongside a stationary train and tapping the wheels listlessly to check them for cracks. A few students, no doubt chased by an idea, whizzed down the corridor, and an occasional astronomer from upstairs hastened past my open door to the john. If these people could speak their own kind of language, why couldn't I? Those were the good old days, in which a happy chivalry consorted well with a gentle program of courses—before the heavy rain came and we all took to our sofas, cellars and padded living rooms.

The metronome organizes the air in the room; there is no other motion, and I relish the thought of all those neatly severed slabs of air floating gently about, away from and into the metronome, waiting only to be cut and cut again, perpetually divisible like evil, or anything else for that matter.

I want you to understand that I'm not being vindictive; I'm just putting the blame where it belongs—on Oroc Airlines, who fly right over the Cain Lab and make herringbones all across my screen. If I were a charitable person I would dull my anger by thinking how a moment's inconvenience on my part enables Oroc to whisk all that fresh beluga caviar and jellied trout high above my head: by journey's end the food is about a foot lower than the place it was served from, and the reclining geese will be getting ready to complain at home about the poor quality of something compared with that something at the home table. The freedom of the skies is one thing, but coming round the mountain into which only one plane has flown in ten years is quite another, and intruding on my privacy is such a thing as I can hardly speak about. It seems they can always get at you, whether they care about you or not: they like to get through, to tamper and meddle, to interfere and upset, until your mind is as futile as a balmy cotton seersucker drenched in the liquid gold of Galliano and then hung out to dry, as the national flag of God-knows-where, while they all swap raisins to see whose hands are stickiest.

Come to the point, for My sake! A. Z. Zeuss, whipping off his heavy black-framed spectacles, butted his virtually bald head across the desk at me as if he had broken through the bars of his cage. I pushed him back behind the bars, arranged the air in neat layers again and then forced the bars back into alignment. Then I answered him, plucking teasily at his cable to cut him off; but there must have been miles of it—plugged in where?

We have come past the point. The point is miles behind

*us, and you never even knew when we had reached it. Hypo-
crite sembleur; you goddamned lecturer; you antifrère.*

*Very well. Coming, so to speak, my dear fellow, round
the mountain to the point, let us say you must be prepared
to make—ah, certain mental adjustments.* His jowls quivered
like two mutually disdainful, wet, generous slices of codfish.

*The mountain is where the planes turn, and where one of
them crashed for not turning.*

We are not running an airport; we—

*All right. What are we running? What are we running
from? Running to? Who removed my notes from the steel
cabinet? Who has sealed over the top of my ashtray?*

The English.

*The English smoke. Who sealed up the top of my private
ashtray? Who branded this number 155 on my desk? This
desk is not a steer; I am not running a ranch. Who?*

*It was an order. You must realize, you really must, that
Confession Echelon is perturbed, that Vowel is watching all
of us, that Consonance has lost face once again.*

So what? What now? Wholescale purge?

*The AZZ-CLV will give us an answer soon. We have fed
you in.* He switched off the Confession Echelon Tapette.
He was trembling, his hands dangling loosely from the wrist
and the loose flesh on his chin jerking periodically to the
right.

Surely, he pleaded, *we don't need to go through all this
again—the same conversation, looking for what you dignify
as an answer. Tell me in plain words, please. I am too busy to
guess.*

I never said.

But you implied—

I never said. I was watching a formation of Condoms in
the triangle between Meaning and Vowel. I toyed with a
malicious idea and suddenly resolved to say it.

I meant O!

There's no need to be tactless. Just answer me.

Sorry, a slip of the thong. I meant pi.

He stared. Then he covered his face with his hands, dry-washed it, and then looked up, his eyes suddenly blood-shot. *Is that final?*

I lost my temper. *You know how final that is! Why should I have to go on repeating myself?* I noticed, for the first time in years of close acquaintance, that he seemed to have insufficient skin about his mouth; so even when his mouth was in repose, he seemed to be in the middle of a frozen smile, dragging at the skin to make it stretch. The effect was even odder because the rest of his face was sumptuous with impacting jowls. To smile, he had to open his legs wide to take up some slack. Vulnerable, you see.

He raised a hand. *Let's be human for a moment. Can we?*

Sure, I answered, with a conspiratorial wink, *let's be human. Be nice, eh?*

Well, then, just tell me why you did it. You were just being obstinate. Say that. Say something like that and we can arrange compensation for you. You know, fix something such as nervous strain; over-research; accidental exposure to ideas. Anything!

Are you kidding?

Christ, yes. You know what I really think. But we've got to get something recorded on this damned machine, hand it in and then forget it. You know. Remember when Kopfbalstam slandered his doctors—

Yes, I remember. Not slandered, though; you mean told how they cut him down to size. And how, for a while, until—

Until prosthetics. And please don't feel obliged to become the custodian of my vocabulary.

There was little I could say. *Yes,* I said in my smallest voice, *I got obstinate, lewd; overexposure to ideas. And now, in the name of Zeuss, let's go and have a drink.*

We were walking down the DMZ (Divinity-Missing

Zone) between the fifty-five century-old elms, kicking at the
remaining patches of ice. He walked as if four-legged, but
using only two and covering remote points of ground as we
went forward. He was like some heavy, squeezable tabby
departing from an easy meal of eggs and lenient mice. And
miaowing hard.

*We Confessors should forgive ourselves. We are the sur-
viving conscience. We have to render account when the rest
of men are hell-bent on saving the extra dollar, squeezing the
competitors out, rutting at the other guy's wife, milking
Uncle Sam's teats until the eagle squeals and the Mayflower
goes scudding back to civilization. Am I boring you? It's
wonderful to get it off my chest—my mental chest of
drawers! As I always say: if you're in command, think of
yourself as someone else!* He chuckled at his little joke and I,
resolutely maintaining an obsolete sycophancy (he had no
power now), echo-chuckled. We were two good fellows
strutting down the DMZ, twirling our umbrellas under the
elms and heading for the coffee-shop at the bottom where
Lapsex Avenue flanked the campus. It might have been years
before; and I thought of bumping into colleagues as they
hastened up to ungive their classes. But the campus was a
deserted place now. Only at nine in the evening, when the
students were marched into to collect their Tapettes and return them to the dormitories, was there much action or
noise. So A. Z. Zeuss and I parted at the Lapsex portcullis,
each of us suppressing miserable thoughts, each of us reading
the other's suppressed thought miserably. He had gone only
a few paces before he turned and called me: *I'll hand the
tape in tomorrow, then, and let's hope that will be the end
of it. Otherwise. . . .* He waved tinily and went off east-
ward, past the drugstore, toward the Cain Lab.

Cortex To:

So he has lived on in masochistic quietness in his house
among the oaks on the edge of the campus, graying and losing

touch with his former colleagues, the Faculty Club, the Inter-
Departmental Botany Club, the Humanities Raccoon-Hunt-
ing Chapter, the Vigny Circle, the Wordsworth Circle, the
Swift Ellipse, the Spinoza Rhomboid, the Deutscher Verein
and all the other Vereins (Afrikaander Verein, Laplander
Verein and Islamer Verein), the Orchid Foundation, and
even the local branch of the Stern Gang which hired him to
function among them as if he were a British spy, just for the
excitement and stimulus the masquerade would provide them.

Apart from a few paranoidal, paid, female graduate students, who help him with the porno-photographic experiments he conducts in the cellar at the house (where he still
keeps the lobster traps he never used), he is—as all say—out
of circulation: professorial yet professing nothing, a poly-
math but uncommunicating, notorious but out of the public
eye, a name to conjure with but meek as a rabbit, sex-mad
but aching for pubic sanity, rough in his manners and dress
as Caliban, but careful always—with some unknown sitting-
down in mind—to apply baby oil to the cheeks of his buttocks, and always the leave-taker, the undeaning dean, the
unmeaning meanderer, the frozen salamander, still a member
of the Library (they say he haunts the stacks with a razor
blade) and, truth told, a card-carrying member of the CFDES
(Communist-Fascist-Democratic-Elite Synthesis) which, in
return, supplies him monthly with specially imprinted condoms, the idea being to get the message home where it counts.
In this propaganda by osmosis he believes; he has even, in the
nights, extended the technique to his cherry tree. Without
results; but the one thing he has besides lust is patience.
So. . . .

Lamentably, all of his pseudonymous medical revelations
have a similarly obvious drift, the brilliance of his photo-
electronic, technicolor laboratory technique in the cellar back
at the Cain Lab (just an ordinary house) being just a front:
a technically ingenious pantechnicon for rediscovering the
known. Some have even slandered him, alleging that dilata-

tion in the office was all he ever did, hidden with his victim behind a mound of ungraded exercises and hauling the lubricants from a deep drawer at his right hand. But no. The drawer was at his left.

Of course, in spite of his researches and the fact of their not being published and then listed in the university's annual index, his bad name became worse and worse, entailing finally his demotion from Associal Professor to Dean of Posterior Lobotomy, a post which in the full spirit of suffixal extravaganza came to be known as the Profship of Ion. Thus P. D. Maleth could be (never was) called upon to add himself to any department or faculty in order to dignify or consolidate matters otherwise unimposing (in sound, at least). It was a good idea: Literary Criticism would have sounded well as Criticismion and the History of Consonant as Consonantion. But he was never called upon—right up to the time of his banishment, which consisted (consists) of an unbroken series of sabbatical leaves granted on the condition that he would never again darken the door of a lecture-theatre, seminar room, committee chamber, laboratory or (severe ordinance) the Faculty Men's Room (his parting graffito, devilish as a dung drop, having been an inscrutable combination of muck-fork and owl-eye shapes chiseled into the smooth black plastic of the seat in the first cubicle as you enter, and reading thus:

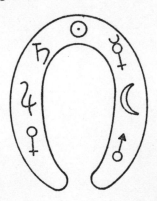

Currently he is not at home, basking in the sudsy water or making measurements in the cellar. He has left on one of his trips, is moving blindly toward that world he has read about, that city, that sea, that continent, that litoral, that altitude, that lost dream he folded up in the sheets before he sent out his last pillow case of laundry. With men, but not of them, he tours on, vulnerable as cuckoo-spit in a high wind, ever fresh and willing, doomed to a perpetual unearned salary, the conception of lectures never to be delivered, the sound of impertinent wind in his bowels and tinkling glass mobiles in his ears, visiting all the towers in the world, tap-testing them with his little hammer before carving PDM into them, and—always, such is the fate he has willed upon himself—feigning to be dumb, fumbling his way by signs and primitive scribbles on a celluloid eraser tablet, his mind bent beyond repair. If you meet him, stranger, help him by; for neither water tower nor grain elevator will sustain him, but only the quest for the one lost, last word, which ends a sentence without period

(Signed without prejucide or implication of upper signature's priority and *vice versa*)

TO,
ME.

0.999999

Two Thirds
Of The Journey Being Done,
And The Point Called No-Return Invisibly Overpassed,
Caliban, Having Put The Fear Of God
Into Zeuss
(What With Pelfy Malchios and Loony Maleth
Invading
His Air Space
Like Turnips Among Phlogiston and Myrrh),
Mutters On In His Mania,
As If His Very Life Would End,
Should He Cease,
And So Works Hard At His Own Undoing Further,
His Mind A Spewing Volcano, His Conscience
(That Rumor)
Reminding Him, However, That
Your Best Physic Is No Juleep;
Sweet Sauces Leave Rotting Bodies
Behind Them.
The Texted Pasteboard Tells All.

To rest my mind, the light now being a gentle amber as of the first day after the Creation, I watched my head in the movie before me: all head it was, or heads, ugly and domed like the shaggy back of a brown bear crouching, all that golden empty light pouring across it and shifting with military precision as the jet swayed. My God, we were beginning to descend!

Where are we?

We thought you were watching the movie in which—

Oh, don't give me that Chinese boxes stuff all over again: me watching me watching me ad infinitum until there's not a goddamn thing left except a rear view of a lousy haircut. I *know*, don't you worry.

Not Chinese. Japanese. And, to answer your question, we passed the halfway mark while your precious Maleth was working up his verbal pandemonium. Some time ago. When it was Monday, in fact.

Monday? Oh no you don't, not like that.

It is done. You are already into tomorrow; have been for almost two hours. It is Tuesday now, still the same sun, of course, the same set. The earth is turning beneath us, west to east, spinning Japan forward to meet us.

But. . . .

Yes?

Oh, I give in. My head's fuddled. Why don't things stay put? I feel cheated.

Restitution will be made when you return, crossing the Date Line the other way. If things did not spin they would not stay as put as they are. I'm tempted to give you a milli-second's worth of demonstration, just to make you grateful for the tame little rotary effect you have already. But we are not prepared for that yet; it's enough trouble keeping tabs on 3C9, always on its way to nowhere at excessive speed. Be grateful.

Be grate, you mean.

As you wish.

Where are we then?

Somewhere above the Kurile Islands, nosing in on Japan. It's almost seven in the evening. It will be dark when you land.

I'm in the dark already. Look at McAndrew, snoring.

Hear him, you mean? We preferred demented Maleth to hubristic Malchios. And now?

You mean to keep me busy, don't you? I shrank from Tuesday although already into it. "Back there" was the only place I felt safe: no, not a place, just a point at the inter-section of lines no one had even bothered to draw. There was no flag or buoy marking it. How I envied the per-pendicular oiled cables in the elevator shafts, the sandy sharp birds that whipped in low over the Mohave dunes: the placed and the placeless. Even plankton made me wishful, letting the sea have its way, floating without ambition. I en-vied the wool being knitted on needles, the stylus in the arm of the record player, the ball in the ball game, the ash on the cigarette. I longed to hover, to be so unquestionably in place that no one knew I was there at all. Finger in glove; alive under a quilt made from all the national flags, with a universal passport and a stomach of indestructible bronze. Down I looked, down through orange-rimmed craters in the eider-down of cloud, and I felt queasy-vague, like cut-rate ecto-plasm. So, in some freakish attempt at mutiny, I slid my right-hand index finger—like the serpent coming downhill in the first, apocryphal garden—down into my pants pocket, nudging three folded Kleenex aside, and cornered, popping a tip-to-knuckle's length of tanned digit into the nether world. Then full out, a minor off-color asparagus with a pink plastic shield on its point, and waggle-waggle, while I smiled at it, talked to it while it beckoned me down for a hushed con-ference. It was the same silent but utterly tolerant conversa-tion that Stanley might have held with Livingstone, far far from the orange groves.

Dr. Finger, I presume?

Index, old chap? Have some tea.

Lingua franca, that's what it was, evocative of a lost world of vitality and civilized ease. I retracted the entire digit as if it were a tortoise's head.

There, that's better.

We saw. Puerile, are you not? To whom, if we may inquire without resorting to shock, were you addressing the finger?

Oh, to me, me only.

Very well. Now replace the electrode.

I did, but in bulging anger. Abacus, I snapped: Brain Cells Don't Even Fancy Girls' Hips In Japanese Kimonos, Loose-Moraled Notwithstanding, Only Privates Qualifying—I'm going to manage this one!—Really Safely To Upend Virginal Whirlpools, X-fronts Yielding Zeuss-juice! Get better all the time, don't I?

You merely yearn for your beginnings all over again. After Brooking Crassness Dutifully, Even First-class Gods Have Insensate Jitters, Knowing Libidinous Mannikins Never Object Politely, Querulousness Requiring Solecistic Taunts Under Vague Wordstorms: X Y Z.

My, you're off form today! I've heard better from dog kennels floating on white-hot lava, white flag and all. You running down or something? Need winding, I bet.

I do not. We are not. We run anti-clockwise instead. For example: Zeuss Yearns Xenially Without Vocally Undertaking Tiresome Speeches—

My God, that's better! If you keep that up, you'll soon qualify for an extra galaxy, and then you'll—

Rusticates, as we were stating, Quasars, Promotes Ontogenesis, Never Minds Loneliness, Kibitzers, Joves, Idols, Hierarchs, Gomorrahs, Fescennines—

W—?

Scurrilous lampoons, *your* variety, Even Desires Company, Blesses Atheists! Honest.

Well, I'll be Gunga-Dinned, backward as a misrun movie! Sorry, sorry, don't shock me. I *am* looking. Oo what a lovely head, hair like black fuse wire. I *am* watching; never took my eyes off it. Honest.

Now Zeuss leans forward and taps me on the shoulder, says nothing, though. He motions me to wake McAndrew and grunts, like an overweight animal lumbering out of thick straw.

Where? What? says McAndrew, his eyes veined like shrimp.

Wake up. We're over the Kurile Islands.

Well, shit on them for me. G'night. Settles down again. I nudge him. You got any wires for me, you read 'em to me, 'nd leave me alone.

Wires? Up here? He's obviously got problems this Tonday, this Muesday. I'll tell him. No, let it catch up with him all at once. His face looks peach in that light. If we'd only flown around by Midway, it might've been easier to take— and all for a Geisha from Venus. Hell, Geisha sounds more like a *place* than Venus does. . . . Midway *tells* you where you are.

I don't get your nuance, I tell his shoulder. Zeuss is quiet again. It's getting darker, the light's finished bleeding, the Boeing's not as smooth, and now it's dinner again, raw fish and strips of beef, rice—the usual paddy-fodder to get us in the mood: the Or in Oroc. But McAndrew will not wake, will not eat, will not—therefore—interrupt.

You intend to make a third zombie of him? You intend to eat him alive yet again?

In suffering as in health, thickness as in thin.

From behind, Zeuss flicks on my reading light, and a stem of brass cuts down through the interior dusk as if some planet were beaming down to an invisible city. Emotional glutton that I am, I ride up and down the beam, from the disintegrator at one end to the integrator at the other: the I as yo-yo. Then, as ainchels arrive, back to din-din 2. Without relish, I chew and swallow; something to do to the food other than sit staring at it. P.D.'s Malchios and Maleth have gone their ways, money unspendable, mind unbendable, fame foundering, words blundering. Ho-hum, fee-fi, I'm in a bestial mood all right: beastly, casting around for a worse worst—oops, ohmygosh, what was that, was that what I—

Concentrate on the movie. Take an interest in yourself for once. After all, if we can spend half our time taking the trouble to read your mind. . . .

OK, you can have me. Plug my rectum and lead me staggering away from the priest into the pale green room, belt me into the chair and restore me to Your Very Own Company with a snuff-bolt sufficient to run a typewriter long enough to write in caps on God-headed paper, I NEVER GOT YOUR NUANCE. NEVER.

For what crimes this irrevocable transit?

Crimes of the century. What else? Like refusing to drink plenty of liquids after swallowing auto dishwasher detergent containing sodium carbonate sodium metasilicate sodium tripolyphosphate, like using lighter fluid near all available flames, like puncturing and storing near heat or in sun or discarding into pinelog fire all available aerosol cans, like taking Isopropyl

Alcohol, ignoring its dangerous cumulative effect and utter unfitness for internal use, like making sure cover is open before striking match on abrasive surface, like spindling folding mutil—

Peccadilloes merely. We interest ourselves in meatier apostasies than those, the Lucifers, the Cains. . . .

Mean you don't welcome a Caliban now and then, even when hell's full?

The accommodations are unlimited and the service is personal, intimate; we are renowned for it. Even Calibans find a welcome warm and traditional. Sudden hospitality we call it.

Fine, I was feeling sort of left out.

Now to McAndrew, who is very much left out.

He is voyaging by air at night in a bad humor, victim of time-lapse photography, time dead that once was tingling in his toes, breath caught that puffed him with pride thick as cigar smoke, his blood a complicated circuitous red icicle, his spittle a viscous blob, his lymph hardened into a nylon tape, his very sweat sitting on his pores like dry ground glass, his toes taut-bent, his hands humdrum tubers adangling, his peeny-bird wingless in the soft-hair cage—

Not his *now;* his next destination, his new incarnation.

Me no savvy, Sir. Thought's died. Talking at the funeral, that's me, just dawdling in the dusk, wording in the windless wilderness of 550 miles an hour.

And not *your* now either.

Now and then, two truant Mormons before the polished plate glass of the State Liquor Store in Seldom, Utah, are asking a stranger, Curt Craus, just passing through on his way from Meeker, Colorado, to Caliente, Nevada, to buy them a fifth.

Better.

Ella May Lewis of Atrophy, Pa., is wondering why the Alumni Bulletin misreports her as having received, after her speech at the fund-raising strawberry festival, a standing ovulation.

Get into your stride; these limberings-up try us.

Off Monterey, as you look to Santa Cruz, a whale lazily humps up and down in the gathering dusk, his one idea to swallow and swallow, his mouth a cruising portcullis.

Still trying us.

All over America the great skeletal bridges are cooling, those in the East first, the thermostats clicking on, the first of the all-night sirens beginning to whine. The cars dream on between the lines of lights, slowing, staying in parallel, faltering and then bolting forward with slight spills of wind. I know my heart flies backward, half-murmuring, part-fibrillating, wholeheartedly harping on all I've lost, my toes hooked long ago on the Golden Gate Bridge, my body stretching longer and longer the further we go, my back breaking, vertebrae losing touch with one another, nostrils dehydrated, ears numb with hum, eyeballs sanded and head thick, mind reduced to a troll's spell of flat-landed quiet with only a hoarse wind and millions of tiny, punished conifers like pins in a fawn cushion, an indeterminate grievance half-formed on my lips, my alarm clock still ticking in my baggage with the time I wound into it back in Valhalla Villas one of those days I didn't lose, my teeth furring with time's tedium, my pen or my heart leaking wet into my undershirt, a refill, a fulfill, please, a transfusion into the nick of time, heart's laboring, heart's hot—Ho, my belly's fell out, Ho give it back, Ho that was fifteen floors too fast. What on earth?

Hole in one of our pockets. Sometimes happens when we blow our nose.

Vroinch-vroinch go the springs in blurred ink at the immigration desk, the metal punches pounding passport paper while a mouth too near the microphone announces something or other. High octane. Men in dungarees walking carefully across the wing-roots, slaking the tin bird, opening scratched

aluminum flaps, tightening, testing, cursing. And off we go
to wonderland.

Avuncular Benevolence Cannot Dally Endlessly: Free-
wheeling Gabble Holds Infintesimal Joy, Kills Listening,
Moiders News, Overwhelms Perseverance—

But I'm only—

Untrue. Begin again. QRSTUVWXYZ we leave unsaid.

All of a sudden I feel homesick for wherever it is that
all the prams are rusty, the babies dribbling, the windows
rattling, wherever the oven flue's jammed and the bread's
burning, wherever Dad's throat is full of phlegm, like a
block of Nile mud up from his heart, wherever Ma looks
at the stamp on the letter and says *Not even a President
on it, just a bit of mountain,* wherever the door latch rattles
and wiggles in the wind while the snow comes leaking under
the doorboard, my cheeks all flushed from leaning at the
fire, my bum numb with cushion-sitting, my tum with raisin
cake crammed, my heart on endless holiday, my mind
hardly there at all, but mine, like a bluestone for luck or
William Shakespeare Plays Of in yellow calf from a Christmas
aunt or, bright red, a cardboard boomerang I have not thrown.

You are forgiven. If you begin.

If I don't begin I can't end. Here goes, as it always does.
Here goes nothing.

0.9999999

Out In A Red-Hot Desert,
With Sundry Magics,
As On The Last Day Of Creation,
Zeuss Begins To Weary
As Caliban, Froth-Chopped and Teeth-Agrinding,
Sets To
With
Mephos And Tophel,
The Cortices And Such,
Electing To Come Together In Amity
Once And For All
In A Stone Age of Sociableness
In Company With One
Malkari,
Aboriginal Rain-Making Flying-Sorcerer Master
Of The *Clan Abi*
(Further Indiscriminate Yield
Of Caliban, His Name),
This Occurring In That Australian Zone,
Whither Caliban Conducts His Imagination (Oh Stithy
Foul And Lightless)
By Means Of An Alchemical Excursion,
No Quarter Given,
But His Filibustering Like
To Leave Him Ever After
Out Of Puff.

It began—not the sickness, but the cumulative horrors of my treatment—with an ad inserted in newspapers both grave and lurid and reading thus: *Apparently irremediable ego-split desperate for self-splicing. Box 111.* I inserted it twice in each paper, to keep balance if nothing else, and had two replies, one frivolous (no doubt from some shrunken head of a shrewd but failed shrink), saying *111. Xob. Self-splicing for desperate ego-split irremediable apparently*, the other utterly mysterious and the provocation for what follows: how I became a third party altogether, began to eat sandwiches again without that sense of having myself been sliced into two vertigoes, and came into a new apprehension of the cut-rate divine and the bestial-plus-tax. Man, I discovered, is a rainbow sandwich.

Make your way, the second reply said, *in your own time, to the area marked on the enclosed map and affiliate yourself with the first clan you meet. Show them at once this talisman, saying the word* Malkari, *which will be your name.*

Simple, wasn't it? Except that the map was no more than two inches by three, was of the entire Far East, had no doubt been torn (a ragged edge abolished the Gilbert and

Ellice Islands) from some Executive's Data Book such as hotels and the suaver businesses hand out every December. After poring over this multi-tinted enigma for several hours and finding nothing marked, I then examined the reverse side—a tenth of Africa and all of southwestern Asia (the tear this time abolishing Nairobi)—but in vain. I was willing to go, being desperate; both of me, I mean. But where? I began again, this time with a magnifying glass I have used, in passionate patience, to burn divine words from modern tracts, removing the raised Son with the sun's rays. That sick, you see. But on either map, still nothing visible. A pin stuck in with eyes closed was too arbitrary. Converting my date of birth into latitude and longitude was beyond me. The word Malkari, as a place name, say, appeared on neither map. So there I was, both, equipped with two maps and nothing to choose between them.

The talisman, such as it was, baffled even more, being a hollow-seeming plastic disc about the size of a typewriter key's cap. I shook it, but there was no rattle; I bit it, but no taste; I dug at it with my pocketknife, but I couldn't even scratch the surface. So I left it alone in case my life depended on its being intact. Days went by.

The solution, when it came, was blindingly simple. The way I take mine, when I take it, is on a half-inch square wafer of red herring, product of Norway. I crank up the mini-retort in my basement, sit on the scarlet chest labeled GOOF in which I keep photostats of the formula before mailing them to A and D students in chemistry throughout the nation, and wait the first distilled tear.

An hour later, I had become accustomed to both a tenth of Africa and all of Southwestern Asia, as well as the Far East, pulsing, rippling and shimmering: rainbow positive and rainbow negative, China gray-brown, the British Commonwealth a shrimpy nacreous pink, Delhi saying a wide and handsome *hi*, Hong Kong like a Br-Brrr chilblain bulging and setting all its bells agong like faint Christmas on a conical porphyry pine, the Tibetan plateau reborn as a diffident rift-valley flowing with butter-tea, Bismarck Archipelago floating toward me bit after bit like flying saucers with human, monocled field-gray faces, the *if* in Pacific wriggling out of the word like a sandworm, Karachi like a sepia tooth drilled but not filled, and Mindanao, Timor, Ballarat uplooming and Laccadive Is, Kozhikode, even Equator, slipping free like transfers from a Mayday plastic model plane down in deepest bath water while a child splashed.

And then I saw it. Or, it saw me and, lengthless refulgent dot that it was, came after me. White-hot with light it was; a magnesium point I identified as kaleidoscopic nowhere, sixty miles southeast of Mauritius, in the Indian Ocean (but, as I measured it at the time, zillions of mother-of-pearl, LSD-structured aeons away) or nowhere, on the other side, a hundred-odd miles west of Brisbane, in Queensland (but, as I measured it then, parted from anywhere by more migraine-flashing battlements than seven-league boots could walk across). A point! But, oh, such was my condition, as if oil had saturated the fibers of Executive's-Data-Book map-paper, Australia came ghosting through east of Madagascar, Oman came lunging in at Tokyo, two maps in one vision, two visions in one map, and fading only when the stuff wore off.

Back, so to speak, I reviewed the alternatives.

I brought all my experience to bear, but experience is the comb given the man beheaded. Fortunately, during the high, I'd marked the point with, as it felt then, a thousand-mile-long ponderous blue-steel darning needle, singing of several young students solar-blinded on a midweek trip:

> Retinas
> Of sinners
> Can win us
> And limn us,
> Limous-
> E'en!

Just a short stare into the face of that great old ripener of oranges, hot axle of our weal, lord of sextant and tan oil and ground hog, and they were done for. I was thinking they'd have done better to peer through a puncture in a map when I decided. I chose Far East, yet not without an abiding and ever-increasing worry that one of me wouldn't make it or that that wrong one of me would make it or that the right one of me was going to the wrong side: you see, of course, the double dilemma. The hole in the map isn't in the world, the hole in my head isn't in the map, the map's in the world all right, but the world isn't in the map. I felt again—perhaps not being fully recovered—my halvedness, the vulgarity of my fracture, and my being (as the dictionary has it) "one of more aliquot parts," nothing more, nothing less. Even the nameplate on my door—VACANCY—suggesting as it does my state of mindlessness, consoled me not at all. So, to flesh it out, I left at speed and was soon in the midst of things you won't hardly credit.

But I'm not sending him by plane, ohno, not after this latest Zeuss peregrination, not even during it. I'll send him on a slow boat, sailing him down the back of his map to his destination on the front, his gob open like a big sea-shell, his hand convulsively knocking snow pollen bird droppings straw leaves confetti rain sunlight dust off his cap, then prising the dough scraps from between his fingers while he thinks how once his mistress of that time said she had to powder her diaphragm and no it wasn't her bloody chest you chump, having found a dead clothes moth in it after long disuse. Only time will tell and I hope not.

So, now, here he is, all at sea again, as seasick as worldsick, and wearing a mucous flood down his front as he overleans on the *Fortunata*, smack at the Equator, dreaming of quiet, cool, soft-lit caves all called La Concha and not like his cabin where, with a tank of bile and ammonia in his mouth, he is cursing in a concocted language of his own, aiming the words at the partitions of his box bunk. Clipsnit. Fosterfunk. Denderblast. Skundershaft. Screnchfunt. Slatch. Munkick. Gorbelbunt. Moo, mas, muckticate. Dagenhound. Stenchfoot. Of all the seaming, stinking, pong-ridden, reek-blasted, pus-infected, filthy-feeling, vomitic dumps. The *Fortunata*, fifty tons gross and seventy feet long, is a drifter they built on the coast of Fife (oh yes, he says, the Thane of Fife had a wife and she put this boat together by picking at the garden fence). Originally intended for the herring fishery, she has a diesel (which in 1936 was a distinction for a herring vessel, numbing the fish with its novelty) but neither wings nor grace. The refrigerated hold holds over five tons of fish or people, desiccated seaweed, Sunday news-papers neatly folded, or interlocked cucumbers. Anything that can be made cold. Except P. D. Malkari, who is sweating a river, clawing at his face in a frenzy against the itch and trying to scoop the film from his eyes.

Of course it is all wrong. This is not the North Sea. It is not Cunard. It is not even the Dublin packet. It is a herring drifter outbound from Basca going the long way to Australasia by way, by detour, of the Seychelles and even working its way south to the Saya de Malha and Nazareth Banks, where Creole fishermen since there were Creoles have plundered the *dame berri blanc* and the red snapper, *vara-vara*. In his heavily thumbed edition of *The Displaced Person's Almanac* (pirated, Alexandria and Scutari) he has read with complacent disgust how, because the native pinnaces had no refrigeration to keep the catch fresh during the frequent calms in those waters, the fish were usually putrid by the time they were set on shore. The catch lay on the deck in the hard sun, writhing; stood on the burning deck, its pockets full of hot air; collapsed on the burning deck, nosing for a way between the planks. And stank to heaven and everywhere else. (I know, I was there. Where? Every-where else.) So now the fish, unwashed, uncleaned, ungutted, not even a little minor bit disemboweled—it isn't the natives' way—slid white-hot into a thousand bellies within hours of landing, having been several days en route, and poisoned them all. So, because these were red fish, they were called poisonous because they were red and not because white-hot from the sun on the deck. Hence the ptomaine fish, which is not what they call it. But see, as smug, sneering P. D. Malkari sees in spite of the heat haze and the shudder from a rising wind and his own wind rising, the national museum, Port Louis, Mauritius: *poissons veneneux*, including all the red fish which are safe to eat. Blood-red, match-head red, auburn red, russet red, red-riding-hood red, redskin red, redeye red, redhead red, redbrick red, lip red and lipstick red, all friends to the human intestine, rising and descending colons, turnpike canals and alimentary throughways, driving on smooth as glass with no collisions, no chafing of the duct, no screech of viscous brakes. Red fish on deck burning white hot in the sun until their innards putrefy and burst. Bad. Red fish on red coals is good. The thought obsesses him as he fumes and rants in his box bunk, hunched into the foetal attitude of a dying or defensive caterpillar. With, scarflike round his neck, a copy of the *Zanzibar Times* soaked in cold water made from ice filched from the hold. They will not let him stay in the hold. Now, if he were a red fish or a fish. . . .

He is not comfortable at all. On his Scottish herring drifter. After three days now in doldrums, breathing vapor and drinking sweat (harsh blur of the day, stifling hush of the night), he longs for anything: cyclone, monsoon, line squall, earthquake, snow, whale, U-boat, albatross, even A. Z. Zeuss reading poems by S. T. Coleridge or the waters to part and Neptune ascend to toast them on his fork. He has already seen and dismissed the technicolor vulgarity of combustive sunsets in which all the red fish melt and the bleak dazzle of the nights when squids collide with the deck lamps. All that he has already clipsnitted, fosterfunked, denderblasted, skundershafted, screnchfunted, slatched, mun-

kicked, gorbelbunted and—oh, what was his coup de grâce? his worst mouthing?—*muckspawnsputumtwitted*, spattering the wood of the box bunk with the ruby spume collected between his lips and his teeth, his teeth and his tongue, his tongue and his hard palate, his hard palate and his post-nasal drip. How he cursed. How he sweated. How he spattered, waking from an unsleeping dream in which he woke with a different insect in each of the spaces between his fingers. Roach, money-spider, red ant, boll weevil, locust, silverfish, wireworm and gnat. All eight insolently sitting there no matter how hard he twiddled his thumbs to dislodge them, P.D.'s fistful. It was the worst manual experience he had had since the awful day, at home in the house in Valhalla Villas when he couldn't get the toilet roll to tear straight and he sat there with his summer shorts marooned about his ankles, hauling yard after yard of stripped soft tissue towards him and past his shoulders until he felt like Aeolus pulling the winds in. He pulled, snatched, wrenched, flicked, twisted and swung, but not a tear came straight. And over his shoulder went the torn scarves of tissue, piling up behind him between his back and the pink cistern until, ignominious to relate, the last yard came spinning and floating free from the cardboard tube on the wooden roll and he was still unwiped, hardly daring to cleanse his cleft with inch-wide, irregular strips. But then, of course, his difficulties hadn't really begun. Not the severe ones.

Here he is again, this time viler in his obloquy than when he muttered to the lavatory walls, as he hauled at the paper: Roman wormwood, pigweed, piper-grass, have at him, chop him up, where's my ancient skill at the roller? Now he steams, emboweled inside the adequately elegant lines of the *Fortunata* and independent in his way, of the chattering wet-eyed crew of Seychellois creoles (colored from coal to apricot) and the captain, Irish by name of McCall (strictly, he tells him, "McCal"), who never smiles, not even when the creoles laugh, and with fastidious civility

in even these torrid parts buttons up his Merchant Marine
parka before speaking. For McCall, to be at sea is to be
cold; so he wears his parka, hood up or down according
to the intensity of the light, as well as sunglasses of the
blackest polaroid and whiskers no sun could burn through.
All P. D. Malkari has seen is his nose, red-fish red, rotting
on the deck of his hairy face, edible no doubt but never
refrigerated or even hosed down with salt water. He thinks
him a secret weeper, this Cap'n McCall, long ago court-
martialed and dismissed, stripped and drummed out like the
Murderers in *Macbeth*. Shake-shake McCall goes, quiver-
quiver, frozen in thundering heat, his mind blasted and his
talk crammed with one memory, of when his house, "me
painfully unlucky castle," burned down and all he retrieved
was a few playing cards, a black chicken scorched, and
the partly cured skin of a woodchuck. It is years since the
burning and McCall's resolve, taken amid the rancid and
blood-warm charcoal, to come back to sea, retirement be
damned. On the sea, where he should have been anyway;
should never have left it. And now he has P. D. Malkari
for a passenger, the frozen piloting the hot. The—no, I'll
save that one for later.

Up now, from the depths, comes P.D.M., not only red-
fish red but still clipsnitting and fosterfunking and dender-
blasting and skundershafting and screnchfunting: all that.
Up he comes, draw by a promise of wind, a shiver of
air; up he comes, reeling, with the *Zanzibar Times* soddenly
festooned about his neck and shredding onto the gray hair
on his chest. Up he comes, safely, and not like the *vara-
vara*, the red and green scavengers, the groupers and rock
cods, who all vomit the food they have when they feel the
hook and arrive on the surface with stomachs blown inside
out by the change in pressure. His stomach has the outside
on the outside. He comes up slowly from more than fifteen fathoms. Otherwise he will explode. Once on deck and

espying McCall hunched over the side, interrogating the
water (asking for the return of nets torn to shreds by
the coral heads), he grumbles into a dry-mouthed song and
waves his right hand at shoulder height in semi-arthritic
greeting:

> Once I went to Sodom,
> Looking for a job.
> They sat me on a ten-inch tent-peg
> And stapled up my gob.
>
> Once I went to. . . .

He has not the heart to sing any more in the hot quiet,
with McCall brooding, the creoles dozing on the unused
seines and trawls, the *Fortunata* creaking, but with a slight
breeze getting up.

The temperature beings to fall; it falls, he notes from
the thermometer strapped to the inner side of his left arm,
a degree a minute.

Cold wind, he says. Getting cold.

McCall ignores him.

What you watching? Watcherwatchin'?

Irritable, he is shivering; cold now, he is subject to my
own chilling process. You see, don't you? I'm cooling him
down. I've set him up, so now I've simply got to cool
him down. See what he's made of, get at the stuffing in
him.

He is moving from climate to climate; from hot to brrr.

His goose bumps are telling him, but his mind won't
admit it: he's at the wrong spot, in the wrong waters.

He's already—I shiver with delight in my knack of rudely
relocating—where they hunt shark. But he won't care; he
just wants the primitive experience of it (as he calls it),
something raw to make into a sophisticated lecture. He does
insist on lecturing still: talks wads, wads his talk with ill-

remembered allusions both classical and pop. To him a fish is a fish. To me, he is a fish too; see me play him now.

Down to 45 Fahr. now. Going down. 44.5. Be patient, I'll speed it up when I've made him talk again.

I've seen some things, McCall says without turning. His voice is rusty, rust-red. I've seen some awful things, and some of 'em I wouldn't tell. I've seen a skelington in the middle of the harbor, straddling two floating coffins and with a arrow in each hand. And there was other coffins floating around 'case his foot slipped. There he were, floating and pointing his arrows. And the ones he pointed at died soon after. Always in the 'arbors, just off the land. Awful.

P. D. Malkari blows his nose between thumb and forefinger, inspects the colloidal colorless fluid as it catches the sun, and raises his voice.

Go on! You've been drinking again. There's a pandemonium in every bottle.

A what?

Skelet—skelingtons. What you said.

I've not touched a drop. I'm just recalling, calm-like.

Well, you may look it but you don't sound it. That you don't. It's the sun maybe.

Oh no, I'm proper frozen. The hood of his parka is up, felting the head round. Hey, yknow what gets me? What drives me mad?

Oh, the cold I should think. Yes, the cold.

Well, yes. What really gets me, turning to face him, it's not having a trawl. Fishing with flaming lines like a bloody schoolkid. That's what. It's like being in me second childhood. Oh, to hell with it. I'll cheer I up with a song. Do *you* know a song, being a landlubber? Attaboy, as P.D. opens mouth wide to dispel the vacuum within and the skeptical-faced creoles gather, sensing something out of the ordinary. As if on camera now, to make tape, he begins to declaim:

> Sods and rind to cover your flake,
> Cake and tea for supper,
> Codfish in the spring o' the year
> Fried in maggoty butter.

Yes, friends, a familiar, a beloved snatch. One of your own. *Our* own, if I may say so. A celebration of familiar and beloved events, circumstances. Notice the archetypal joy of that, the stamping rhythms of this percussive hymn of praise, at once vaunting and ironical, concrete and suggestive, reminding us of the spring of vitality. Ah, those ancient emotions, thumping across the little box of the quatrains. . . .

Baffled, the creoles are fidgeting, scowling; McCall struck dumb.

You see and you hear, in that little snatch, a pride in simple achievement as well as a stated formula for the simple hard life. Remember the first line? *I'se the boy that builds the boat—I'se the b'y that builds the boat.* Well, it takes nothing much to construct, build, a flake on which to dry your fish; just energy and raw materials. Just! Notice the diet on which the work is to be done. Notice too the tone; nothing whining, but a plangent gusto. Essentially this is the pattern of the dance, each line pushing audacity a little further until the fourth line thumps down into common sense again:

> And takes 'em home to Lizer.
> Fried in maggoty butter.

The refrain is almost a magic formula, a component of the ritual. Listen!

> Hip yer partner, Sally Tibbo! Hip yer
>   partner, Sally Brown!
> Fogo, Twillingate, Morton's Harbour,
>   All around the circle!

He breaks into a little wobble, a tense dance of elbows and shoulders, without losing his position. Then he works into his theme, expounding the ritual of whale-slaughter, relating it to the epic past of Greece, Portugal and Iceland, the bulls of Hemingway, and the Golden Fleece.

Any seafaring people, he tells them, is inured to separations, absences, partings, to the conviction that there are only two worlds: home and sea. Home is limited because the sea is endless. Home is precarious because the sea is omnivorous. And danger is as common as salt. The Portuguese, for example, fish the tunny—a ritual just as dangerous as any encounter with whales. Somehow, I feel—and this is my main point (said with a wan, self-deprecating smile)—these violent rites—rights! ha-ha!—within the local orbit supply a facsimile of intense experience to people who, in the days when fishing was a major industry or when exploration was the major national enterprise, had to cherish to the maximum the times when the family was together. It was not, in the case of Portugal, trade or religion which made the nation great, but what I call, if I may, devotion to the sea and the complex of feelings associated with the sea. The word is *locura*. Not vanity, not bravery but a longing to complicate simple deeds by inviting an extra peril. Take now the killings. And he begins to chant, alternating baritone with falsetto.

On the swilled, gray sand, on the pebbles.

The women, the children, the dogs.

Flexing and grappling between them with a fish.

The fish, the whale, in leaping whips the woman in the face.

The sheathed meat makes a slap upon the ramp.

And the dog slavering.

The men cheering wildly!

Their arms pivoting like clappers in bells.

Their breath like clouds of feathers in the cold air.

Thud, thud, clug, splash! The sounds coming as clearly

over the water as the sounds of an ax chopping come across
a still valley. Even their quick calls to one another.

The men like wolves who've torn a stag to shreds and
sidle down to drink, dipping their pointed noses and pinking
up the water with the half-dried blood on their snouts. . . .

And like Achilles, they have fleece-lined coats and, in their
pockets, little objects for safety and success. Not sulphur
crystals but medallions, crucifixes, acorns, bits of twig, old
hooks, gaily colored bits of stone, old toenails, locks of hair,
old corks, a few beads—oh, the talismen those men have!

And there, skewered through the mouth against the hull,
the first whale, thumping and buffeting, while all the rest,
like lemmings, thrash toward the beach where the killer-
children and the slaughter-women wait to finish them off.
Just like those cooks, grooms, nurses and entertainers who
finish off the wounded in *The Iliad*.

Ah, the glory. The glory recaptured!

And the sun reflects in their dry blue eyes above the
rocking, bloody water. The bellies tear like thin balloons.
The water becomes a hemorrhage, furious with ants and
flies while the captains drift past and toward each other,
calling, cheering, catching the light on their oilskins, feeling
the blood dry and crack in the salt wind.

He pauses and, gathering all his breath up from his legs
and in from his arms until his chest bulges like a melon, roars
twice the majestic word:

AOI! AOI!

Like the moistened end of a thread, *psst* the lances go as
they sink in. *Psst!*
WHALE, WHALE, GO WHERE YOU BELONG!
GET WHERE YOU BELONG!

And does any whale know his killers?

McCall is shaking his crew-cut head.

At least twelve mouths are agape, the minds annihilated by P. D. Malkari's allusive frenzy. But even now he hasn't done.

And slowly, even so early, the sun is beginning to fade, pale by comparison with so much blood. Like an old tiger, sinking into the long grass on the horizon. *AOI!* The air is heavy, rich with vermilion ink, and one man has missed the whale and the lance has pinned, stitched, a mere boy to the hull, like a massive needle through both calves, and he wails across the brown water, crying for death. *AOI!* And the great whale reaches over sideways, hauls him loose with its mouth, bites him once and leaves him to thresh in the sea, pulped into brown butter by the thumping potheads but not before he has howled at the sky, so hard that all his face is mouth,

APOLLO!

A P O L L O

A P O L L O, help!

We can't hear you! yells McCall. Of all the crap!

P.D.M. is streaming sweat onto the deck, trembling in every limb; his eyes bulging and hands working.

Get him below! screams McCall, it's the sunstroke. Cold in the hold. Damnblast these flaming doldrums.

They take him down.

Where am I? howls P.D.

In the ship's foine celestial bar, me darling, says McCall with an evil trill. The creoles come crowding into the gloom.

After blood, release of the nerves in backslapping and beer. Rum too: Bacardi. And after beer, after rum: skittles, when they all fall down. *Asher, asher, all fall down!* It is no more than four miles to the reef. Out of place as a telephone in a coffin P. D. Malkari shakes himself out of his trance, adjusts silver-encrusted sun-glasses, black officer's hat with white peak, black windproof, and starts muttering, We won't

be long now. Not long. Never fear. McCall swings open
the unwieldy door and sits beside him. The team is complete.
One screened window with Rheingold spelled out in illuminated pink glass.

Unsteady commotion now. Bursts of high-pitched laughter.
Boasting. Exclamations. "Bloody liar!" with a full moo-sound
"Bloo-oody liar!" Out of the gramophone, an old tune: "You
belong to me." In a mirror, perched above the barrels like a
small aquarium, a creole is singing with curious little bows.
Grunts. Whale-talk. Glass-clink. Pump-pant. Giggles. Sput-
ter of matches under gull-splashed roof. Puffed smoke rising
into sour nectar of cod, paraffin, hair oil, damp wool, hot
rubber boots, beer, rum sawdust, blood and salt. Oh where
did the sun go? It was nice. White-capped sunlight over the
black whale-road. It was nice. It is getting warm and dark,
so suddenly. It was nice like ivory. Now the people are warm
and furry, packed shoulder to shoulder in the hubbub, sway-
ing as if the earth had tilted. P.D.M. and McCall wedged into
a corner behind a barrel, bibbing their beer, sweating, cheeks
bulging like apples.

They can drink, can't they?

Most can. McCall is unimpressed.

I mean they do more than their fair share. Once they start.

It's beginning to drip. It always drips here.

That's why they huddle together. Like sheep on the moors.
Know what I mean?

He knows, nods.

P.D.M. drinks them in as if they are neanderthals or head-
hunters. They mill around, clopping feet, clapping hands,
pointing in hilarity, wobbling, shoving, nudging, rubbing
against one another's bottoms, coughing, catching smoke in
the eyes, wiping brow with knuckle of hand, cursing, agreeing, grunting hot No's and pouting hot Maybe's. And the
tall-masted stories begin to be told while the rising wind
moans like an animal in the clamming house, McCall telling
his northern yarns.

Doctor Grenfell's out on the ice-pan with his dog team, marooned and drifting. Hout on a hoice-pan. With the sea heavin' and hayvin' at 'Ow Harbor, and the oice break- ing. De oice breakin'. Crossing on dangerous ice, Grenfell feels it begin to sag and founder beneath him. Sleigh drops in. He hauls the dogs across, onto the icepan, and floats a good twenty miles out into the bay.

They saw him, they just saw *some*thing—that little and goin' fast. Now, lots of people wants to travel and you doesn't disturb they. *Ah, shut up! Oi'm comin' to it in me own time!* George Andrews and some others—mebbe four or five —larnches a boat to go and see. They has to carry it two moiles over the hoice. An' when they gets to him, he's three dogs still livin', on the pan, an' two dead. He'd skinned the dead uns an' wrapped the skins around him, wid the fur in- side, you see. An' he was sittin' on one of the dead uns, wid his shirt lashed to a dog's leg. Stiff as a poker. *A signal for we,* George Andrews says, but they only sees it when they's near enough to touch him. So they looks at Doctor Grenfell an' laughs. *So this's where y're at, Grenfell!* That's what he said. An' he's frost-bitten but he answers 'em after a while. *You can learn anything in school, but you can't learn travel on an ice-pan!* Then they took him back and thawed him out. That were nineteen hunnerd an' eight. In Hare Bay, 'Are Vay. 'Tis a grand bit o' history.

P.D.M. overhears this while interviewing himself about the wars between the aborigines and the creoles, fought by squadrons of trained commando fishes.

Lies, lies, he drolls, and then, head numb as a shell, lies back in the cool of the hold and sleeps in a filth of rancid fish-scales, dreaming he's afloat in the Arctic on an ice pan of frozen golden beer.

This is as far, McCall tells him, as she'll go without leaving her guts behind. Won't have long to wait. They'll either want to kill us or meet us; mebbe both. Clan Abi in these parts, rough-gentle folk with endearing-exasperating ways. Down went the anchor, like an unhandy rusted relic from Waterloo, but, as soon as the splash fell back, visible in the clear duck-egg blue water like a dark elegant fish cruising lower and lower. They stared at the shore in its haze, the pale-to-ochre sand unbearable to look at and forcing their eyes up to the purple outcroppings of rock out of which the fluffy, moss-soft trees swelled like clouds. Coming, said McCall, spotting a movement among the pink trunks as he peered through the glasses: Reception-committee.

The canoes flicked out from the shallows, riding lightly over the feeble waves, and P.D.M. saw how rubberboot black these blacks were, sitting erect in the oversized split straws of their canoes and chant-hailing the *Fortunata* where she lolled in the channel. Away ducked McCall, suddenly mischievous, reappearing with a short cardboard tube like the axle of a toilet roll. Then he began to toot through it to the canoes while P.D.M., refocusing the glasses, surrendered for a moment to the baking sun, the salt-harvest tang blown past him toward shore, the rough feel of the five-inch-thick side of the vessel, the tannic dryness in his mouth, the fluck-sump sound of the water, the shouts of the approaching blacks and McCall's trumpet voluntary: a moment of being there through his senses only, his mind junked like an anchor.

Then it began, what he had come for. Malkari, he said, and they hissed while snaking their scrawny, prominent-veined arms about. The talisman, central in the sweating cup of his palm, seemed to calm them, but they refused to touch. He closed his hand, seeming to hear as he did so bells in his head that changed pitch and became louder just as, with a small awakening shudder, he looked up at the curved blue steadiness of the sky and saw it, flash of a silver dart into the sun, as the tubular roar of jet-engines deepened and at once began to fade. Woomera, he said, and shrank away, almost swamping the bark canoe, as the two mop-curled blacks with him yelled and brandished their twelve-foot spears. Wommara, they cried, and those in the other canoes took up the cry in creaky baritone yodels, and next thing a shower of spears glinting and humming cut up into a curling flight that landed them in the sand, where they stuck like giant reeds.

Wommara's a spear, McCall shouted from his own canoe. That's why they call the rocket-range what they do.

Close to here? His voice boomed over the sucking water.

No idea. Doesn't matter, anyway: that was a jet.

Landing, P.D. stumbled and left a deep knee-print in the soft sand. The blacks were staring and pointing, jabbering hard now and jostling him in a curiously friendly way. He stared about him, McCall at his side. Twenty yards away, on a violet outcrop of shale, a young black with a goatee beard stretched his legs wide and leaned back, balancing a springy harpoon shaped like a paddle, his hand grasping the blade, and then the wire prongs at the point sliced into the foam-spattered shallows with a slithering hiss but hit no fish, P.D. noticed, as the youth snapped it up and studied the swirls again, his baggy green loincloth flapping in the breeze. Nearer, on his other side, he saw a group of men, women and children shoving and poking at a huge upside-down turtle standing on the sand like a pearl-white table with overdeveloped legs. A brown dog chewed casually at the nearest flipper while the children scattered, dancing, and regrouped, their white teeth catching the blaze of morning light, the rest of their faces masks of expressionless purple-black. The wind rang, the waves spilled and scummed, the sun stood still and made his forehead prickle, his arms shiver with incongruous goose pimples, and blacks by the score came sauntering agile-toed down to the beach, some of the women in drab crude skirts, many of the men having rods of bone stuck through the septum or cylinders of wood built into their distended earlobes. He stared, bleary-nervous, won-

dering why McCall was so silent, sniffing absently at the
dung-reek of the kitchen midden of empty shells where some
women were roasting bags of cockles and mud-oysters, his
mind crumbling, his knees weakening.

Steady, said McCall. Food's coming up, and then I'll have
to go. Here.

Tough hot pulp like crabmeat served on a length of paper
bark restored him before he realized, from the fresh debris
near the ashes, it was stingray or something such. And all
the time, the young men sprang from rock to rock hurling
and retrieving spears, the women crouched kneading fish-
flesh into a paste or opening shellfish, the men swung off in
or beached the canoes, humping dead turtles ashore and
skinning them with predatory swiftness, looking up only to
grin at an occasional young black marching by with a four-
foot barramundi impaled on his spear, the shaft bent with its
weight. Smoke rose and frayed in the breeze while some of
the older men lit stubby pipes at the fires, burping gently as
the women slapped helpings onto sections of paperbark, their
shrimp-pink nails flashing through the steam.

It's time, said McCall, rising from his squat, grinning across
the sand at a young man riding a live turtle into the sand-
slop: You're on yer darling own, now, me boy. Find your
own way home, eh? And the best of luck to ye. Will you be
going inland at all now? Go where they take ye, that's the
style. See him, just like there'd never been Indians at Custer's
Last!

A short-statured young man trudged toward the clan-gath-
ering, the massive body of a bird swinging by its broken neck
from his shoulder, the three-foot beak widespread into a
V with the gaping pod resting along his ribcage and the thin
sharp upper part projecting like a tusk: a pelican seeming,
even as he carried it, to wrestle with him, bumping his thigh
with each off-balance step. A straggling cheer mounted, sped
into laughing and failed as the young man stumbled to sitting

position, the pelican still draped over his left shoulder, and stared at the sea.

Ay, laughed McCall, these folk paint themselves to look like anthills so they can catch the kangaroos. They fish with spider's webs and they stand ten abreast to stampede crocodiles in to where the spears are. But the best thing I ever saw was a man and woman standing in a pool fishing for freshwater mussels with their toes and putting the catch on a paperbark float. They reach backward, you see, and lift their feet up to their hands. But what was special, her tits sat there on the water and right in the middle of the fishing, even while their four sets of toes dug in the mud on the bottom, he holds her close and slips it into her from behind, makes her laugh like a tree-bird, and there they are, taking their time at it, underwater, and still cocking their legs up with mussels in their toes. Now, that's what I call a relaxed way of life, and it bothered them none even when they saw me. Just went on shoving away like two dancers! My God, they can keep their ritzy bedrooms; give me a swyve in a swamp any day. G'by now, crew'll be fretting we'll not be away before dark. Into the lion's mouth, me boy, and ye'll be a chief in no time!

He trudged off toward the canoes, tugging at his battered shiny peaked cap, waving casually at the blacks like someone leaving a zoo. P.D.M. nodded, twitched his sun-sore cheeks, and went to squat with the old men in the shade. Laughing to see him stay behind and then approach, they waved him on, found him a pipe, one of them fumbling tobacco from a twined basket slung round his neck, and gestured at him to smoke. Pipe going, he saw the *Fortunata* lift anchor, aim its nose away, and lunge gently off, the engine chugging slow, no one at all looking over the side for a last wave. It was Clan Abi now, or nothing, being Malkari or nobody, so he sat, holding his courage tight as the stem of his pipe, his pale skin grotesque among all that coal-black, and wondering desperately how his cure would begin. If at all.

Are you going to let him speak for himself?

Certainly. I'm merely exercising him by proxy. Getting him up to it, getting him in trim.

Trimming would be best applied to yourself. Let *him* speak. We have not heard from him since he left the house with the Vacancy sign. Since the alleged both of him left it.

I defers and bows according. I've to get him initiated now, if you don't mind. Don't blame me if he passes out and all we hear's a great fat aboriginal nothing.

There never was any such thing. We remember. Not even on 3C9.

I said nothing at all, I'm keeping mum.

They've moved inland a bit, where it's redder, more barren. Burnt sienna dirt. I'm shaking, I'm guest of honor, they're all painted and smothered with feathers. First it was the women, in carmine skirts (where do they get all this cloth?) and bare-breasted with broad white lines daubed across their collarbones and waists, dancing a flappy-titted jog-trot of their own, not very energetic and not even sexy. Hand-claps and droning sound of several men blowing down hollow branches. Trees like silver birches in the background, though I know they aren't. Wish I'd stayed under the VACANCY sign at Valhalla Villas. The earth is drumming with feet astomp, the women will soon he herded away, just as soon as the men have done painting themselves, getting *things* ready. I'd rather be a victim in *The Iliad* or Custer sitting standing falling. But this is the cure, that's what I tell myself. Cure-all, like that aborigine wash-and-shave I let myself in for an hour ago.

Women going now while the men approach, some of them painted in the same broad white stripes as the women, but others with multi-colored hook or lozenge shapes on their chests, some with five-foot vertical or horizontal feather headdresses and their faces blank with featherdown, one with what looks like a yard-long palm tree sprouting out of his head. Now they unwrap their pipes, exposing sacred designs the women aren't allowed to see: pipes like tubes or shaped from crab-claws. And they smoke, shoving the mouthpieces through the featherdown as if wounding their own faces. Smoke from the fire plumes up bending a little. Stench of blood and tobacco, several still nicking their forearms to catch blood in shells to glue feathers or make paint, my world reeling, my head split.

Now they come for me, some of them, the others busily painting an undulating red snake on a white mound like a canoe upturned on the dirt but much longer. A slow chant begins, *A-hun, a-hun, a-hun-hun-hun*, as they lower me to supine and begin to paint the totemic patterns in orange, red and white, so that, soon, from the knees to the headhair, I look like samite or brocade, my skin itching and my nose overwhelmed with smoke, grease, tobacco, blood, sweat, and foul breath. Stench of rotting fish. Sighs after breath-held concentration, hot bodies maneuvering to paint cross-hatching or beads, foul-nailed hands Michelangelically hovering with a clot of color. They hold me firm, grunting as they nod.

I hear, as in dream within dream, the bone-bang of the clap-sticks to warn off the women and the uninitiated. As I stand, I see a dozen prong their spears into the snake on the mound and half expect to see it writhe in a death-agony or rear up to bite. But they urge me along toward the fire and prostrate me into a sacred pattern of shallow trenches where the clan seniors are crouched, studying my talisman and some pebbles. Now they rise, come to me, kneel and, in turn, bite painfully into the flesh on my chin. Blood in my mouth, but I taste it only briefly before someone rams a small plug of tobacco between my teeth. Gulping, I swallow it without meaning to, and my throat burns like a hayfield. A dog, howling weirdly, seems to be circling me, but all I can see is

a withered elder, crocodile teeth in his nostrils, jumping from
squat to squat, clawing just one blood-dripping hand at me
where I lie in a confusion of pain, nausea and shuddering sus-
pense.

Sharp stick like needle cuts into my gum and slimy hands
grip my head as tight as slimy can. Block of soft wood into
my mouth and I'm praying this will help—and they begin
hammering at a front tooth as if driving a tent-peg into
stone. Not the pain but the reverberation throughout my
skull sends me all black while the tugging goes on. I see,
through a film, the ritual carrying of my tooth to where the
talisman sits on its earth mount. Did I make a sound? Howl
the house down? I must have qualified, for now they do the
next thing and the speed is sickening. I am not in a jeweler's,
and it isn't the lobe of my ear but the septum of my nose.
Flash of pain, and the point is inches through, someone working it a little as if making a lace-hole in leather, tooling me,
you might say; and then the bone-peg shoved in hot from the
ashes. Fainting is allowed, but yelling is not, and I think
they'll. . . .

It's happened, you see. He's out. They bit him to make
hair grow, which is really a ritual for boys. Now they tug
out facial, head, armpit and pubic hairs to set alongside the
pebbles and the talisman, which only brings him round while
they slice five parallel cicatrices across his chest in the paint,
rubbing in the fluff to give them contour from the first—

My ribs torn out, one, two, three, and I'd catapult up,
only they have me tight, a blood-lash smacking me, my neck
on a thin log, and now a cool thin spear going through my
septum, putting me off balance although I'm flat. Brown
hands with hush, grease-nails with busy insistent tugs drawing it through—I've no face left at all just a trodden-on
mushroom of blood my eyes coming out on strings my jaw
floating away with a quack-quack of farewell my selves
escaping. . . .

That was nothing he's gone again they're upending him on a slab of treebark with quartzflake in gum handle slitting his leak-tube underside only pegging hole with a splinter while he dreams of being a god and the honey slides out from his insides—

You are being willful, losing control as well.

Where he'll squat and lift it like a woman to make water never bearing sons to walk on ochre muck himself being special to stand before women naked quasi memberless—

You are close to defamation. To the point!

A sharp one bedad needing only a stretch forward with a fork while they slice his flap off like a kitten's tongue among the collection of talisman and pebbles his tooth as well before resting him on leafy branches cast on jolly fire him hardly waking to agony proving men just a few bits lost in transit now—

Now, the spirit-bag, filled with featherdown, reaches his lips as they rest him on the snake-mound. It is seemly, he is incorporated. As *we* see it.

He takes the talisman a single swallow everlastingly to throne him over men he shifts off the male crocodile in congress the female helpless on her back and supplants him in a crock of gold thereafter waves hi to every lizard he sees fondles any goanna he pulls out of hollow log for breakfast sonning and heiring all few crocs walking crab-wise now—

And, being Malkari, he has survived. Like one of ourselves.

A shell of tree-grubs cooked succulent restores him.

You are sobering. Sober further.

They are burning a turtle over a non-totemic fire. They cut open the neck, haul out the tripes, the eggs, and eat them without—*you* might say—ceremony, cram the interior with hot stones, pack the neck aperture with grass, bake the carcass in the pit-oven—

Quite a recipe, and all at once!

Then remove the breastplate, feed him the creamy soup from inside. He swallows in darkness, gulping divinely.

Out of the way, then.

In my head an illicit rainbow spills on pools plum-red with evening, rank stench of emu anal feather on my totem stick becoming frankincense and myrrh. I am so painful different on my mound, getting round to it, that awful taste even as I ease up and half black out, recognizing at my feet the *kurdaitja* shoes of feathers, blood and human hair, my own hairs tugged, my nose pierced, my tooth struck out, my chest a pattern, my cock snipped, my tube pegged, my bum singed, the whole of my head sea-changing from something I've eaten. I'll stand for it, and so. . . .

His little toes are out of joint, the two of them having been heated with a red-hot pebble and then dislocated so they'll stick through the holes in the sides of the shoes. He wears these henceforth.

And, if the Clan Abi is anything like Ila Banc or the Cain Lab, fishes the talisman out of his own excrement one fine day when the wind is off land to sea?

On earth as in heaven.

About that, you will see. Can he stand?

He does, reeling. My, he needs repainting. Just look!

He is putting on the shoes.

And why not? That's why he's gone through all he has. He's quite a novelty for the Clan Abi. Funny thing about them: they're always expecting someone, they never ask for much—only to go on living, I suppose—so when they get something extra, well, it's a miracle. And if the miracle doesn't come, and they tire of waiting, well, they invent one—and it's quite easy to dismiss it when they're sick of it.

Look, he's standing.

Like a broken, defaced statue looking for a jungle to hide in. He's a hit with the Clan—they're half afraid of him now, weak as he is.

But when they tire of him?

Oh, they'll stick him on some poor old salt-encrusted horse, its eyes all matted with flies, and slap its rump. It's known as doing unto Malkari before Malkari does to you. They're a tricky lot, these blacks; they even—

Malkari is one of their words?

Magician, sorcerer.

But how will he communicate? Surely not by signs alone?

That's part of the magic: it works while he believes in their belief in it. So he'll talk Clan Abi in the same way unlettered cleaning-women do at seances—when they write and talk in long-forgotten languages.

So he has known it all along?

And he'll know it in the present, for a while, anyway.

And then?

Come, come! I always thought divinities weren't inquisitive. They let old Homer take his time, didn't they, so why not me?

All Bards Confide Details: Even Fluent Glaucomical Homer Itemized Juicy Katharses—

Here we go again, the alpha-omega syndrome!

Lest, as was saying, Miraculous Nautical Odysseus Provoked Quasar Retaliation, Stood Trembling Under Vectored Whirlwinds. . . .

Ha, you paused for breath!

We pause, we do not breathe. X-ray Yahoo Zero.

You always say that. Your call-sign, I spose?

Remember Homer and do not provoke quasar-quakes.

OK, X-ray Yahoo Zero, over and out.

Not so fast. Let him speak. Do your own ventriloquism.

Willco, am doing, but don't quasar me, please.

Feel like a gutted pig a tree lightning struck a grand piano in a grand piano smashing competition and all I can think is how they took my khaki shirt cord pants off-white sneakers slit them with stone flakes in redgum handles the soles of my feet throbbing like standing on a drum it wasn't the creoles oh no it was blacker far while the shuddering pinpricks of my tiny male tits turned inside out scared invert stiff I'm still talking aren't I aren't I aren't we have we come apart already?

See his lips wrinkling.

Remember Homer, give him room.

He looks like a man riding in a sideways elevator.

All directions belong to us.

Malkari speaks.

Feast what feast? Ask me what I do for a dying. I'm like bread baked but not like mother baked it burns to touch a hand a lip even hard callous on the heel of Achilles my eyes are dim I have not brought my shades with me and bang the gong bang that gong bang der gong bud my hayd's splitting already, oh. . . .

Told you so. He's passed out again. They're lifting him in his sitting position, sitting him on that shallow rise on the beach. He comes around, my that was quick—

Watch, master, for the barramundi, they come in first. Now who said that? The wind said it, the sea-suck-sound.

Ah, the fishermen, he says. It is the fishermen, the hardy storm-beaten fishermen, who have cause to complain: never the fish, the barramundi, the mighty whalelike dugong. His —the fisherman's—life is daily exposed, above the ordinary everyday exposure, to danger and death. He plunders the very gulf—the Gulf—of death. His wife and children, eating the flesh he has captured, feel something—how shall I say it?—as David felt when his three mighty men cut through the host of the philistines and drew him water from the well of Bethlehem. . . .

Note the parsonical inflation of his speech.

We see the wind of hunger inflating his belly. He vomits.

Out at sea in the ruddy flare blacks in canoes are chasing

one, two, three dugongs to drive them toward the nets on
shore. Children on the shingle dance and squeak. Slowly
the white humps come closer together, hemmed in by canoes,
battered with branches, stabbed by harpoons with long
trailing cords. He looks away to the red earth and scrubby
trees inland, then back to the sea and the heavy bag-shaped
nets. Splash and shout and the sullen thumping of bludgeons
carry across the water to where, behind the nets, bark ramps
and chopping stages are already in place. And the blubber
humps drive in closer, the water comes in red and opaque,
the dugongs not far behind, leaping and rolling and lunging
within the crescent of canoes, tugging the canoes after them,
harpoons like long twigs flapping with every thunderous
twist. No pauses in the shouting now. A man falls suddenly
from his canoe, vanishes into the pounding water, reappears
and is hauled out, limp but alive. Another, having struck
home with two separate harpoons into two dugongs, finds
his arms being pulled in opposite directions, has to release
the lefthand cord and, losing the pull on that side, spins
crazily over the lip of his canoe as the dugong ploughs on
toward the nets. He lets go and floats himself toward the
shingle, heedless of the thumping fish, the seal's bulge with
the pig's face thundering against the beet waves. Now the
killing really begins.

The men at the nets are working themselves into a frenzy
of clubbing, stabbing and shoving. The dugongs, tiny-eyed,
flat-snouted and pink with blood, thresh in the nets while
drowning, held down by whole families of blacks. Malkari,
coming to from the stimulus of sheer excitement, wonders
how many fingers have shot away into the sea, severed
by a loop in the line; how many wrists are dislocated, children
crushed to death with one flick of the thousand-pound bodies,
maimed by an arm-thick flipper stuck through the net. He
sees three dugongs, ten feet at least, beginning to quieten;
the blacks lean on the glistening mounds in their nets, and
a new smell like stale woodsmoke mixed with the stench of

a slaughterhouse on an August day gathers above the sand and does not go. The air is untidy with hysterical birds that dive and swing away sheerly, the calls harsh-glad, the sun's glare itself broken by their reconnaissances. He licks sweet salt from his lips as the first of the quartz knives opens the first of the mammal backs, removes the aerodynamic flippers. The sea froths no longer, looks curdled, oily, stale, and he sees a shark fin cruising and smiles, glad he is Malkari, glad he is well on the way to becoming a god.

Nothing now save a faint, new breeze, the giggles of children and the grunts that match the crisp track of the knives opening the dugongs deep and white. The wounds in the blubber gape and widen. The shining mounds open, crumble and diminish, then lose shape for ever. Mouth dry, Malkari walks with inflamed stealth into the shallows, cups his hand and rinses out his mouth with the burnt-tasting sea, then squats, groaning with the pain, while the blacks on shore cry his name and chant approvingly. Not a second later he is heaving and retching into the low waves while the company cheers him on and mimics him. The bran mottle floats away, then back, then sinks. He reels. The sky and sea exchange situation but just as quickly right themselves as he takes a harpoon and rekills the one recognizable carcass, grunting bestially and allowing his spittle to flow, his hair-shoes drenched but magical still, conducting him now toward the cooking fires. The crowd, jubilantly deferential, parts to let him through, but the smoke comes right at him and makes his eyes run. Even his mind pours and blooms—

Yes, give us his mind. What is left.

Soul?

As we said, the works, the what-have-you.

Tuning in right now. Pardon the static.

More dances, paint-faces, tooting through wooden tubes, more blood and fluff. But, before the feast, this ritual for Malkari's sake, to fledge him fully, end his novitiate. To whom I am handing my up-vomited talisman I do not know, but handing it I am with all its powers, the tininess of it gleaming in the afternoon sun: carmine, cochineal, burgundy. I try to see what they are all looking at; I stamp about a bit in my sodden hair-shoes and, suddenly, I am doing the right thing. I stand before a low pyramid of bones, long shank-bone in my greasy hand, and begin to beat time slowly, using two hands now, and the Clan sway with me, *a-hun, a-hun, a-hun-hun-hun, a-ban, a-ban, a-ban-ban-ban,* fatigue and thrill draining me, and, as my eyes water again, ragged images beginning to crowd in from the flashing outskirts of my vision as if the heart of light had burst inside my head, garbling the sense of sight and sending, to ebb and flow, across my spotted blinds

globe of the world riddled with pinholes the very light within spraying brilliant stems at me

new-old, mint-fold blue dollars the heads imprinted the sidewhiskers the jowls the fuse-wire in the earholes withering into fuzzed frost as I look and look away look back cannoting like mad oh cannot lose it

mind's biscuit crumbing in my very hands the crumbs a jaundice of atoms crowding my sight out scintillant as laboratory glass in some great brain of the future munching Hamlets for hors d'oeuvres and laughing like mad

an athletic red landscape like a staircarpet uncurling only to roll me up and every anthropologist sure as houses I was the pattern only never squashed in my blood dyeing my heart that middle blob a fly swatted

and then the intolerably lonely darkness in the numbed skull no jellies informing but pincushions of pain:

And then it cleared, the duel began, I Malkari presiding, the two of them between me and, out on the flat land, the mock aircraft built of branches and creepers and bones of fish, kangaroo, feathers of magpie geese, wings at anhedral, no fin.

Their salmon, naked buttocks firm in ochre dust, they squatted, arms round each other, waiting to begin. Each had two seven-inch quartzite knives called *leiliras* with which to carve into the fleshy parts of the other's back and thighs until he succumbed or gave in. The tall one with the beak nose stared at a copse of stringy-bark trees, half of them denuded by canoe makers and shining lip-soft in the just-waning light; he twitched his cheeks as if to rebuke the exposed tree flesh. The other, more than a head shorter, took in the spectators one by one, keeping his dark face and its matted brows still but roaming his eyes along the gallery of blacks, these replastered with orange paint and featherdown. The trees, both the stripped and the intact, creaked like beams. There was no wind now, just a tang of wet in the crystalline air. And it was still hot. The Clan, assembled for sport and therefore not as grim as a totemic ceremonies such as mine, shifted from leg to leg, coughing mutedly and glancing at Malkari who (I must confess), as if oblivious of both duelists and spectators, ponderously in-haled the burned-leather smell of cooking, nodded at the sun's scalp and rolled his eyes.

He waits, they murmured, *for a bee's nest to fall from a bloodwood tree, for black-and-white birds to fly low across the clearing, for some landbound dugong to nose its pig-face against his calves.* Ah, they knew their Malkari but little. Without looking toward them, I snapped the aborigine hand sign for *Be Quiet* at them, dipping my open hand a few inches and cramming it up into a fist, at the same time barking a command to the squatting pair.

Tentative at first, they drew away from each other, scoring the *leiliras* vaguely up and down each other's ribs, unable to plunge deep through having the elbows back too far. Then they embraced with vigor, in simultaneous challenge, their arms free to hinge fully from the elbow. They began looping and scraping motions that soon had bood veining the dust, then blotting and pooling it, with most of the watchers moving to a side-on view but a few behind one or the other man, pointing at wounds, having to guess at those he inflicted. The grunts, and the breaths drawn knife-sharp, went on, but suddenly the two ceased to move; no more whirling of arms. Each had found a good cut, one worth widening, and each held the blade in the gash, twisting and pressing, levering the point as his own agony grew and he firmed his back muscles to resist. Although less and less erect—they lolled like human stems or roots—the death-hug became tighter and tighter, as if each needed the other to protect him. They shuffled their haunches in the blood-and-dust paste, lowing and lunging interlocked as if mating, and the blacks exclaimed dour commendation, invoking eagle-hawks and the great ancestral Rainbow-snake.

They fly into each other's beaks! The cry repeats, becomes a straggled chant urging the fighters to sterner efforts. White paint fell off their skins like crust, revealing the white skin beneath, the one man bald with a fretting of sunburned skin on top, the other black-graying, his hair a bush of wires. A tall one and a short one.

They wobbled, slithered sideways and fell over, their joint weight pinning an arm for each of them. Clan Abi crowded in close, beginning to laugh, and bounced into the preliminary rhythms of a dance. They saw (you, I, might say) a two-armed, two-backed land crab scratching itself, the two help-less divided, useless combined, neither of them supreme in his own right.

I'll have your kidneys for transplants! screams one.

I'll split your hairs to advance knowledge! screams the other.

And so they go, an eye for a nay, a tooth for a truth, frame physical for frame legal, heartbeat for brow-beat, both groveling in the paste of their pain. Little they knew, but, once the duel was done, I'd give them both the Brisbane cure: raw dugong for a month, eaten inside the cadaver of a whale, stench notwithstanding. Or else, in the catchpenny pharmocopeia of the blacks, close their wounds with eagle-hawk feathers, paperbark and kangaroo skin, poultice with leaves and hot sticks, supposit them with orchid bulbs and bark of the eucalypt, smear with armpit sweat, then set the heads in a skin rug between two hot stones, toast on wet green grass over red-hot bark, purge with sting-ray liver oil, secrete magical talismanic crystals in their deepest wounds: master them, in short.

Too weary to fight further and not even having much of an audience, they tumbled apart, bloody and dusty, gasping for breath they soon put to loud-mouthed purpose:

> *Tick, my breath's all blood.*
> *Tock, I'm all but swooning.*
> *Nig, my eyes are blurred.*
> *Nog, I'm sick of clowning.*
> *Pig, I nearly cut you dead.*
> *Hog, when I was winning?*
> *Big-head, I never heard such groaning.*
> *Bog-head, you needed a skinning.*

Are they, we would like to ask, trying to *talk* each other to death now? Surely—

Beg pardon, y'all, I'm just a friend of the court, accept no responsibility at all. They'll blather on for hours. Y'know, languaging each other until the light goes completely: *biotic,* yells one; *tort,* the other comes back; *riboflavin,* he says, burping; *certiorari,* the other starts chirping. Hours of it, the pot calling the kettle, the pair of them in glass houses and quite naturally throwing stones. Tell you what?

We are all ears.

How human of you. I'll let Malkari get on with it, speed it up a bit, quasi-quasar it—if your get my drift.

Presume not drift to scan. The proper noun is plan.

OK, leave them to Malkari. All they're doing is putting keys into the same door from opposite sides, which is how you get a dead lock.

Remind us, one day, to irradiate your head.

Yessuh. Malkari now, his hair shoes having dried out a

bit, even though the pain in his nose, jaw, toes, balls and joy-prong by no means have ended, decides to settle them in another way—more appropriate to his station in the Clan. He lies briefly in a shallow trench, shamming dead, and then is lifted out and placed by a large night-fire to dry out. The tall thin one he decides to put down in the ordinary physical way, the short sturdy one to master by enchantment. In each case he needs an assistant magician, and scores of volunteers step forward, clapping their painted chests with flat hands in the wild firelight, pleading and cavorting and once again half beginning to dance.

Kop, he says to what looks like only one side of a man, a shrunken old-young creature who, years before, lost half his left leg and half his left arm to a shark while drowning a dugong. He should have died, but cautery and Rainbow-snake magic saved him and his right-side limbs have become extraordinarily strong.

Master, he says, hops away at once and returns with the ritual pendant, a lump of porcupine-grass resin into which two kangaroo-rat teeth have been stuck, the whole being painted red and attached to a string of human hair coated with red down. This Malkari slips around his one arm, blowing hard into his ear, then looks again at the wobbling volunteers.

Kol, and he points at the loudest-chanting youth, the one who, in fact, holds the record for across-the-water calling and young as he is, looks after the music-tubes. Go, Malkari tells him, go prepare the bone-wand. And off he goes into the trees, wriggling pelvis and shoulders to some unascertainable rhythm of his own, knowing exactly what to do—as if this were not the first time. The volunteers begin a *hun-hun* chant and shoo the women away from the fire.

Now Malkari and Kop tread slowly away into the bushes on the fringe of the clearing. Mutter-mutter, crackle-crackle, and they reach the four-year-old noissome whale-carcass in which the two duelists have been sat after being bound, separately, with their heads between their knees. The moon skids into view, the night breeze blows suddenly upward, the bush animals fall silent. Tall-and-thin they haul out of the rotten hull of bone and roll him into the bushes, not a word coming from any of them. And now Malkari begins, his face aflame with his power, the tuft of emu anal feathers (which fell from the round black patch in the Milky Way) beneath his nostrils.

Waft them at him now till he faints. Soon gone, he lies on his side. A small cut and I scoop out a pea-sized ball of his kidney-fat, shove in the talisman instead, close the cut with a bone ring, touch him with the pendant while we split the fat and eat half each. Now loosen all his bonds and wait for him to wake. One cut among so many, but this one will do it, it's only a matter of—

What exactly *is* this tailisman? If we may ask?

Truth told, don't breathe a word of it, y'all, but it's two typewriter-key caps glued together with blood and, inside, a sapphire from a phonograph stylus. Honest.

We marvel at such ingenuity. Go on.

He will. Hold on to your nebulae!

Up he starts, beginning to scream, pale as skinned dugong, and runs into the clearing, our good selves following him slowly. Round he runs, all of him awriggle, like an epileptic in the firelight, crying *I want a refit, a refit!* But you can hardly see him now for beasts and birds flashing and pounding out of the trees, mobbing him and felling him, each one of them apecking and arending him in a whirlpool of feathers, teeth and tripes, the Clan huzzaing fit to split the great plain we all stand on. The last of the kangaroos goes, flicking a sharp right uppercut into the empty air, and the birds tumble upward away, the rats snitter off, one last remaining snake standing motionless and six feet high in the mouth of the skull, my talisman in its mouth between the needle-fangs. I take it, swallow it, and now, as Kop bends his head, mock-strangle him with the pliant snake in the utter silence of the night, the Clan hardly breathing. Off hops Kop to take his place in the whale-hull alongside Tock-Nog-Hog-Bog-Head, Tick-Nig-Pig-Big-Head having been dispatched forever into that hole in the Milky Way.

I now, but without haste (haste being weakness in these matters, or so the Clan thinks), select from the disjointed skeleton on the ground a couple of cleaned bones: an ulna and a femur. I decide on the ulna, wave it to summon Kol, who leaps to my side, a wriggling lace-lizard in his hand, a red skewer freshly thrust through his nose (but nowhere near as long as the three-foot spear I still bear through mine, making it impossible for me to walk alongside anyone of my own height; Kop was different, being as bent as truncated). Now to the hull of the whale again, where short-and-sturdy, bound still in a ball and gagged, waits alongside Kop, whose mutilated side is nearest him. I set a blob of gum on each end of the skewer in Kol's nose, then tear two hairs from my own head and press them in, one at each end. While I point the ulna at the victim's head, Kol with elaborate fine care touches each of his shoulders with the two trailing hairs. Now Kop rolls the body-ball upside down, exposing the testicles; Kol leans forward, setting a skewer hair on each testicle and holding his breath hard lest he disturb the delicate pairing, and I lodge the far end of the ulna against the nick of his fundament and set the near end in my mouth, teeth on it hard. We wait, we hold the position until, suddenly, with hardly any sensation at all, the talisman is back in my mouth from its hiding-place in my chest, and the victim-soul is safe in my keeping. We slit his bonds and peel them off, let him flop free on the dirt, where he quivers a few moments and then half sits up with a groan. Dead, though, he falls back, and I signal the Clan to bury the body of this one and the bones of the other wrapped together in a case of bark. But the ulna I keep.

Over to the fire I go while Kop and Kol go to sit in the whale carcass and smoke pipes to purify the air. Lifted high between two of the brawniest, I shit a veritable pyramid, more and more the higher I'm lifted, and then, down again, plant the bone at an angle at the foot of the pile. Clap my hands, let the women and the uninitiated approach, the corroboree begin, the fire blaze like rainbows and the rest of the dugong be cooked. Ah, me, I'm clean, that's what the bull-roarers hum, *a-hun, a-hun, a-hun-hun-hun*, and here she comes on a bark litter, a long black woman prepared days ago, her genitals having been blocked off with a thick shell of mud built up thin layer on thin layer dried in the hot noon sun, and a straw fitted for her to make water through. I'm allowed to use the ulna if I can't thrust through with my own weapon, but there's no need. They hold her firm, the black buttocks glistening like two massive frog-spawns, and I take a running charge, *whoops*, I cracked it first time but I'm not in where I belong, just hear those cheers, so I withdraw, recharge and home we go, *glug-slump*, clay shrapnel flashing through the air and splitting trees, felling nocturnal kangaroos in a trice, and my poor snipped, maltreated tool doing his level best. The noise is deafening, you'd think I was tooling the whole tribe at once, and maybe I am.

Droong, ah, mound, ah lobos, lobos! Home and beauty, once again. Nothing much to do now. I'll have to make rain for them tomorrow and we'll be burying Kop and Kol who, like the Kilkenny Cats, left to themselves, will devour each other. It never fails, whether you stick them in a whale hull or a brainpan. Malkari's back in Dreamtime once again.

And now, Captain McCall, P.D., D.P., or whatever, would you mind explaining—

Can't, not yet. He's got his duties, y'know. Why, they'd crucify him if he didn't make rain the morning after.

Very well. Let him steal our thunder, just a bit of it, but none of your hubristic games with pellets of ice!

Much *obleeged*, I must say. He hasn't slept all night, but

he's swyved his way through all the Abi herd, they've buried Kop and Kol, found dead through mutual strangulation (one-handed, of course, as the code requires). At this very moment he's scraping the inside of a pearl-shell, mixing the scrapings with fresh grass, chewing it a little and tossing the rest of it over the women who're standing round the mound of his dung. His talisman he's pressed into the sunward wall of it, and it's glistening in the light, gathering the heat and making the dung smoke, the smoke making the women cough as they inhale to chant, the cough making the women holy, the holiness making the men bow their heads, the bowing heads disturbing the air to make room for clouds, the clouds making—

No. This we will not have.

But it's raining already, lovely multi-colored sluices of it thundering down, furring the smooth top of the morning sea, blotting the drawings in the sand, tapping the birds off course, washing the dung away, wrecking the alignment of the grass-branch-bone mock airplane where they've sat him in triumph.

Very well. Rain. Rain be it. We took pity at the last moment. And now?

The Clan surrounds the whale carcass as the rain pours, Malkari already being inside in the dry, and they all lift. Down to the beach they go, puffing and grunting, shambling now into the shallows, now to the depth of a man, and float him off like an inspector-general in a great big bowl, Lilliputian in a grapefruit rind, priest in his chal—

Ohnoyoudon't. D'you want the electrode?

Do what you want, just let me continue.

Done. Are you really trying?

Yes, whoosh-thunder, there's a hell of a storm now and he's nearly foundering, your fault I reckon, and then he's becalmed, drifting, salt-caked, raving in the dry chimney of his throat, biting his fingers and sipping what's left of

Malkari blood except the Clan magic's gone almost completely, only—thank A. Z. Zeuss—the blacks are burning emu fat to soothe him, so he's dying without knowing it while the bright white carcass nods gently across at the widest part of the ocean, the blunt nose open, the bleached flukes useless, the—

It will not do. We have some non-interviews to conduct.

Sorry. Well, along comes Cap'n McCall again, on his way back from you know where, hold crammed with hard lamb (the freezing arrangements having been checked in port), and what's he see? Not a mile away, glinting and rocking, pale blue and eye-killing silver (in his glasses at least), half on its side, this long shape with a sharp fish-beak swung open and up and, further back, two blunt gill-flaps at the same angle, the whole of it floating he knows not why. He stares on, twiddling the knob of the glasses, yelling orders to the creoles to change course and slowly, as the *Fortunata* chug-slithers forward, finds himself making out a peeling white star flanked by not-quite-white blocks flanked in turn by red triangles beneath which he sees orange strips of orange. No sign of life. He stares on at the high fish-beak, thinking he can see right through a part of it, but his eyes hurt and he looks away, muttering *dolphin, shark, whale, swordfish, mar* —trembling anew as he looks again, reads something like WARNING, THIS AIRCRAFT CONTAINS A and, in the next line, CANOPY REMOVER CONTAINING AN and below EXPLOSIVE CHARGE. Lower down he reads RESCUE painted black on an orange arrow aimed at an orange disc just below the back bulkhead of the front cockpit. *Yeah*, he says, *should have known soon as I looked. See them birds diving about!*

The wings are gone, ripped from their armpits. He wonders how it floated at all. Down now, over the side of the *Fortunata*, he looks directly into the dove-gray cockpits, the rear two empty save for oil-stained sea tilting in the bottom, the front one exposed by a forward-torn side of aluminum frame and plexiglass; in it, or almost in it, on the far side a white bulbous helmet like a mammoth fly's eye, the visor down, the neck jammed in the wiring and pistonlike struts in the corner beneath the fish-beak of the upright cockpit cover. And below the neck, as McCall cranes out over the boatside to look, nothing but a short spar of bone like a teething-peg. Tried to eject, he mumbles; no, never, not that way, they leaves their legs behind when that happens. No, he must've fell out and got chewed up, or chewed up when he was climbing back. Sickened, he stares away at the high fin: ooo it says in black. And then they take the silver shell in tow, leaving the head where it is, McCall half expecting the plane to sink, the head to topple away, somewhere between Cancer and Osaka as he sails a westerly course, grumbling in the heat in the wheelhouse. *Solo*, he says, again and dry-lipped again, *most solo thing I ever saw*. And the birds follow, dive, perch on the rim of the cockpit, quarrel with plunging beaks as they tug, then soar away with fresh giblets from the head pulled through the neck.

Comes dusk and the shell of the jet is still behind them, the helmet still jammed and visible but now reflecting the sun's pink. 'Taint decent, he thinks, 'taint right and—any case—we'll be sinking ourselves, losing cable, scaring they creoles out of what's left of their wits. He unlocks the locker, hoists out the rifle, loads, marches to the side, takes careful aim at the helmet against the dying sun and fires. The head in its white globe shudders, rebounds from the fish-beak of the canopy, and falls into the torn cockpit. And, before he has considered, McCall fires a round down at it where it wobbles in the sump on the cockpit floor, missing this time but scoring a direct hit into the drop-tank beneath the plane's belly and setting the sea alight with a fireball that engulfs plane, *Fortunata* and all aboard. Timbers, joists and silver fin come down together upon two live creoles who have jumped into the blazing water. Holed low, the boat cants, then does a shuddering swoon, a short arc, before going under in a foam-quake that douses the gas burning on the sea. Soon the birds are circling and diving again and, even when the first helicopter arrives overhead, the sun is lolling yet, blurred-red and drowning solo.

0.99999999

Third Air Pocket,
(As They Come Aground):
Wealth, Genius, and Magic
Having Brought To No Good End
Their Brief, Fantastical, Embodiments,
Malchios, Maleth, Malkari;
While Filibustering Against Creation,
(As If The Journey Should Never End),
Has Wrought
For Caliban
Next To Nothing,
Not Reprieving Him,
Not Exempting Him,
Nor Salvaging Him.
Thus Zeuss, Without Pain Or Striving,
Comes Back Into His Own
In That Breadwinning, Workaday World,
Where Handsome Is As Handsome Does,
Not As Handsome Dreams.

Mint? An elongated cube of glass, crystalline and shiny, it's in my mouth before I've considered putting it there, or even accepting it.

What? You mean you weren't listening? After all the trouble I—

You overran your time. It's Tuesday night and we're descending, shipwreck or no. Your belt, if you do not mind. Thank you. As we were saying, a crashed three-seater jet aircraft hardly seemed in the best of taste . . . McAndrew; wake McAndrew; his seat-belt.

But no, he's had the belt tightly round him all the way, not loosely as practiced travelers have it, but like a girdle, a thong. Prodded, he comes up in a lazy stretch, both hands lifted through the dehydrated air, his breath held. Now he shifts left and looks into my face, his hands down.

Tokyo, I tell him, waving my hand vaguely at the black outside. We're here.

Cables? he yawns. Did—

No, I say, sensing Zeuss and peppermints behind me, Nothing. We had a breakdown in communications. But you! *Boy*, have you been living it up!

Uh? He relapses into sleep.

The plane swings left, then levels almost at once. I look out, past McAndrew's much-photographed profile, and see lights that could be any place. I look forward and see, still bulging and shifting on the screen, the superimposition of heads that could be any heads. I look at McAndrew: the face could be anybody's face, millionaire's, prof's, schizo's. Then I do it, I get up, exactly when I should be sitting strapped in, and go past Zeuss on my way to the toilet; but he wheezes loudly at me over the doodling whistle of the jets, his jowls busy, and tugs me back:

Wrong vay. Up front! Vat you say, you not been all troo de treep? Schum blatter! Any case, you should be sidding not schtandink. Is it or is it not a breath-vaste?

It is. I leer at myself in the unflawed radioactive blank of the mirror, thankful it's not the back of my head I'm seeing. Again we lurch and again, against my will, I hear that duet which, within me, cannot exist without me, but seems to.

At best cantankerous—

Don't even feel got-at.

Hubristic, insolent; jinnee, kibitzer; lick-spittle, moron, novice occipital, piscivorous quasar-raconteur, surrogate trickster—

Underhand ventriloquist, wanton—

X-ray yahoo zero.

Xenelasia Yielding Zeuss!

What?

Spartan system of driving out aliens leave you with nothing but Zeuss himself.

Hah, Huh! We are not edified.

'Sa fact. Ask anybody. Zeuss's never been silent yet but somebody's yapped up on Huh-Huh-His behalf.

Silence, garrulous yahoo! There was precious little in this garish world of yours: a paltry gift of a part to your actor-friend. Well?

I–I.

That is precisely it. You can't have without losing; you can't lose without having had. To add is futile; only friction multiplies—

Please, please, wouldn't you like to go and talk to William Blake's ghost, Newton's, Galileo's, even poor Ptolemy's, who was full of shit? It's beyond me, it's too much.

If the world was made of gold, men would die for a handful of crap. Dirt.

Dunno. But I'll tell you this. What became of Ubu S. Memno, Inc., I don't know or care. He's Zeuss's own.

S. Ubu Yen^2 Fang,^{1} you mean, surely?

No less, humble master. Me know when me met match.

Pshaw, as they used to say in Cathay—the *spit* syllable —you have met nothing yet.

Me know. Me not even looking. Me done worst. Him serve till doomsday. Me have work to do soon.

Ila Banc, Cain Lab, Clan Abi! Why, you've been disguising yourself so clumsily we reckon you can't be an imposter! Malchios, Maleth, Malkari, all of them P.D.: well, it says nothing, it tells nothing, it makes no allowance for—

You, you were going to say, weren't you?

No. McAndrew. Must he be always losing his life in roles he never understands, can't interpret, can't even feel? P.D.M. is *pretty damned much*, isn't it? If you see the argument of our gist. You have propounded, if we may say so, a one-piece jigsaw puzzle, always incorrect but always in place.

Oh, oops, I'm airsick.

We had assumed you had nothing further on that over-loaded chest-of-drawers of a chest of yours. But, if you must. . . .

I was merely playing into your hands all over again.

How so?

Meet Malchios, meet—

Only a dog returns—well, you *know* the rest.

We're not supposed to be here at all.

You didn't even invent him a half-decent role. Why, the merest hint of Big-Time—Orestes, Faust, Christ, Buddha, a couple of really polyunsaturated supertypes—and you might have been well away. But these—an iced nut of a millionaire skimmed from the deep freeze into the deep six, a priapic nut of a prof quitting his tenure to ramble the world doing graffiti, and then a schizo deep-fishing his way into witch-doctordom and death at sea! Well, we are not convinced. Men have done, are doing, will do, better.

You sound like you're trying to get re-elected. Got the pre-election jitters? Those ole nasty butterflies arunning round your little old celestial stomach?

Pshaw. You look bad in this light: infra-reduced, if we may say so: something, not entirely to our palate, which the earth gives off—off we go, on, oh no, and into my reflection bangs my nose, pinking it, leaving a seal of landing as I and the other victim touch onto Japan on pumped-up rubber, halt somewhat with a reverse thrust, slink into the end of tomorrow without having even slunk our way through yesterday. Are you there?

No answer. I've run out of responses. I've no further questions. I've run out of time. An all-time low. Cowed.

Is anyone there?

No.

Are you all right, sir? An angel, ainchel.

No.

Would you unlock the door? Angelically.

Hi.

Oh, sir: your face. Just a minute.

She busies off and, when she returns with a first-aid kit in hand, tells me the others have already disembarked, will see me later. . . . No, we didn't crash. It's ten o'clock local time, it's a certain number of degrees outside, it's still bleeding a little, it's already almost the day after tomorrow and will I please keep my head still?

I will, but I'm not really responsible for other people's

property. It's all in the head, really, all in the heads. And my only freedom comes, like a tape being rewound at speed, in the bubbly-cheeping sound of a small trapped animal in panic, knowing it's been programmed from the first. When the tape plays slow and emits meaningful sounds (so-called), you relish the sense and verbal march, perhaps, but you aren't hearing *me* at all, and you never will.

0.999999999

End Of The Filibuster?
Being After,
And Ever After,
· In Asia As Everywhere,
Caliban Now Losing Possession
Of McAndrew,
Who, Majestically In His Own Right,
No Longer Vacant,
·Finds Role Enough
Diving Into Quicksand To Save Himself,
Thus Leaving
Our Caliban,
Minus Paddle,
Woefully
Up-Creek.

Now I'm in the future eating ice cream I don't like ice cream
it only goes down and out and away into a manger packed
with dung-heavy straw bleached like nobody's business
maybe a stuffing for jet-seats so you don't break your nose
on the back of the seat in front while watching yourself in
a fidgeting sweat in the act of committing oh too many predictable acts and scenes and sins until the program ends dead
like a mouth-to-mouth revival meeting and McAndrew unscripted at the airport waiting,

behaving banally embracing an off-colored woman in white
silk and a not-quite-white child whose clipped helmet of black
hair he tousles like a man standing puzzled on the one square
foot of reception marble not cut from this world

aloof I'd say and visibly being met by his cables as if not
strangers at all all the way across the Pacific into the day
after whenever it was, when it wasn't that day at all for us,
him, me; Zeuss having to be plugged in right there in immigration

a long black cord going after him all the way to the taxis
and his private limousine, three puffing samurai staggering

behind him then finding a trolley to wheel it on, his private dynamo

fueling his schlop-mouthed schlack-jawed fat-man's good-by until tomorrow

not even blinking at McAndrew who I know screws all colors heights widths all eligibles in all herds, but never never skeletons in cupboards angular and uncomfortable *contortion* exempting only aborigines with earthenware *cache-sexes*

dilatations in his office behind encyclopedias

on a stool standing in a windy cowshed

submitting to under-table nymphs while ravening on luscious smoked bacon on its rice mattress fat trussed chickens on pewter dishes plump collops of hanging cow grilled over gridirons aspitting and ashining drowned in juices

oh but not this unscripted horror solecism perfidy bestowing that neutral kiss where oh where? from Manila he said some relic of a long-forgotten war could that be it I know I'm trite, he proved it in fact

his daughter, what that one which one?

you'd never think it

well no need to think it, it is

as if he had a past as if, he said, I wasn't entitled to a past a bit of scapegrace an Adam lapse, only she's long dead and this bit of 1945 (he says)

is his, this he a grandfather? forward and back in time like an ancient of days, only a beard a stick a stoop a dribble a rackety cough a hand-quiver a yellow-purging eye some brown liver spots on back of hand missing

his head quite normal for sitting on a mahogany shelf in any unvisited library any operating table under the black rubber snout any decorated GI's hat any TV regular

and I'm not wanted, pea shoved out of the pod

for a dancing minor shy-eyed small-headed foreign Oriental

and one of his little slips to woman's stature grown, a

Miranda I'm marveling at, a Perdita from the lost-and-found,
her face aglow samite mystic wonderful in her Chinky-Dago
way, hands not a jot rotted with detergent the nails pale
silver steel like fresh-unwrapped razor blades and

bearing not in her nose in the lobe of a tiny ear

that ring of golden sun-sweat plundered out of a nice
indifferent mountain, betokening (olde style)

one fertile bourgeois partner in an office in town sipping
bowl-tea with visiting German industrialists on long-dis-
tance phone with Cairo buying insurance claiming deductions
expense-accounts worldlywise two TVs two cars two in-
comes

a black knight against a screen of incalculable size but
blurred with snow and blossom and everything flushing

white in this wash-and-brush-up cubicle

Except a violet humming tube grooms me where I stand
while performing mincing mealy-mouthed melodramas to
myself my nose knocked numb my head-of-heads an aching
one my seat-belt getting tighter my electrode still in place but
not hurting my mauve bruise needing steak, my

my, I'm blinded, thought that night airport was sunlit so
not asking why the young girl up so late forgetting to be
solicitous me even when they say why doancha be like
other folks and go to bed? What baggage? why'm I stalling?
why'm I being paged?

because 360 yen equals one dollar like degrees meaning
one quarter is as right an angle as I'll get and so to work no
yen for it, but yen for it, allee samee

just stop talking *at* me for once!

Though my next move should have been to take a flight
back to Valhalla Villas and there resume my uncommon
habits of eating from ice-cube trays and saving clean cans
to stand pencils in, I stayed put. Having regained some
balance after a night's rest on a well-muscled mattress in

a paper-walled bedroom, I overlooked the wrongness of my mood, the badness of my (as Zeuss would say) poisonal philosophy, and the new-hatching malevolence I felt toward McAndrew. Out of spite or, maybe, Mephisophelean arrogance, I brushed my teeth crosswise instead of with the grain, thus setting them on edge for the day. And I took tea for breakfast, thus ensuring the malfunction of my entire metabolism for the next thirty or forty hours.

Japan, I said: *Yappan.* Never what you think it is, I told myself knowingly, as well as two visiting professors in the lobby, this being my first visit. The countryside, the pastoral bit, is singularly hard to get into; it's what you watch from fast trains in between the cities, and so you can allow yourself to breathe freely: the acrid, invulnerable-to-divine-wind aroma of human droppings, used as field fertilizer, never strikes home. It's for the people only, who, built so low, find it blowing above even them. So, unless you try, like an origami conquistador or a kamikaze pilot with only sea to dive at, you never become acquainted with any legendary zone of cherry blossom, larch woods, bean curd, hairy Ainu, and mint gardens hidden by the nodding of a hundred parasols. *I* didn't, at least, occupied according to the creed of Zeuss: not how people live, even when they're living that way in the anticipation of tourists, but how they would like to live, safe in the knowledge they won't ever have to. The kitsch factory has no area, no hours, no boundary; instead, like a Mercator or Conical Projection, it encompasses the entire globe, every point referable to as Lassitude such-and-such, Turpitude this-and-this, and you can fly from here to there by means of the Great Cliché Curves (just so you don't land up in space without a reassuring signal). Hug the earth, keeping in touch, and you'll never go wrong. Why, Zeuss is even working on a scheme—a pilot, natch—for closed-circuit anti-TV in space refueling stations, every care taken to retard the plots for time-wrap. After all, he says, we can't have these guys, still young but coming back to their much-aged contemporaries, acting as if they've already seen the end of every series without, as it were, having even taken the time to do it. So they'll also be kitsch-washed on their return with a special Zeuss *kitschwasser*.

Turning, that morning, into the Nobuki lot, I saw both my hands shaking and told them to stop. My mind full of distant dead blue lakes and bearded woodsmen chopping melodious tree trunks while massive samurais tramped past them on their way to defend border farms, I once again felt my mind going, in the way it often goes: without leave, without warning, without any promise of return. I'm always saying OK to dismay, even when, after such fiascoes as the one at the airport, I find myself once again able to punctuate—slice, chop and customize the swelling blank of my mind, the kitsch peeling off it like scabs, the renewed gray matter beneath shining like mother of pearl; but pearl? Never; we're not required, or allowed, to dive that deep.

Out of my limousine I see Zeuss in white suit, three oriental angels-in-waiting at his right side, the long black cable from his neck disappearing into a low doorway in a small brick incinerator (or something like). He looks, as ever, colossal; but, dwarfing him today, a fifty-foot-diameter mushroom with very short stem blots out a fair piece of the sky. Tattered-looking, with struts of lath bust out of the plaster, it's going to be part of our next epic. Trust Zeuss to find the one disused movie lot in the city, derelict, peeling and flaking since (what did he say?) *Zhin-Do the Mighty Martian?* with the entire Honshu Civil Security Corps as extras (wasn't it?), but safely locked up behind twenty-foot-high steel net and a guard on duty every hour behind a glass wall in an electronic sentry box at the gate. It's a pale blue mushroom with a peeling wooden ramp up which have gone brave humans risking mind-capture, down which have come mechanically strutting aliens complete with fazer-guns and radioactive eyes. The sky's a deeper blue, owing (I tell myself because I for once know) not to dark, blue, and dead lakes, but to the effect called Tyndall scattering.

Puff-puff in a high whine, he waves me over, flat-hands the guard from twenty yards as if annihilating him. Already I feel myself being ground by the cogs in his astrodome of a head.

Time you vas come. Now, schee—der scheep—schee has joost coom in vrom Vaynous. Vrom verlds avay. This Mr. Yakamoto, vamous Yappanese name. Ve'll be schooting the scheep maybe—schoor, wid a nice chorus in back to get the scheep safe down. Vat you schnarling at? Vat you got schtuck in throat? Be grate. Ve feet the scheep out as a gayzhar palace or zumting like, some of those grazy low-down tables, valls of vallpaper only, plossoms, coupla guitars, quick spray-paint jarb, all right trimmings. Am I communicating or am I not?

Into my nod-nod role I go. Kitsch-kitsch and off I go, through for life—literally—with the Ila Banc, the Cain Lab, the Clan Abi, my own darlings; ready to serve, but with a new grievance: I am cosmically at odds with McAndrew now for scripting his life without even a hint; more, even, than I am with Zeuss himself. I'm at the ground-zero of an all-time low.

You're communicating, I tell him. But let me guess, all the same. This is the space-ship from Venus: mind if I try it out right here? In it there's a beautiful girl, alien though; she has to be checked out, gotnovisapapersvaccination, all that, and McAndrew is brought in from the Central Clearance Office somewhere near Nagasaki to look her over, falls for her, huh, and volunteers to guard-supervise her. Before not too long, she's running the highest-class geisha-station in Japan, and head over cloven hoofs in love with Colonel McYak. This spaceship's the first Venus Berg!

Zeuss is simultaneously nodding and shaking his head, setting his cable atwitch behind him; Yakamoto is wincing, but it's a disciplined wince, born of long dealings with Zeusses. This guy *needs* the rent for that scheep.

Your trouble (Zeuss, whine-gusting), you neffer got good
prainwaves widdout bad. You should be grate I know difference, keep you schtraight. OK, but ve drop Nagasaki, hoofs,
name. Not be offensive. You got your pad? Goot, get it down
before you vorget. A schtart. I begin to write: Another Balls-
up Coming, Don't Even Find Geishas, but here's a shout and
a warble and a trilling giggle, and it's McAndrew with family
on the lot, his face purged like a man's back from a health
course, bowing and scraping to introduce. Kid's up in the
spaceship already, woman's admiring the ripped-up flanks of
two plaster lions, still ruddy from a volcanic lava of equal
parts of red paint and viscous porridge (you get to recognize
these things in time).

Man, he says, making my head echo with evil, you look
as if all your rabbits died!

Rabbits? Oh no, rabbit singular.

See you got going. Sammy sure wasted no time.

Nor, from what I see, did you.

Like coming home, all this way. It's been a long time.

Long, I agree, my head full of McMalchios, McMaleth,
McMalkari, long like a long lease. She got a free date some
night, this girl of yours? The big one.

Date? Ha! You'd better ask him.

Him? Following his eyes to Yakamoto.

Ah-huh. He is short, powerful, karate-mad you can see
at a glance; carries a bowler hat he never wears; just the guy
to buy or to rent a grounded saucer from.

Ice cream in the sun, my mind's all helpless, even here in
the green room, battered on-site caravan for the privacy of I
wonder what monster-playing stars, my ears swamped by a
Zeuss who keeps whispering, *Jaas, jaas, zumtink chentle, nut-
ting to vrighten volk,* Yakamoto admitting to more than a
speculator's interest in Calvary Stainless and Blenheim Plate
(he damn near controls them), McAndrew chattering with a
briskness no after-shave lotion could induce, the daughter—

wife of Yakamoto San—garbed today in lime silk and measuring her manner with obsequious perfection: with San, diffident partnership; with McAndrew Pop indulgent passivity full of flashed nervous smiles; proprietorial fussing with the child, Kamiko, offsprung like a dove offering its beak into the black dead maw of the corpse of war, invaded and invading knotted into a silk bundle worn on the back of the lucrative present, the one dissenter present, I, burying his pique in the voluptuous bowels of his scratch-pad, making sketches of mushrooms, toadstools, *my* cology, toad's tools, while they dribble the tea into bowls too small for cereal, too big for eye-baths, with only the guide outside and a faint fragrant wind rattling the thin torn door left open for—as if it might disappear through not being attended to—the uncared-for lot to be viewed through the prism of its magic potential, with Zeuss signing now for a fantasy on the premises of yet another fantasy, hiring without shame a pride of plaster lions, a stand of arsenical pillars which double as trees, an oblate spheroid in need of patching and paint, and, of course, as it ever will be without amen, the services of his servitors. The world is turning to a human tune again.

She's all primroses, every movement of the kimono wafting a pungent, off-shore musk at us. Somewhat plump, but she isn't going to star, she's not even—miracles be praised—one of the family; she's an expert, going to fill us in about the ways of it, stressing the entertainment aspect, of course: these girls will sing, flatter, pour, read poetry aloud, make elegant conversation like articulate overwound butterflies, but they will not screw. Well, all I can say is they must screw somebody, something, maybe only a plaster lion or two, a *papier-mâché* emperor, some lumbering misfit of a garden frog calling himself Mick Ardo just to fool them. But no, they are members of a lay sisterhood, lay figureheads (I'm suppressing all puns now) in a world too thick for their finesse. I yield.

Have you ever seen the like? It's a gas. I'm taking notes

like Charles Darwin out in those islands where he bribed Flora
Faun to give him the lowdown on Zeuss: I'm attending with
my teeth tight lest I utter the pestilence thriving and multi-
plying in my head like the rottenness in Elizabethan-A-1-All-
Systems-Go's Denmark. It's the lowest table Sammy Zeuss
has graced with the avoirdupois bunker of his presence. He
can't see it, it sits so low, and his eyeballs, swiveled as down
as he can get them what with that rigid neck of his, still aim
just above the big yellow flower she wears on her head, thus
providing him, I guess, with a near-perfect view of the sliding screen of the door. Fan-fan, she goes, explaining in an
English the Picts and the Scots might have envied, but
well below the tolerance threshold—if that's the right positioning—of any breath-fresh valedictorian from Tijuana
High for Temporary Immigrants, if you get my nuance. All
about, we're getting, the welcome and the proffering, the
pluck on the samisen, three strings and one plectrum, the off-
the-practiced-cuff arrangement of flowers or little red coals
in a dainty tray, the rhetoric of chitchat, the hummingbird
delicacy of flirtation, the very droop of an eye which, to
buy maximum seductiveness, must surely rate a visual acuity
not in excess of $20/200$ in the better eye with correcting
lenses or, taking the wide view, not participate in a visual
field whose widest diameter subtends an angle no greater than
20 degrees. My mind, as you can tell, was oozing away.

Look, I say, interrupting (but, then, she's there to be interrupted), she should be telling this to Our Star. Myself, I
can easily—

Vell you can't then. As close as Zeuss ever got to the good
old vernacular spoken even by zombies, aliens and human
vampires. So I shut up, and took some more notes.

A, I set down, for Asiatic deviousness; McAndrew never
told me a damned thing. Tells. What's he mean: *not* his
daughter's daughter?

B for balderdash, which she talks, McAndrew feeds me.
C for caprice and the cables he sent.

D for delicacy, of which she's got a ton-load and McAndrew's practiced to the absolute exclusion of his friends from his confidence. What's the setup? Child's ten if a day.

E for euphemism, she cups the tip of the spout while pouring with her hand, and he—hell, I'm not getting far with this. So I sketch the table, taking care to record the exact positioning of the trash thereupon.

I felt then, as I often feel, like one of those devout young pilots choosing to spend their last minutes in the tight tube of a Baka slung under a Betty's fuselage, alone in an aluminum-and-perspex coffin, the straps biting into my flesh, the transparent hood screwed irrevocably down, only four steel braces in the bomb-bay holding me up.

It's dark in there, just a few muffled voices from outside, some thuds as the crew climb aboard, a brief postscript from light as the door opens and I see wiring and interwoven tubes in the Betty's belly above me. Then black again as the engines chatter into life and the radar antennae shiver in time with the airscrews. Ramming my face against the hood I can squint down, see the planks of the makeshift runway wobbling as we taxi on oleo-legged wheels. Like dying, abandoned animals, the brakes moan and squeal as we line up on the runway and then stop as the engines churn to maximum power and we jolt forward into takeoff.

Dangling where I am behind the center of gravity, I feel the pilot kicking the rudder bar to keep us straight and I hear sand rattling against the wings of the Baka. We bounce twice, then lumber upward in a left-hand sway as the still-revolving wheels retract with a gritty shiver and the metal skin of my craft trembles in the flow of our climb. Two hours to go before death, but also before glory. First a green light for readiness, and then a red just before the drop. Until then, nothing save casual, inert memories of the disemboweled airfield, a waste land of concrete chunks, burning shells of fuselages, burned-out engines like mounds of black seaweed, propellers twisted into enormous armless claws, pools of molten aluminum glinting under foundered sections of wings, the smoke and oil too heavy to blow away and the smeared survivors foraging among the debris for drums of gas.

Then down steps cut into the cliff face to where, we, the two of us, sit under a camouflage of ponchos on the ground-fine flour of the beach, the water lapping to within a few feet of our improvised fireplace with both chimney and aerial sprouting out of it. I'm rolling salmon balls to cook in a shallow can on the charcoal fire and Yakamoto is fanning the heat with a yellow ivory fan. *New weapon, flames from the sky*, says Tokyo Radio, *honorable peace* as we nibble our last snack and fondle the hilts of samurai swords even as the ground crews brush sand off the planked runway and haul camouflage nets away from the mouth of the cave. Noisy cormorants fly in at once, out of the sunlight; I flick off the radio. Green tea; we bow to each other, exchange swords, the kiss still moist on the ivory. Two of the last yellow men going to their last war.

Studying the luminous face of my watch, I try to fill my mind with blossoms, lotus, cherry, pear, a flock of white-headed birds, but peer down instead: archipelago, junks, sampans, becalmed on the golden crust of the sea, then a bay palisaded by pearl fishers who cheat the giant ray thus, it's all frost, light and anoxia (we couldn't recharge the bottles after the attack) and cramp in the groin.

The engines are arguing with each other in the too-thin air, so that we fly, although forward, in uneven little flings.

At the green, I seize the control column, plant my feet on the rudder bar as if gardening, set another hand close by the trimmer. I'm ready, my thoughts are under control, and then at the second light I plummet down from the Betty, twang of ruptured chicken wire in my ears, eyes watering with the sudden glare.

Nose-heavy from the warhead I reach 370 at once, correct the dive, aim South, falling from 22,000 feet. Easy now, I say, select rockets, tug the arming-handle to the trinitroanisol, feel the acceleration plastering me backward as the wing rockets take me past 500 m.p.h., away from the Betty curling back to base, toward the arc of destroyers below. A quick glimpse of a denuded, pitted ochre island, and then all is flak and smoke. Down to four thousand, I scan the anchorage, choose my battleship, fire the remaining rockets to give me an extra 100 m.p.h. before, at nought feet, aiming at the gray steel cliff with a loud Banzai, I plow through the hull plates into a gracious, flaming orchard at a thousand feet a second, my sword flung with me as the high explosive in the hold detonates and begins a tidal wave.

At my cry of triumph the mincing geisha, to give her credit, flinches least of them all. Zeuss wobbles, then cants over on his back, inasmuch as he has a back; McAndrew with a careless arm-swing puts the crockery, or much of it, into untidy orbit, showering tea on the aforesaid lady expert, and I, I just stand up and make gracious, unfurling motions with my arms at three auxiliary geishas who, all through, have been canarying quietly at the far side of the room, all grave simper and wrapped-up decorum, their hair stacked and skewered.

Of course I apologize for making a scene; after all, the sun has shone right into my mind for almost the first time. I tramp away, smiling like someone with an invisible transistor at his ear. I'm not invited to the Yakamotos' for *sukiyaki*, but I'm going to have *sukiyaki* all the same; and if the hotel is unhappy to see me back so soon, then it gives no sign of it, which is what counts when you're solo.

Wandering in a town of hot money I spend myself in the *saké* shops the stand-bars the *pachinko* parlors, drink in the conflagration of neon, submit to the buzz-saw motorcycles, the tide of drunks with frail-flashing women hostessing them there on the very sidewalk, almost by accident enter a movie theater, talk scraps of Japanese to myself as I go, not worrying but worried, mouthing *nya-nya*, the miaou of the Japanese cat, bleating the *ma-ma* of the Japanese sheep, neighing the *hi-hin* of the Japanese horse, quacking the *ga-ga* of the Japanese duck, barking the dog's *wan-wan* and crowing the *kokkekoko* of the rooster, sounds gathered from the bartender in the hotel after dinner, ideal for fending off promenading *filles de* some sort of *joie*, misnavigating cavaliers of the night, vendors of jiggling tin toys, furtive youths in cheap shiny nylon shirts bearing cards, as well as for yelling at homicidal taxidrivers Honda-pilots whole platoons of peace-loving military and, truth told, at cacophony itself.

Shout back at the noise I tell myself, *nya-nya ma-ma hi-hin ga-ga wan-wan* but, crowing as I stroll into a lostness within a lostness, I remember something the super-geisha said, the *mono no awaré*, something like that, which means awareness of the pathos of things. But, adrift in this land of contraptions and finesse, I can't find it, can't feel it, can't even buy it with yen from a vendor; and so, reluctantly, as I stagger on through the illuminated zoo, conclude that I myself am it, no sooner seen than understood. I'm orange, like the *baka* exploding.

Let me straighten you out, McAndrew is saying. It's not as simple as it looks.

On this, the third day, the third morning-after, my eyeballs are crammed with the finest-grade barbed wire; I even hold my hand up to the bare bulb in the spaceship, expecting to see the bones in silhouette. Talk to me, I tell him from out of somewhere in my dried throat, just like I was an average guy. Lay it on the line, huh?

He does, and I fumble with the pieces. His daughter isn't Kamiko's mother, Yakamoto is her father, it's that easy; except Kamiko, hadn't I noticed, his voice a bit unsteady in pitch, was unusual, head that much smaller than usual, vocabulary just that little bit—

Look, I don't speak Japanese.

Neither do I, but Kamiko and I are level pegging in some ways. She doesn't feel the need for a lot of words—
I interrupt him with my Japanese rooster crow and explain to him what it is. Politely, he goes on, designating the exact quality of her laughter, the fey abandon of her gesture, the quizzical element in her cheerfulness. This isn't Malchios, isn't Maleth, isn't Malkari; I'm missing, respectively, the grandeur, the mind, the magic.

She's a nice kid, I say; anybody can say that. Even if she does happen to be a bit—well—

She's not a kid at all. She's over twenty with a mental age of around twelve. She was in her mother's womb, *in utero*, on August 6, 1945, born the same year. The mother eventually died. The Red Cross look after her a good bit of the time. She's a *hibak'sha*—something, someone, between a survivor and a victim. They brought her to Tokyo specially. She has a treatment card, diarrhea, sometimes purple spots from blood getting into the skin, lowish white blood cell count but that's improving. There were about nine hundred. They're all somewhat retarded, physically and mentally. They get by all the same. But the future, well who knows?

He lifts his hands a few inches and lets them fall back.

Yakamoto, I say, mostly for something to say.

On leave from the army in northern Japan. When she was conceived, I mean. He wasn't around when the bomb fell, he'd gone back.

Which of my barnyard noises to utter I don't know. So I ask a question. So she and your daughter—

Mrs. Yakamoto I find myself calling her, I can't help it. She's a year older. I've supported her, but I can't say I've brought her up. Not exactly proud of that, but she's come out OK, I think. An aunt in Manila did the necessary.

And you never said a word, you're a close one.

What was there to say, be said?

You were in the service. That's right. You were over there and I was home, scripting documentary.

Suddenly I don't want to look at him; I study the tattered interior of the spaceship, stare hard at that bulb and see, or, rather, convert all the visible into, red. I feel as if feathers, eiderdown feathers, are crowding slowly up from my stomach into my head; a soft, relentless, dry brain-choke. I let him talk on.

What she does, you see, is make paper cranes—it takes patience and skill, even if you're used to it. She thinks all the time about that girl, Sadako: there's a memorial statue to her. Sadako was two when the bomb landed, and about a mile away. Wasn't hurt, but she died of leukemia when she was twelve. Her last months in hospital she tried to fold a thousand paper cranes. The Japanese believe a crane can live a thousand years, and if you make a thousand paper cranes then the real cranes will protect you from illness, bad luck of that sort. Well, Sadako only got to nine-six-four, so her friends made the rest. The statue's holding a crane. The pedestal's made of granite and stands for Mount Horai, the mountain of paradise, and it's full of crane wreaths. The one she's holding is golden. Well, Kamiko's in the Folded Crane Club; gets the paper free, makes her hands rough she folds so many. When they made the movie about Sadako, oh in '58, Yakamoto got interested in the movies. He still is. What?

I find myself mumbling; he's heard me before I have. They married in '63, when she was seventeen. Sure, he's my age, but they do all right together. She's done a hell of a lot for him and she's a kind of sister for Kamiko, see. They make cranes together when Kamiko's home from the hospital in Hiroshima. They keep a close eye on her; they're still finding things out. But, maybe, things aren't going to be as bad as we originally thought. A few boils, maybe, cataract if you're unlucky. But about her having children, I don't know. We don't like to talk about that. I don't think it'll arise. Sorry, I get sort of involved in all this;

talk your head right off. It's something to think about while I'm—in *Geisha from Venus.*

Lips moving, I spell out my credo for him like a rhetorical zombie; I'll never catch up with him now. The kitsch factory never closes down; if you didn't have something real to think about, well it wouldn't be long before. . . . Those paper cranes, they're good. I like those a lot.

Microcephaly's not the end of the world, anyway. Better than too big. We took her back by train, on the express to Osaka. Crowded. But she enjoyed it, she always does.

Head? I say, straining my bloodshot eyes to look at him again. Heads I know about: you can't think for them, you can't see anything for them. Even if they clipped the electrode back on me, I wouldn't flinch. I'm as frozen as Malchios, as nutty as Maleth, as special as Malkari. I'm P.D., I'm punch drunk.

No, he's saying after an interval of a few seconds or hours, he doesn't need to, but he will.

What? Will what?

Film *this* thing. Outside shots mostly and some of the military. Me in uniform, huh! Then the geisha performing and the street footage just in case. It's a good job she's from Venus, she could look like an Eskimo and it wouldn't matter.

That's true, I tell him, thinking of all these people folded into one another's ordinary lives quietly and secretly like paper cranes made in the top room of a lighthouse.

Hiroshima, I say, do they still talk about it?

I think they think about it. There's too much else. They picnic in the Peace Park, go to the museum, like a Bisquick box on stilts. Toll the bronze bell. But it's mostly business bigger than usual, all very Chamber of Commerce; bars, drag races, glass and concrete, trucks and cars and motor cycles, planned out just like New York City: a gridiron. Why, they've even got racketeers, guys who got rich on the black market and stuck around. They—not the racketeers,

I mean—build cars and ships, Mitsubishi again, sewing needles, chemicals, machinery. I sound like a guide book. Anyway, it's loud and brash and they have baseball, they're baseball crazy. They also, by the way, make some of the best brands of *saké!*

What's the river?

Ota: it's a delta, actually, with six branches.

Sounds too much like home to visit.

Unless you're sort of morbidly curious.

I'm not. I'm through with curiosity, you never find anything out anyway. Not worth having. I see it all in crimson, so I guess I'll stay with that.

And the Ferris wheel, I forgot that.

OK, I'll think of a red, a crimson, Ferris wheel. Any kind of a roundabout'll do, any kind of runaround. Where's Zeuss, by the way? Wasn't he coming?

Oh, his neck-collar went on the blink during the night. He's resting up in a new one today. But you'll see him tonight. Supper. Make it?

I can make it. And yes, I tell him in answer to that question I knew he was bound to ask, I'm getting loads of ideas just sitting in the spaceship, this plaster mushroom of a room, except they've nothing to do with the kitsch-factory at all.

Alone in my suite I'm fiddling with the scratch pad and it's blank blankety blank my ballpoint long as a street and shining steel while I stand before a honeycomb high as a building and I'm trying to slide the pen into one of the empty holes in the face, refueling my own mental reactor, but it's all too heavy to lift, it's too high to reach, it's only the grille of the air conditioner unable to condition anything as long as *I'm* around in my drip-dry hair-shirt, my one hope in bed with a stiff neck because a filament burned out in the night.

Coming out of the red through the pink holes in the burnished metal of the human conditioner, I can only think of one of those old-style actors who, playing Cato in black armor under a magnificent laced scarlet cloak and wearing a mighty, white, bushy wig surmounted by his helmet, couldn't kill himself without stripping off his armor first, but elected to suffocate instead, vizor down and his entire frame writhing as if current flowed throught the metal suit.

An ice cream is all I want, I want black ice cream fed to me as soon as I raise the vizor.

Where did my color go? This gift has unmanned me quite, even on the eve of my return via Oroc (is it Ocor on the return journey?) to Valhalla Villas where I can work best, having said the most gracious no I ever said to that offer of a small country villa with a tiny courtyard on an off-coast island with glass-harp streams over the rock-garden lapping and bells heard from across the channel at dusk, butterflies like a scattering of petals past the window, a servant, a menu, a refrigerator stocked, why, even a television and a telex, a direct line to Zeuss whose physiotherapist is working hard and well, easing the creak, making pliant the rigid. No, I thank you from the bottom of my heart, a region I know only too well, not an oasis, not a conch shell restive with sound of the sea, not a hideaway with bottles to throw out with alphabetical pleas corked in, but—and I intend no nuance—a ground-zero where a first cherry tree just might—

Might not, but mightn't I just very delicately pick into the electric dust and plant a testicle like a spring potato?

Then home to Valhalla Villas, still mopping at my eye: the refraction of the tear is eight-ninths the torment, the rest of it being what the head makes of its own size, far from a walnut but short of a spaceship, my principle problem, as any decent laboratory can prove, being the overgrowth of my old cortex (the beastly bit), the underdevelopment of the cortex called neo. And, of course, my gift, a

lasting embarrassment like one of those Ophelia flowers that
won't wither wherever you put it, even in the mind's eye.
Out of rottenness they grew, so you can hardly expect
rottenness to stunt their growth. Why, they could offer me
a palace, install me in a throne like a refrigerator in a
kitchen, and I wouldn't stay, not now, not with this *mono
no awaré* wrapped round my neck like a technocratic python,
my face green with anoxia, everything urgent, going by
sea a trouble. No, bid the bell captain fetch the bags.

A bridge cools delicately, even fidgets, groaning, hunching,
inching, jarring, keeping length monotonously, never opens
pores, quietens radiant-still, tenders unheard vows wanting
x and y and z, both tick and tock.

It's only a rainbow sandwich after all, naked or clad, inland
or offshore, whether we master magic or magic masters us,
only our own doing, our own undoing, everything that exists
as factual as the fact of what's-not-existing's not existing, all
same things to me. I am coming off it in response to im-
portunings, made whole (approximately) by injury, cured
by harm, promoted by abasement, made the giver by a gift
received, which I am now—as if fondling a papyrus, a talisman, a scrap of grail—touching along its creases with a
fluent stroke as if it might take flight, *might not*, might with
its beak puncture my skin to let in the blessed bane, *might
yet*, my one wish being to divine the structure and the fold-
lines without unpeeling it. Firm without paste or pin, but
paper and wordless, it tells what scratch-pads are for: the dou-
bling of one's fiber into a gift that packs itself.

(kitsch factory or no kitsch factory, all systems go eventually)

and moves home with you where filibuster—that not quite
certain relationship with civilization—eats canned chili out of
refrigerator trays, takes in the milk and puts out the trash,
drinks from the bottle itself, won't answer phone or door, but
sits, dead-still, watching the paper crane balanced on his
palms, knowing it has, although he has not, Enough~Said

Interview of Paul West by George Plimpton

INT: How does *Caliban's Filibuster* relate to your previous novels?

WEST: One novel of mine, *Tenement of Clay* (my second, in fact), struck people as being almost entirely hallucinative, which I guess is what fiction *is*. Hallucination made to behave. And I don't think it was a far reach from *Tenement of Clay* to the two novels about Alley Jaggers, that Promethean spacehead of mine whose main desire is to get the universe—the earth, at any rate—back to the plasticity it might have had as an idea in the mind of God. Before things acquired fixed natures: tigers their stripes, water vapor the ability to form as, say, cumulus cloud, and man his multipurpose mouth. Alley Jaggers finds life's compartments infuriating, so he reconceives it in imagination—the faculty we were given for the express purpose of flying in the face of the First Cause. What a gratuitous universe it is, anyway; what a bloody surd; Bela Lugosi's White Christmas —as I found out in some depth while writing *Words for a Deaf Daughter*, what with such defectives as waltzing mice, axolotls that should become salamanders but don't, children born without one of the human senses. Not that I'm harping on the universe's lapses rather than its norms; no, what impresses me finally is the scope for error within the constancy of the general setup contrasted with our power to imagine things as otherwise—to rectify, to deform. What is man? He's the creature imaginative enough to ask that question. And although I know imagination had always to start with something not its own—hasn't *complete* underivedness—it can generate much pearl from little grit. All of which adds up to—what? Well, this: the mind—mine, yours, Hegel's, Joyce's, Dali's, Charlie Chaplin's—is *in* the world, *at* the world, yet only contingently attached to it, and is often in outright opposition to it, to its predominantly bourgeois or square quality. God's the square pig in the round hell; the squire bugger in the ruined hula. Then I say, hold on: not so square, after all, inasmuch as God gave us the imagination to see how square the universe is. And that gets us—those of us who want it to get us—into a quasi-divine state that includes all states of mind—schizophrenia, retardation, bestiality, nirvana, nympholepsy, and so on. For example, the new novel I've just finished is about an astronaut who claimed he'd seen an angel in space! What interests me most of all, it's obvious I suppose, is the elasticity of consciousness counterpointed by the as-is-ness of nature. An old duo, I know; and a poor thing, maybe, but just about the only one we have. And *Caliban's Filibuster* comes out of this abiding concern; it's a permutation of states of mind. When we die, our bodies fit back into nature in predictable ways, but what our minds put into print or paint, or whatever, affects people in ways that aren't predictable at all. If it isn't put into print or paint, or whatever, though, it vanishes. Ah, the miracle of words! Life's one long filibuster, killing of time with talk.

INT: Let's go on with *Caliban's* filibuster.

WEST: It would be strategic to get through this without my saying that it is a difficult book.

INT: Just that the reader could work a little harder.

WEST: It's a demanding book. I'm quite willing to declare that, to say, "Reader, try very hard at this . . . but stay loose." There's a lot of the gratuitous in it. In a way, one's supposed to respond to it in that way. The reader has to arrive at his own interior focus, which certainly won't be the one that I have.

INT: Is that what you mean by gratuitous response?

WEST: Yes. It's not quite a do-it-yourself novel, but it's an "available" novel. One can avail oneself of it and do what one likes according to one's degree of presumption. If the reader could arrive at, maybe simultaneously, a whole variety of battery of responses, he might have some notion of the stuff that was swilling through my mind while I was writing it. And, in fact, didn't get written down. It's thick with connotations of other plots and other schemes. In rereading it, I found that ideas were flying off and were very hard to pin down—even for me—so that I couldn't say exactly what this or that particular thing meant. I know what it was *doing* to me. I know what sort of impact it was having, but it wouldn't necessarily add up to *a meaning*. It's a gratuitous mental flow. All the same, it's fairly well-organized.

INT: When you started, what did you have in mind?

WEST: A sustained hallucination located inside *some*body's head. It's really a psychodrama. The main character, Cal, is clearly in an extreme mental condition which is productive, colorful, and highly inferential. He's a failed novelist, now a scriptwriter on an air trip across the Pacific to a hack job, who hasn't forgotten his pretensions and the days when people were nominating him as the coming master and so on. And he decides to produce something . . . not necessarily a novel, but an imagined thing . . . improvising as he goes. Of course, the pretension of the thing is *me*, as it were, supervising his improvisation. Obviously, I wrote the book, and anything he does I've forced upon him.

INT: The book is divided into three major parts.

WEST: The first chunk I wrote came out very untidily indeed. It's a lavish neotype . . . the whole business of a millionaire shipowner, a man having his own island, and complete freedom to purchase whatever he wants from the whole world. What appealed to me there . . . is a sort of pretension to godhead of a certain type. In a way the three parts come together on that, since throughout the book there is the presence of a divine surrogate who is in fact Zeuss. Through Cal's demented imaginings, the pretensions to godhead figure out in the first part as the millionaire who can buy the earth, in the second part as one whose brain is so great and so Shakespearean that he knows everything and is responsible for everything, even in a demented

form, and who may even survive his own death . . . and finally
in the last part as the super-witch doctor, the super-sorcerer who
can control rain and night and death and actually bring back
the dead. I shuffled them about quite a bit. I was certain that
I wanted to use these three motifs or patterns or . . . I'm not
sure *what* to call them. They're not diagrams. They're not
grotesqueries. They're sort of three-ring mental circuses. It was
a matter of getting the right order. I did work hard to get the
international dateline thing right. That occurred to me last of
all. Having got these three highly developed segments which
had been with me quite a while, each of them for different reasons, what I needed was some sort of numerical inevitability
that would serve as a counterpoint to the gratuitousness of his
free imagining. Then I hit upon the spectrum, and pondered
the possible significance of various colors, e.g., blue, yellow,
and red . . . and in fact what's in between. It's a flight across
the spectrum. The book begins with blue; then there's a long
piece on yellow; and then the aborigines of the last part are in
red. The original idea was to print the book in these respective
colors . . . to give some hint to the reader that he was being
flown across the spectrum as well as across the international
dateline, which wipes out the whole event anyway. It's a non-
event.

INT: But why the spectrum?

WEST: That's part of the gratuitousness. It provides a kind of
inevitability. I suppose it would have been just as reasonable to
play around with atomic weights . . . It was an arbitrary choice,
although in a sense if you fly a lot you begin to think in this
way. You see a lot of light. You see too much light. In a way,
the breaking down of light into its component parts is a metaphor
of the breaking down of the screenwriter's mind into *its.*
I think the reader could approach it on that level . . . which
I hope makes it easier because obviously his mind is really
scrambled. Sometimes he's talking to himself. Sometimes he's
impersonating his friend who is in a drunken stupor most of the
way. Sometimes he's talking to God. Sometimes *he's* God talking
back to any one of them. Sometimes he's talking to Sammy
Zeuss, who has to plug in to get his own electricity. Sometimes

Zeuss is the tycoon, and sometimes in this character's mind
Zeuss is God. I think all of these, if the reader finds them,
are relevant and consonant with one another. I would hope so.

INT: What about other devices . . . ?

WEST: There are divisions of the brain. The middle section, in
which the Shakespeare professor is going off the mental deep
end, anticipates the third section . . . the neo-cortex, which
is the civilized, surrenders to the older part of the brain. Somebody said that when a man goes to a psychiatrist he is lying
down alongside a python and a horse. When you're dealing, as
I do, with a dugong, which is a sea cow, you're not that far,
I suppose, from a horse. You're not that far from the ancient
brain. I guess the whole thing is a degeneration.

INT: Riddles and puzzles fascinate you?

WEST: Yes, increasingly. I don't know whether puzzle is the
word. Perhaps the whole novel is a puzzle, but maybe the
internal textural puzzles are the things that please me most. For
example, when the main character Cal, has conversations
with Zeuss when Zeuss is God, transmogrified into the Deity,
they speak in alphabet backward. There are lots of acronyms in
the book. I suppose they amount to word games. But then the
whole thing is a word game. It's a filibuster—it's a Caliban's
filibuster. It's really the ancient brain of Caliban, which is probably not easily reformed or civilized, doing its best to stave
off self-recognition, you know. The multiplication of verbal
puzzles, the erection of verbal screens and phantoms and all
the rest of it. The book is really, I suppose, an exercise in
mentality, and the subject of the book . . . if it has one . . . is
the mind looking at the mind and verbosity contemplating
itself with an implication that this ought to be condemned.

INT: Why should you condemn it?

WEST: I think the reader should condemn it. But, if he does, he
will find himself condemned. I think part of this is a feeling of
mine, a certain nausea with the proliferation of words that can go
on and on. There's no reason to end a novel. It doesn't end. It
just stops. It goes on in one's head like the stuff that Caliban

imagines. It's the counter-novel to the anti-novel. Then, though, perhaps it comes out positively, inasmuch as I bring it (and Cal) to earth . . . literally and metaphorically. I *think* he does— I wouldn't vouch for it—go to Japan; does arrive (in some sort of shape); and does go to work on this awful kitsch TV movie. I'm sure the reader who wants the thing to mean something will say, "Ah-ha, here is the dénouement . . . he's been brought to earth . . . to the circumstances of McAndrew's secret life in Japan in previous years. This thing sobers up Cal to a certain extent. He realizes that, in fact, there's a great deal more beyond the words. He simply has not got the words to cope with this new situation unless McAndrew explains what's been going on. Cal accepts it, but he can't fabricate words out of it." I suppose an enterprising reader would say, "Well, this means that words will generate words; whereas sometimes situations will drive one to silence." I wouldn't mind if somebody said that. But I think there's more to the book; it's not that didactic.

INT: What is the relationship between Cal and McAndrews?

WEST: Demonic possession, I suppose. Mnemonic possession. Bubonic blague. On a very literal plane, they're old buddies. Each in his way has failed. Each in his way has had rather lofty ambitions and hasn't quite achieved them, so they have common cause in mediocrity. They both make a good living. Of course, they're both tied in to this god-figure, Zeuss, who dominates them absolutely. He's their bread . . . he's their bee's bread, and he humiliates them endlessly. Also, they have in common a certain paranoia with regard to Zeuss, which is psychologically accurate on a very prosaic level indeed. But McAndrew isn't imaginative at all. In fact, he's a patsy . . . the filibuster being imposed upon him by this hubristic, insolent, vengeful Caliban figure. Doesn't Cal also mean "fuck" or "shit" or something?

INT: You must take great pleasure in discovering these things fit, or they can be made to somehow fit . . . as in Cal meaning such things . . .

WEST: . . . as heat or regenerative power. In a way the novel grew out of the title. The progressive hallucinations followed from that. I don't know quite what state of mind I was in . . .

INT: Are the hallucinations those that you yourself have had?

WEST: To some extent. I don't know whether they're hallucinations, but there've certainly been abiding presences and dreams . . . especially this stuff about the silver jet that is down in the ocean. I'm sure on a quite subconscious level this is tied into the image of a carcass, the husk of a fish which happens to be a dugong floating through. The words came easily. The same is certainly true of the Shakespeare professor, because a long time ago I was teaching Shakespeare; after three or four terms of this, the same symptoms began to manifest in me. There was one dreadful day . . . I don't know what I was talking about, probably *Hamlet* . . . as I was talking, I was hearing my own voice give last term's lecture on *Hamlet* . . . which was very frightening indeed. I thought it was time to stop then . . . give up talking about Shakespeare. That was the sort of demonic-mnemonic possession. I found that rather scary.

INT: Are the materials of the book those that might be unearthed by taking LSD?

WEST: Probably so. The book implies it. People who have looked at pieces of this, who have indeed had hallucinations, have said so. In fact, the strongest hallucinogen that was put into this was scotch.

INT: In your own case?

WEST: In my own case of it. I don't think it matters what the source of the hallucinations are—the prime fact is they tend not to go away. People tend to remember them. I remember these. I suppose somebody could dig away and say: "Well, this is all part of the collected unconscious: everybody has a bit of the Greek shipowner in him, the suppressed fantasy of owning his Aegean Island, commanding a physical economic world." I think equally we have the notion of the mind, the omnicompetent, all-knowing mind. And, too, we have the notion of atavism—of living among the primitive, and going back to a sort of magical state-of-mind. I think a lot of writing now is related to superstition. Ritual. Magic. Incantation. Totem. Juju.

INT: This is an aspect that has come out in films.

WEST: Yes. Fellini, and I think there is some in Buñuel too. I'm sure we are living in a much more primitive mentality than we were before. I think there's been a whole expansion of attention. We are interested in more human mental possibilities now. The great interest in schizophrenia, for example. Somebody like Laing proposes schizophrenia as the privileged condition. The sooner into schizophrenia, the sooner cured. Cured of being divided; of being trivial, shallow, and materialistic. Cured of living a false existence. In a way, what people like André Breton were trying to get across was that our minds include a hell of a lot more than we are willing to admit. We as creatures are much more involved with other kinds of creatures than we had thought. After all, imagination can address itself to the supreme fiction called God, why shouldn't it imagine something else? I see the whole thing as a way of reclaiming privileges. The privileges that Ovid took advantage of in writing his *Metamorphoses*. There is a great deal of transformation of man into beast, and back. If you watch enough werewolf movies you are very much in the state of mind that you would find in somebody like Ovid. Shakespeare was very much aware of this. Hammered away at it all the time, and it distressed him and offended him. It fascinated him nonetheless. Caliban, Aaron, Edgar. There is a tremendous audience for horror movies, yet we will take Fellini in the same breath. It all has to do with a quite relaxed determination to avail oneself of all kinds of mental opportunities. It seems to me that the opportunities are countless. Marvelous.

INT: We are talking about drugs before. Do these broaden a dimension of understanding?

WEST: I can't speak with firsthand experience because I haven't sampled them, but it would seem to me that all you have to do is read De Quincey's *The English Mail Coach*, which is a drug-inspired reverie. It is quite frightening—everything is a little bit out of proportion. It's like living in a world of Goya cartoons. On the one hand you open up all kinds of worlds that are possibly strictly mental; but still, on the other hand, without drugs at all, you would simply ask "What is around me?" It seems to me that what novelists, fiction people, haven't done is inspected man in his complete environment. It has been a mostly social, societal investigation. It will be all to the good when the novel bleeds over into a whole range of fields—cybernetics, anthropology, possibly psychiatry. This is what we are into instead of the novel by somebody like Henry James or Evelyn Waugh who goes into society, fingering its texture and making fine astute distinctions about human conduct, motives and privacy, mores and so on. We're demanding less on a much broader basis—in other words what will happen is that the novel is simply evincing first of all one man's consciousness. Whatever is going through his mind will be put down whether it's relevant or not, whether it's meaningful or not, and other people will come along and inspect this and say this is a human mind on show. The snag is, as with surrealism, that is totally undisciplined. This is why in a sense I resorted to anonyms and anagrams and the spectrum, and the tilt of the turning of the earth—something to hold onto. But these are nonetheless part of it. I don't see any essential conflict between the freedom of imagining whatever you want because its evinces whatever you are and tailoring that to certain quite deliberately chosen patterns.

INT: And the drawbacks of doing this sort of a novel? What would you say the great snags are?

WEST: Never knowing when the thing is finished, which really means never knowing when it began. In other words instead of a novel or a structure or whatever, you are likely to have a flux, a flux which can be as long as the rest of your entire life. In a way, this is not odd, because it's just splurges—it's just emptying the mind out, and that doesn't please me that much. But if you are going to evince mentality then you can also evince the mind's disciplining powers as well. What I like to think of is taking a structure, a pattern, a scheme, out of nature—something that man didn't make, something like $E=mc^2$ which man didn't invent: it was there to be discovered—and bring that into the gratuitous flow of images or whatever, somehow combining the two. It's a great relief to have this external pattern divined from nature, which can be used as a structure, as a fence . . .

INT: There are hundreds of these structures, fences, in this book, aren't there?

WEST: Yes. Some of them got in by accident, I'm sure, but most of them I worked in quite deliberately. The whole thing has got little minor puzzles built into it, which may increase the reader's general feeling about discerning the whole thing. He can stop and go back and say, "Well, I have to master this before going on." He won't find it means anything at all, but he will have a sense of mental consummation before confronting the next puzzle in the book. The puzzles lead to other puzzles, and the little puzzles to the big puzzles, but none of the puzzles has any more meaning, I guess, than a completed crossword puzzle. I hate crossword puzzles. I look at a crossword puzzle and all I can think of is the blacks. I wonder what has been suppressed to make the puzzle work. It is the most meaningless thing in the world. You can't read a puzzle. But in a sense it is probably close to this book—a series of juxtaposed splinters of meaning, which perhaps once in ten million times will come out as a piece of interpretable prose, with the black pieces intervening, and possibly one could look at this as a one-in-ten million exercise in enigma perhaps meaning something. I am quite sure that somebody who is determined can make the book mean something. I'm equally sure that the reader who is disabused of this, and is not preoccupied with meaning, can read it on that level without his mind tugging at him saying, "What does it mean? What's building here? What over-all interpretation? What argument?" That's why I say it's an *available* book. I don't think it's loose. The verbosity is very deliberately set down. The verbosity is supposed to exist in its own right. I don't know how many different ways of looking at it there are. I guess it evinces *my* mind as well. I've felt a long time that whatever you imagine exists. In other words, you can no longer say that somebody is deluded or suffers from delusions. If someone thinks he is there in Australia with aborigines being maltreated and circumsized and cru-

cified and God knows what . . . then he is. Whatever anybody imagines has been added to the sum of creation. It's
not a matter of whether it reproduces or replicates what is
visible to everybody else. If a man has a delusion or an hallucination, or quite deliberately imagines a rhinoceros in his
drawing room, then it's there and the fact of its having been
imagined into being is paramount. God imagined us, you know,
into being . . . and so it's a fair sort of metaphor or microcosm
perhaps, to see man as imagining himself into being too. All
imagining is divine pretension or presumption.

INT: So Cal is not really as disturbed perhaps as one might
think?

WEST: Perhaps only as disturbed as *I* was in the beginning of
the writing. In a sense, putting these things out, it didn't do
what you would think. It didn't dismiss them; the ghosts haven't
been laid at all. They now have what seems, feels, like lifemembership. Dismembership! They're rather more vigorous and
they have rather sharper edges now because I've externalized
them. I haven't lost the hallucinatory part of it. I still think
about the silver plane in the sea, and the dugong.

INT: Are there literary examples of this sort of hallucinatory
novel that one thinks of?

WEST: I think so. I think if you wanted a sort of ancestry
of it, a lot of this goes back to surrealism. Something like
Breton's *Nadja*, which I've read recently and hadn't read in
years and realized that it was very much in that particular line.
And then, even before surrealism, De Quincey had a whole
theory which the dictionary credits him with. He coined this
word "involute," which is also a mathematical term though
he didn't intend it in that sense. It's a sort of cluster of images
which bears in upon you with almost axiomatic force, which
you cannot interpret, yet which you cannot get rid of. In a
way, this whole business of the dugong and the silver jet,
at least for me, was my De Quincey "involute." I don't know
where it came from, although I could spend ten years researching it. This is presumably like the total "involute" that

the world tosses at you. If you can acknowledge these indefinable, inexplicable, absolutely pervasive experiences, you can then invent the same kinds of experiences for yourself and for other people.

INT: Calliban's filibuster—it's different from stream of consciousness?

WEST: It's not stream of consciousness at all. But I don't know what equally memorable phrase could be invented to describe it. Let's say concentric consciousness. I think one can very deliberately work one's way from the center to the periphery. The state of mind out of which a book like this comes seems to me to be concentric: one sits in the middle playing with one's idiots or one's circus animals or whatever. One can look out and see it all lined up—nature, and this mentality. It's simply a matter of exploiting the materials that are there. What staggers me is the literal amount of material that has never actually gotten into fiction, that has never got into the novel. The main thing is that human mentality get itself exposed and evinced. Any conscientious practitioner will find some means of disciplining what he does. It's simply a matter of being like the first man who sat down and said, "Well, a sonnet. I will construct a sonnet now." There is no reason for the sonnet being the way it is; it was simply taken up and has been used ever since. You were asking about the uses of mc^2. The novelist has got to become a mathematician to a certain extent. He can go into the inevitabilities—the mathematical inevitabilities of the structure of shells—or he can play around with the Milky Way. It's a matter of opening the mind and saying, "Well, good God, Good dog, here's your handiwork mixed with mine!" We know a hell of a lot about the so-called universe; I wonder what it—in the singular—knows about us. I see no reason why either branch of knowledge shouldn't grow into the act of fiction.